Praise God for Pasties

PAMELA G. HOLMES

PRAISE GOD FOR PASTIES. Copyright © 2026 by Pink Crow Press, LLC.

All rights reserved. Printed in the United States of America.

For information, address Pink Crow Press, LLC., 1510 Airport Road, Panama City, FL 32405 or visit www.pinkcrowpress.com.

Cover art designed by: J.D. Justice | @art.by.mr.j

Author photo by: Louis Columbus Photography | lou1492.com

Spotify playlist compiled by: Paradigm Logic Studios | paradigmlogicstudios.com

ISBN-13: 979-8-9948295-1-6

Ebook ISBN: 979-8-9948295-6-1

Special thanks to Rob.

You are a god damn delight.

You are my muse, my inspiration, my kick in the ass,

the wind beneath my mothafuckin' wings.

I will love you until we're bones.

Content Advisory

This novel contains depictions of human trafficking, kidnapping, sexual violence, physical abuse, murder, and the psychological trauma associated with these experiences. It also includes explicit sexual content, strong language, and scenes that some readers may find disturbing or triggering.

While this story is a work of fiction, the realities it portrays are devastatingly real. In 2021 an estimated 27 million people worldwide—men, women, and children— were trapped in human trafficking,[1] with approximately 199,000 incidents occurring in the United States each year.[2] Florida, where this story is set, ranks among the top three states for human trafficking cases. In 2024 alone, researchers estimated that more than 200,000 people in Florida were victims of sex trafficking, with minors making up half of those exploited.[3] The state's tourism industry, major ports, and seasonal labor markets create environments where traffickers prey on vulnerable individuals. Human trafficking affects people of all ages, ethnicities, and genders and extends far beyond prostitution into entertainment, hospitality, and restaurant industries, as well as domestic work and forced marriages. No industry or economic sector is immune to human trafficking.[4]

My awareness of human trafficking began when I worked for a high school where Freedom 180—a state-mandated health curriculum covering mental and physical health awareness, substance use and abuse education, and child trafficking awareness— presented to our students. I was shocked by what I learned—not just the staggering statistics, but how many myths I had believed based on Hollywood's portrayal of trafficking. The reality is far more insidious than dramatic kidnappings by strangers. Human trafficking often involves coercion, manipulation, and the exploitation of trust by those closest to victims. Traffickers frequently use gaslighting and psychological manipulation to break down their victims' sense of reality, making it difficult for them to recognize their situation as abuse or to seek help. This psychological trauma can persist long after physical captivity ends.

Recognizing the warning signs can save lives. These may include someone who appears fearful, anxious, or submissive; shows signs of physical abuse or malnourishment; lacks control over their own identification documents or money; is not allowed to speak for themselves or has someone who speaks for them in all situations; or works excessively long hours with few breaks. This novel was informed by the testimonies of survivors who have bravely shared their experiences, and it was written to illuminate these often-invisible realities and to honor the resilience of those who have endured them. By bringing these stories into the light, we can better recognize these warning signs and support those who need help. Human trafficking thrives in silence and shadows. If you or someone you know needs help, please reach out:

National Human Trafficking Hotline
Call: 1-888-373-7888
Text: 233733
Available 24/7 in more than 200 languages
Online chat: humantraffickinghotline.org

Additional Resources:
Polaris Project: polarisproject.org
Florida Alliance to End Human Trafficking: faht.org

Reader discretion is strongly advised.

Notes

1. International Labour Organization, Global Estimates of Modern Slavery (2021).
2. National Human Trafficking Hotline, Polaris Project, Annual Report Data.
3. University of South Florida, Trafficking in Persons Risk Index (2024).
4. United Nations Office on Drugs and Crime (UNODC), Human Trafficking FAQs.

Part One

I Put a Spell on You

CHAPTER ONE
CANDYMAN

Spotlights flooded the stage with blinding, white light made brighter by the inky black bar surrounding it. From behind a red velvet curtain, Bella Valentina saw the stage, speckled with the glitter her burlesque troupe had haphazardly thrown throughout previous performances during the night. She heard the clinking of shot glasses against the bar in the back and the popping of Pabst Blue Ribbon beer tabs. She took one last stretch, arching her back like a cat, and inhaled deeply, breathing in the aroma of tequila and cheap aftershave. The room then fell quiet except for the hum of the bar. And that was her cue. The first few beats of Nina Simone's "I Put a Spell on You" called to her, luring her closer. Bella felt the vibrations coursing through her body like tingling waves of energy flowing from the tips of her gloved fingers. With her heart pounding like a drum, the tease began. She slinked her way around the stage, making love to the bright lights and the black beyond. Flirting with winks and smiles for a lover she couldn't see. Every sultry caress, every seductive shimmy, every layer of lingerie she peeled off was an invitation addressed, stamped, and delivered. The wolf whistles, the cheers, the claps, and the cash all brought her closer to that perfect moment of euphoria. Bella artfully inserted her long middle finger into the edge of the glove. The sleeve glided down her arm like silk. One by one, she placed the black fingertips between her teeth and gave a gentle tug until the glove was off and twirling above her head. She flung the glove to the whistling crowd.

This stage and these lights were her drug. And not like the cheap weed you bought from your cousin at the family reunion that had the seeds and stems among the nuggs. No. This was the good stuff. The sticky, crystallized florets of weed that set your brain on fire with one bong hit. The perfect high that made you feel like it's the best time every time. Bella felt as though she transcended into a burst of pure white light. The incredible euphoria of the happy drug cocktail that her brain had just poured for her made her feel invincible – powerful – celestial. She felt the double shot of endorphins and adrenaline raging through her from center stage, her brain prickled with intensity. Breathless and euphoric, she gazed into the inky black beyond, waiting for her heart to burst.

She took her final bow to the roar of the drunken, now raucous crowd. With that roar, so came the bursting of her heartstrings.

Sasha, the stage kitten, pounced on the stage as Bella strutted off. She was young and dramatic and fancied a future as a Hollywood actress. She chased after bits of lingerie like a playful kitten after a ball of string. With a grand flourish, Sasha tumbled around the stage like an acrobat at the circus. She flexed her lean muscles and accentuated her long legs as she bent at the waist. Like a hinge opening a jewelry box, she glided smoothly up, stuffing crumpled $20 dollar bills that had been worked long and hard for, but given away quickly, into her cherry-red sequined bra.

Bella slipped past the red velvet curtain that led to the girls' changing area, which was really just the supply closet at the back side of the stage. As unglamorous as it was, it was the best the club owner had to offer the troupe on short notice. But when a gig opened up, you took it, even if the club owner was a bit dodgy. Bella stood at the edge of the short staircase by the stage curtain, leaning against an unopened stack of beer boxes, watching Sasha collect her tips. Bella's pale skin was flushed pink and reflected the dewy sheen of perspiration as she peeked through the thick curtain.

Bella was high. Drunk. In love. But this was no ordinary love, not like the love you have for a partner, or your family, or friends. It was the kind you could only get from living a passionate life, taking chances on the experiences that made you whole when the world tried its best to tear you apart. Bella was drunk with the liberation of her mind, her body, and her heart. When she was on stage, she was no longer held back by what the world had to say. Instead, she was in the moment; vibrant, alive, intoxicated.

But there was no drinking on the job, at least, not as far as Desiree, the show producer, knew. It was a gamble deciphering where the conviction came from—maybe it was Desiree's firm belief in professionalism as a performer, or her desire to control an unruly group of young girls, or maybe it was just a remnant of her days in Alcoholics Anonymous. Desiree Barnes was a long-time lush who had a college degree in something mundane that she never planned to put to use and an unquenchable thirst for control, like a well-seasoned dominatrix with a riding crop in hand. She hovered over the set-list as the lights from the stage peeked through the velvet curtain, revealing delicate lines that creased her furrowed brow. In this lighting, she looked every bit of 40, but it wasn't the lines along her forehead as much as it was the bitterness behind her brows. She had the disdain of a 40-year-old. She had the jaded, broken perspective of a millennial with a life half-lived and an oppressive realization that had been met with the inherent tragedy of an unfulfilled existence. Desiree looked up to see Bella peeking through the curtain like a child on the other side of a candy shop window, salivating for a piece of fresh chocolate.

Desiree chided, "OK, Bella… you don't have time for standing around. You need to get ready for Candyman!"

"Oh… yeah," Bella said, "I guess so." Bella took one last look at the shadowy crowd beyond the bright stage lights before turning away with a sigh. Halona pushed past her and anxiously glanced beyond the curtain as she fumbled with the hooks on her corset. She watched Sasha working the crowd, jingling the tip jar in rhythm with her shoulder shimmies. Bella paused beside her, watching her struggle with the metal clasps on her corset.

"Do you need help?" Bella gave Halona a hopeful smile. "I don't mind."

"Huh," Halona was lost in her view of the stage. It seemed like her eyes had glazed over, and she hadn't heard Bella speak to her. Bella leaned in to ask again, when Halona was shaken from her distraction, "Oh, nah. I got it. Thanks, though."

Bella wondered if Halona had also felt the lure of the shadowy unknown calling to her as well. Perhaps other women in the dance troupe also felt the same exhilaration and freedom that she felt when on stage. Maybe that was what united them.

A short man in suspenders stepped up to the microphone. He twisted the tips of his dark chestnut handlebar mustache and adjusted his tweed newsboy cap as he announced Halona's act. He bellowed into the microphone, "Up next, put your hands together for the scintillating sensation of the Sioux Nation. All the way from South Dakota, welcome to the stage, Turquoise Cloud!"

Halona's iridescent peacock feather fan fluttered just past the velvet curtain announcing her debut. Like a shy schoolgirl, the ruddy umber of her ankle teased the audience of her imminent arrival. As she leaned forward, the gap in the curtain revealed more of her warm skin. With a bold left kick and crescendo of drums, she twirled to center stage while the iridescent gleam of peacock feathers hypnotized the audience.

Bella stepped past a wall of wine crates to find her best friend, Clementine Sullivan, tucked behind the make-shift divider. She swiftly handed Bella a bottle of her finest discount supermarket wine, whispering, "Quick! Before mother sees."

Bella cast a look over her shoulder before taking a long swig of the blush pink liquid inside the bottle of Arbor Mist. Bras and fishnets were scattered in an array along the top of the wine crates that constructed their makeshift dressing room. With only two minutes before their duet, Clementine took the bottle back, upended it with a gulp, then screwed the metal lid back onto the bottle top and hid it in her suitcase. Desiree paced in front of the pallet wall, unaware of the intoxication that occurred behind her back. Hearing Desiree's footsteps, Bella scrambled to jump into her costume. For their Candyman performance, the duo wore matching blue sailor hats, black back-seam thigh highs, a sequined bra jeweled with stars and stripes, and crimson red lipstick. Clementine helped Bella fasten the quick-release snap on the back of her sequined bra. The girls smiled appreciatively at each other with an unspoken understanding. There was a sisterhood backstage. One moment they were strangers with little in common except their curiosity, and the next they were half-naked, gluing on pasties, taping up back-seam hose, and straightening thong straps for each other. The intimacy of the action wasn't lost on them. But they didn't let that stop them; they helped each other with professionalism and efficiency.

Desiree continued her laps around the room, micro-managing the dancers as if she were a sheep dog herding a flock of lambs. Without taking her eyes off the set-list in her hands, she walked into the pallet dressing room and announced, "Candyman! You're next! Halona's act is almost up." The girls nodded a confirmation without realizing that Desiree wasn't even looking at them, and had already continued her lap around the room. They rushed to make their final touches and gave each other a quick twirl for quality assurance.

As Clementine applied a second layer of red lipstick, Bella's mind wandered for a moment, lost in the reality that she lived in now, and how it was so much different from what she had envisioned for herself. She wondered how her family would react if they knew she was doing burlesque — something so tawdry and vulgar. *My poor mother*, she thought. She imagined her mother pressed and dressed in her Sunday best — a fine upstanding member of society — with a look of disapproval permanently etched on her face. Envisioning her mother's pursed lips and furrowed brow sent a shiver down her spine, and a feeling of guilt crept over her. She scanned the room for Desiree, spun the metal cap off the wine, and took another long drag from the bottle. There was no time for sadness now, but at least there was wine, thanks to Clementine…as long as Desiree didn't find out. Bella gave her breasts a swoop and scoop to make sure they were perfectly situated in the cups of her sequined stars and stripes bra.

"How patriotic," she said, "I think Christina Aguilera would be proud." She gazed into the small, speckled mirror that hung from a loose staple on the wooden crate.

Clementine smiled briefly, "You ready?"

A big smile crawled across Bella's face. That familiar unseen lover waited in the inky dark shadows again, lurking just beyond the bright lights of the stage. It pulled her forward, and she hovered at the velvet curtain, waiting for her moment in the limelight. Her brain had already begun mixing her favorite cocktail — oxytocin, endorphins, serotonin, and dopamine, with an adrenaline chaser.

Halona hastily pushed past them as she exited the stage after her act. Sasha had already pranced on stage and was working the crowd with a lusty bend and twerk, as she grabbed a crumbled five-dollar bill.

Sasha's smile radiated as the crowd hooped and hollered for her. She adored the attention.

Bella heard the din from the bar and felt the buzz of the crowd's excitement surging through her. She just knew they were calling for her. Begging for another tease. They whistled and clapped and shouted for the next beauty to tempt them from the stage, edging them closer to sweet release. And she was just as hungry for it as they were. But the crowd didn't know that behind those perky sequined breasts thumped a heart that still mourned her dead brother. Her mock patriotism and star-spangled breasts were hiding the trauma of losing her brother to a war in Afghanistan, one he fought even though he didn't believe in it. Bella was struck by the duplicity of the moment. It was bittersweet to long for the freedom of dancing all while knowing her brother gave his life for her right to do so. She closed her eyes and thought, *My poor brother.* She envisioned his young face, a remote sweetness upon it, even though his brown eyes were glassy and his skin was speckled and smeared with dried blood. His husky voice echoed in her head, *They say the 'good die young' so I guess I'll live forever.* She scoffed as she thought of him as good. He was far from it. A scoundrel in every sense of the word, but he was as good as a martyr in the eyes of Bella's staunch family.

The hipster MC was finishing his monologue, "Put your hands together for Bella Valentina and Crimson Delight!"

Just as Bella started towards the stage, she looked down to realize the bottle of Arbor Mist was still in her hands. She sloshed the contents and drained the last of the wine bottle before hiding it in the velvet folds of the curtain before joining Clementine for one more thrill on-stage.

CHAPTER TWO
YOUR LOVE IS MY DRUG

After the show, fans scuttled toward the stage to snap a selfie or buy the dancers a drink. Maybe it brightened up their drab little lives for the Southern belles, or maybe the redneck boys in the audience thought they'd get their dick sucked in the alley behind the bar. Who could say, and why shouldn't they? After all, the woman in front of them was "Bella Valentina," the stereotypical fresh-faced good-girl-gone-bad with a heart of gold and tits the size of cantaloupes. And certainly not Rebecca Coleman, the almost 23-year-old college dropout from Bum-Fuck-Nowhere USA. And for the redneck regulars and the curious tourists brave enough to enter The Treasure Cove in Mossland, FL, with its dilapidated bar, sticky carpet, and peeling walls, she was the belle of the ball, and this was 'The Best Little Whorehouse in Florida.' After all, 'stripper' or 'dancer' or 'burlesque performer' was synonymous with 'whore.' Like the Puritanical voice of America's ancestors spoken through the booming voice of John Proctor echoing in her head, "once a whore, always a whore." But, sometimes a free drink from an over-zealous fan was the only score of the night, especially if the tips were lean — at least the working girls got drunk for free; "Love the drug, not the dealer."

As the fans in the bar started thinning out, Rebecca looked to pick her target before it got too slim. Placed squarely in her line of sight between a lingering poly couple who stopped her for tips to help spice up their sex life, a silver fox appeared from out of nowhere, seemingly manifesting at the end of the bar near the exit from a plume of smoke that also accompanied his cigar. He was an older man with dark, chaotic eyes, a warm tan, and silver patches of hair at his temples. He appeared to be in his late 40s or early 50s. But he had a certain refinement to him and a deep sense of control – like he was well-traveled, well-read, well-funded... or at least, distinctly not the traditional Conservative White American male that she was accustomed to. He was unlike anyone else in the ramshackle bar, well out of place like a smoky beacon of culture in a sea of unwashed masses. Rebecca caught the man's eye and gave him a flirtatious smile. There was no reaction but the continued gaze. This stirred something in Becca; no one could ever resist the 'Sly, Flirtatious Smile,' and it almost made her leave him alone. But something was alluring about the way he gazed at her, like the dark, tumultuous sea in his eyes found the deepest parts of her and wanted to devour them. He had a twinkle in his eyes that seemed as though he was mentally summoning her, pulling her toward him with an invisible thread. She excused herself from the over-sharing couple and began to step towards the edge of the bar to introduce herself when Desiree loudly nagged about penis-shaped confetti on the floor and empty wine bottles in the trash. Her high-pitched complaints cracked the spell Rebecca was under. As reality crashed in, her eyes drifted away from the handsome man seated across the room. Desiree jabbed her in the side with a broom handle, which further snapped the invisible thread he had on her. Becca swiveled her head quickly to meet Desiree's stern glare as she thrust two straw brooms into Rebecca's hands. She reluctantly took the brooms. She glanced back for another look at her silver fox, but as quickly as he appeared, he was gone, and so went any possibility of an Old Fashioned.

Rebecca shrank from view and met Clementine's gaze with a sigh. They both knew the confetti came from their grand finale in Candyman when they simultaneously fired bright pink penis-shaped guns filled with bright pink penis-shaped confetti at each other; their wanton mouths open as the result of their climax showered onto their faces. The proverbial money shot. It was their show-stopper. And it always, always raked in the cash.

"Dammit. My free drink took off. There won't be anyone left before we finish sweeping up dicks," Rebecca groaned to Clementine as she handed her a broom.

"It'll have to wait another night, I guess. Anyone here in this dump probably would have gotten too handsy anyway."

"Or put molly in my drink."

"And really, who wants to be raped or murdered on a Friday night just for a free vodka cran?"

Becca snorted, "And made with nasty-ass Popov vodka!"

"See… not worth it anyway!"

Clementine and Becca giggled as they swept the sticky gray carpet in an attempt to collect the wayward glitter dicks. But the action seemed to adhere to them instead of releasing them. The sticky carpet served as a glue, firmly cementing them to the floor. The girls laughed harder and harder as they realized the task was hopeless. Everywhere they had walked after their performance was sprinkled with a path of sparkly pink dicks.

Halona stood in the far corner of the room, packing the remnants of Sasha's costuming and props. Her own gear was strewn across the floor, haphazardly dumped after her performance. After packing Sasha's gear, she organized her own. She was lost in thought as Clementine and Rebecca tidied the room. She repeatedly glanced toward the back exit, waiting for Sasha to return. But it had been over 30 minutes since she saw Sasha disappear into the back alley of the bar with a man. Halona waited another 30 minutes after packing up before grabbing their bags and heading to the parking lot. She huffed as she pushed past Rebecca and Clementine, only stopping at the exit to get her pay for the night. Desiree meticulously counted the bills twice, ensuring that she didn't overpay her. As Halona stepped into the gravel parking lot, her shoulders were strapped with luggage, but her face bore an even heavier weight as she scanned the parking lot looking for her friend. But Sasha was nowhere to be found. Halona schlepped the luggage to her compact sedan and stuffed everything in the trunk. As she slammed the trunk shut, Sasha appeared around the corner. The man zipped his pants and handed her money before going back into the bar. Sasha walked over to the car where Halona waited. As she approached, she waved a $50 bill in the air.

"Waffle House on me!" She exclaimed and jumped into the passenger seat.

Halona was visibly irritated, but shrugged it off as she got in the driver's seat of the sedan and drove off.

Watching their car turn onto the highway, Desiree stepped out of the back door and lit up a cigarette. Her pale skin looked vampiric in the sallow light of the street lamps. The tip of her cigarette glowed orange as she took a long drag. She held the smoke in her lungs for a moment and released it in a slow exhale. A plume of gray rose above her head as a man in a suit appeared like mist out of the shadows. He waited at the edge of the building, as a neon sign blinked twice before going dark. Desiree saw him standing in the shadows, took a final drag from her cigarette, smooshed it into the gravel, and walked out of the glow of the street lamp, toward him.

Clementine and Rebecca realized they were the only dancers left as the bartender slowly turned out the lights. They grabbed their bags and headed for the door.

"I hope Desiree doesn't notice a few unswept dicks on the carpet," Rebecca said as she and Clementine stepped into the cool night air.

"Where is everybody?" Clementine glanced around the nearly empty parking lot. The neon lights of the bar continued to flicker and turn off one at a time.

"Um, looks like Halona and Sasha are already gone. I don't see her car. But Desiree's is still over there," Becca pointed to a beat-up Chrysler Sebring.

"Yeah, I'd kinda like to get paid. Sooooo," Clemmie drew out the vowel for a moment as she looked around. The flick of a lighter and the orange flare of a cigarette in the dark caught the two girls by surprise.

Startled, "Oh, there you are!" Becca said.

Slowly, Desiree stepped out of the shadows. Desiree smoked the cigarette in two long drags before grinding it into the dirt. Blowing smoke from her crimson lips, she said, "I guess you want your money."

Her face was placid, even though beads of sweat creased her thick makeup. A cool night breeze sighed through the trees, sending a chill down Clementine and Rebecca's backs. Goose pimples covered their arms as Desiree counted out their cash. As they walked away, Desiree shouted, "And don't forget we have a photo shoot at the old Copacabana tomorrow morning. Be there early! We're meeting a new photographer at nine."

Just outside of earshot, Clementine mumbled, "Who could forget? We all know we'll catch hell if we're late."

"Nine sharp!" Desiree's voice echoed from a distance.

"You mean you'll catch hell, Lil-Miss-Sleep-Til-Noon. Besides, nine a.m. comes early, and the camera isn't forgiving when you're hungover and wearing bits of last night's makeup."

"But then again… neither is Desiree."

The two girls cackled as they got into their cars and went in two different directions.

PART TWO

COPACABANA (AT THE COPA)

CHAPTER THREE
CENTERFOLD

It was a crisp Saturday morning in early November. The breeze whispered a chill through the trees. Half-brittle leaves floated to the ground and collected in piles along the roadway. The sky was a clear blue canvas with thin, delicate strokes of white clouds. It was the kind of day Floridians lived for; the only time of year when the weather wasn't trying to kill people. No oppressive heat. No sweltering sun. No ravaging winds. No pounding rains. No sand shifting surf.

The beauty of the day was offset by the dilapidation of buildings in the original part of Palm Dunes. *This can't be the Old Florida of our dreams,* Rebecca thought. The street was lined with rusted, sun-bleached metal lanterns from the 1920s. Across the street, there was a run-down brick grocery store. The windows had been smashed out. The doors had large sheets of plywood with "No Trespassing" spray-painted in bright red. The building was surrounded by a chainlink fence that had broken 'for sale' signs barely hanging on. What the incessant marching of time hadn't done to damage the neighborhood, the constant rolling of hurricane season after hurricane season had. All that was left in the once beautiful town of Palm Dunes were the empty shells of once bustling businesses, and the active tent city located behind a warehouse a few streets down. It was a local haunt, reserved for the homeless or addicted, who were willing to venture to the other side of the canal.

Rebecca stood in front of the old Copacabana nightclub on the corner of Levine and Third, staring up at the faded neon sign. In its day, it was probably modern technology and the envy of the business block. Now, the glass tubes were discolored or busted. As Becca crossed the street, she could hear Desiree monologuing to the photographer about angles, poses, and what lighting was best for her fair complexion. Her burgundy lips appeared gothic in the pale morning light, like dried blood and vampire teeth. She looked beautiful, ethereal, dangerous. The rest of the troupe were awkwardly trying to be inconspicuous with feather boas and plumed headpieces. Clementine walked up carrying a large duffel bag full of makeup, costumes, and props. The green feather plume on her head teetered as she struggled with her luggage.

"You look like the slutty remake of *The Great Gatsby*," she said with a Cheshire grin. Desiree responded with a cold, sardonic smile. Her vampiric lips were reminiscently pursed with disapproval.

"You look like you're late as usual, I see. It's 9:30."

The photographer used the distraction as an opportunity to finally break away from Desiree. Walking quickly, he disappeared behind the building.

"Uh… yeah. Sorry about that, boss," Clementine remarked sheepishly. "I… uh… got held up."

"Save your excuses for someone who believes them."

Desiree turned her attention to Halona, as if picking up mid-conversation from a previous argument about costuming. The two women fiercely gestured with their hands as they walked toward the entrance to the abandoned bar.

"This place is sketchy. It gives me the creeps," Sasha said, looking over her shoulder, as she scanned the parking lot like an estranged ex-boyfriend was going to jump from behind a light pole. "How long are we gonna be here?"

"Oh, don't worry, Sash. We won't be here long," Becca attempted to soothe her paranoid mind.

"It's a nice morning for a murder, though," Clementine said as she wiggled her eyebrows and flashed a mischievous smile. Without waiting for a response, she hustled toward the building in an attempt to catch up with Desiree and Halona, who were several paces ahead.

"She's just teasing. I'm sure it's fine. You have nothing to worry about," Becca chimed. She awkwardly patted Sasha on the back and motioned for her to follow the others toward the club. Sasha gave a weak smile. It was clear to Becca that Sasha did not believe her.

"Ha. Ha. Very funny," Sasha shouted at Clementine. But Sasha was not reassured. She continued her search for unseen danger as she slowly wobbled toward the deserted club in her stilettos. Becca continued to reassure her of their safety, even though the neighborhood was a rough one.

Reaching the large double doors, Desiree whipped her head around and shouted, "Can you guys stop chattering!" Her disapproval was still ever-present and as evident as always. Her face was contorted in discontent. She glared over her shoulder, watching to see what the holdup was.

"S… sorry, Desiree," Sasha apologized, trying to walk faster in her high heels. As she approached, she hung her head and stood in silence. She had the most bubbly personality of any of the girls in the dance troupe, but she also had a crippling desire to appease. Desiree's nagging schoolmarm routine left Sasha in shambles more often than not.

"We MUST get some decent photos today," Desiree continued rambling to Halona, ignoring the threesome of women behind her, as if she were leading a group of rookie new hires on an office tour. "Otherwise, we're never gonna get the good out-of-town gigs that you've been begging for! We only made $400 last night, and that's before the owner's cut. I don't know about you guys, but that's not gonna cut it for me. We need to try other avenues."

Halona interrupted, "Have you contacted that club in Tampa, yet? The Velvet Rooster, or something. They said they were booking shows."

"Well, no… I can't very well book a decent gig at a nice club if we don't even have promo photos. I've been on you guys for weeks about this. There is an order to these things, Halona."

"I get that, but I thought you would have at least emailed them or something."

"This isn't my first dance troupe. I know what I'm doing. I assure you, I'll pass along any information that you need to know about upcoming gigs."

Halona threw her hands in the air, "Fine." She backed away from Desiree and stood by Sasha. The two seemed to have an unspoken conversation with the quirks of their eyebrows. No one was happy with Desiree's management style. But also, no one was bold enough to really challenge her on it. Halona was the only dancer to push back. And even she knew when to pick her battles with Desiree. In every conversation, there was a teetering line when Desiree's stubbornness exceeded the other girls' capacity for patience. They knew she wouldn't be swayed, no matter how logical the argument.

Distancing themselves from Desiree's open contempt, the girls stepped away from the door and back into the sunlight of the parking lot. Clementine hovered close to Rebecca, whispering, "Where did she even find this photographer guy?" She pointed toward the building, where he was last seen. Even though he wasn't there, she hid her pointing finger behind her other hand, concealing their attempt to gossip.

Mark or Max or What's-his-name, Becca thought, and shrugged. "No clue. But I hope he isn't as awful as the last one. Remember that brilliant idea?" Rebecca snorted.

"Oh, yeah. The infamous milk bath photos. I swear that photographer copped a feel of my tits."

"Girl, he probably did. He was making me uncomfy the whole shoot. Just kept looking me up and down. And you know—vibes don't lie."

"Uh-huh. Vibes never lie."

"Oh, Jesus… what about the time…" Becca was cut off by the sound of shattering glass. It caught everyone's attention, but the women didn't move. They listened intensely for another sound. They strained their ears for the approach of footsteps or the creaking of a door.

"Did you hear that?" Sasha said as she grabbed Halona's hand.

"Uh, huh." Clementine said, "I'm pretty sure someone just busted a window. Think it was 'What's his name?'"

"I don't know, but this doesn't sound like such a good idea after all. Why are we even having a shoot in an abandoned club? What's wrong with the club we danced at last night?" Halona gripped Sasha's hand tightly as the two edged further away from the door.

"Don't we have permission? You don't think he broke in, do you?" Rebecca paused, unsure of whether they should question Desiree about the professionalism of the photoshoot and whether or not it was entirely legal.

"It's for the aesthetic," Clemmie said, mimicking Desiree with air quotes and a Southern drawl.

Suddenly, the side door cracked open, and a hand came out. The photographer stuck his head out and waved the girls over. The clickety-clack of high heels echoed down the corridor like the incessant clomping of an early morning horse-drawn carriage on its way to a funeral.

The eerie creaking of a solid wooden door revealed heavenly white light as it poured into the dark room. Flecks of dust were afloat. It smelled like mold, the earthy bite of murky river water, and stale, burnt cigarettes. The girls coughed and choked as they stepped inside the club. Stirred by the smell of muddy water, some unpleasant memory flitted and fluttered at the edge of Rebecca's consciousness, but it was gone in an instant.

The vestibule was once luxurious with sweeping red velvet ropes and expensive furnishings. Tall columns lined the dance floor leading up to the stage. There was a thick layer of delicate dust covering the tops of the velvet ropes. It hung from the folds of the sheer drapes and fell in great clumps at the infiltration of fresh air. The floor was a neo-Byzantine mosaic with small tiles depicting a lion among beautiful gods and saints encircling a golden R in the center.

For a moment, as she was walking into the room, Rebecca was transported, like a moment of time travel or astral projection, to the nightclub's heyday in the 1920s when it bustled with mob rats and showgirls. For all of society's growth, maybe things weren't so different – there were still showgirls and mob rats. Rebecca wondered, *Were they like us? Did the girls dancing on that stage with their feather fans and exquisite costumes ever worry about what the neighbors would think? Did they fear the truth coming out? The reality that they weren't perfect cookie-cutter schoolgirls? Did they have an over-controlling mother like mine?* Becca was lost deep in her thoughts as they walked through the club, marveling at what once could have been. It seemed so romantic to her. Like some Gilded Age of the past, where men were suave and women were stunning. She slowly dropped her things on the floor, still marveling at her view, and slid her short denim skirt off.

Noticing her disassociation, Clementine crept up behind Rebecca, reared back her open palm, and swatted Becca hard on the butt. She jumped with a yelp as the daydream was broken.

Clementine cackled with a witchy laugh as Becca rubbed the throbbing handprint on the curve of her rear.

"I hope he doesn't take any pics of my ass! Now that your hand print is on there like a bright, neon sign!"

Clementine chuckled loudly as she went about preparing for the shoot. Becca also went about getting ready. It wasn't long before the two were lost in their preparations.

"Hand me that other headpiece, huh?" Clementine asked as she pointed absentmindedly to a large blue feather plume sticking out of her bag.

Halona and Sasha were unpacking props on a nearby table, whispering intently, momentarily glancing up at Desiree and Photo Guy, who were poking around on the stage, presumably looking for good natural lighting. The two girls continued to fiddle with boas, while Desiree and Photo Guy continued to look up and point. They seemed to be in a deep, heated discussion.

"That wasn't part of the deal...," Desiree blurted, before realizing her voice had risen. Halona and Sasha paused, startled by Desiree's assertive tone. She looked behind her to see if anyone had noticed her outburst. Halona and Sasha awkwardly scuttled away from the prop table and began adding the final touches of glitter to their makeup.

Rebecca and Clementine barely noticed the commotion because they were fussing over each other's hair. After Clemmie's final hose down of hairspray, Becca quickly unbuttoned her shirt, revealing her ample bust. She went about making the final adjustments to her costume nonchalantly. She turned to face the small mirror she brought with her. Her nipples had hardened as they met the cool air. The filtered light cast a soft shadow against the curve of her breasts, like storm clouds heavy with condensation. Clementine paused for a moment, watching Becca fidget with her pasties. She took special care to position the rhinestone star bursts strategically over the anatomical parts the State of Florida (and her mother) would consider indecent.

Clementine moved forward, "Here, let me," she said as she took the pasties and spread the liquid adhesive on the reinforced back. A lump of glue remained on the tip of her index finger. She inched closer to Becca, and felt the heat radiate from her skin. She bent forward and gently spread the remaining adhesive in a circle around Becca's tawny areola. Becca shivered as Clementine's cold hand touched her warm skin. Her areola constricted even more, making her nipples harden like thick butterscotch candy kisses.

"Hold still," she jokingly admonished, pressing the glittering stars onto Becca's breasts. She held the pasties in place for a moment. Looking up, she smiled at Becca. A twinkle of light in her eye caught Becca's attention.

"I... I got it," Becca said awkwardly as she covered the pasties with her own hands, "Thanks... for your help." Her cheeks blushed as she fluttered her eyelashes.

"Sure," Clementine flashed an embarrassed smile, "Uhhhh... can you check my thong and back seam? I... I don't want them to seem wonky." Clemmie stepped backward and removed her black wraparound skirt. She turned her back to Becca and twerked her butt for a moment, trying to get a laugh. "All good?"

"Yeah, you're good," Becca chuckled, "But you could use some spray tan on that white booty. Lookin' kinda pasty," Becca giggled.

"Ok, first off, rude! And secondly, it's ivory, not white," Clemmie flirted, "And thirdly, not everyone can have Halona's sun-kissed complexion." She said a little louder, trying to get Halona's attention.

Halona looked up, "Yeah, you right." She laughed, "We can't all be blessed with this much melanin."

Sasha burst out laughing and shouted, "We also can't all have a huge ass like you either, Clem."

She snorted and called back, "Y'all just jealous because I'm blessed." She folded her hands in prayer and winked at the other girls. They all cackled.

CHAPTER FOUR
NOWHERE TO RUN

A thunderous pounding fractured the merriment of the girls' laughter in the abandoned club. It echoed through the decrepit building like a church bell calling the masses to prayer. No one within earshot could ignore the forceful intonation thudding from beyond. The girls screeched, like demons shrinking from holy water. Halona jumped and spilled glitter everywhere. The purple flecks floated through the air before landing on the dingy red carpet. She looked toward the sound and watched in horror as the double doors shook violently. Rust crumbled from the aged metal hinges. Dust flurries exploded into the air. Light pried its itching fingers through the thin cracks of the wooden door and forced dried slivers open. Bright light clawed into the dim club. With every attack against the door, the hinges threatened to break. The wooden door bent and trembled against the forceful blows.

"What the hell was that?" Halona cursed.

A loud, cracking pop and metallic clink resounded in the background. A light flashed from backstage. It was the beam of a flashlight cutting through the darkness. The stream bobbed up and down as the person carrying it neared the vestibule.

A gruff masculine voice called out, "Alright, everybody freeze!"

Sasha jumped behind a large white column that was as thick as a palm tree, "Wa… wa…was that a… gunshot?" She was quivering as she pressed her back against the cold, white column. The cool plaster touching her bare skin made her shiver.

"What the fuck," Rebecca said as she froze in place. Her gloved hands covered her bare breasts like a shy virgin who'd been caught naked and unprepared on her wedding night. It was a pitiful attempt; two cantaloupes in a mesh grocery bag would have been more modest.

Praise god for pasties, Becca thought, *because they are all that remain between me and indecency.*

Clementine's gaze darted across the room, looking at each of the girls. Terror filled their faces as they scrambled to understand what was happening. Confusion and panic summoned their lizard brains.

Seeing the fear in them, like a silent whisper, she mouthed, "Don't move."

"Oh my god, oh my god, oh my god," Sasha gasped as she tried to make herself thinner in an effort to completely disappear, not just behind the column, but altogether from the situation, and ultimately, from reality. Sasha clutched at the plaster column with her sweaty hands. Tears immediately welled up in her large brown eyes.

Clementine dropped to her knees and began to crawl. She inched closer to the white column. Her hands motioned for Sasha to stay calm. No one else moved a muscle. Their eyes just continued shifting from one another – from Rebecca to Halona to Sasha and back again to Clementine, unsure of what to do next. It was like a terrifying game of round robin.

"I said, FREEZE, DAMN IT!" The voice roared as it came closer, "The next person who moves gets shot!"

With a final crash, like a great log ramming into the doors, the hinges clattered to the ground. The doors toppled inward. Two men pushed through where the large wooden doors had once hung. One of the men held a red, metal battering ram in his hands. The other man held a pistol at the ready. The sharp metallic scrape echoed in the room as he cocked the gun. The two men stood poised on top of the abused door. The light pouring into the dimly lit club made it difficult for the girls to see the faces of the men who surrounded them. The man who entered from the back of the building shouted at the two men who had broken in, "It's about fucking time! What took so long?" The men jumped, as if commanded. "Get a move on, ladies!"

A voice echoed over a bullhorn, "Everyone outside the building now!"

Oh god. This is real. Be cool! Be cool, Rebecca!

Becca's mind was racing as she tried to calm herself. She didn't want to react out of panic. But instead, she was spiraling, her feet were frozen in place, and her body was rigid with fear, like she had awoken from a night terror. She begged her legs to run. But they didn't budge. She clenched her eyes tight as she tried to picture something calming. *Mind over matter. Mind over matter. Mind over matter,* she chanted to herself. As she opened her eyes, the men had pushed further into the room, and there were more of them. The squad was approaching the stage area, where the girls huddled. They had their guns aimed at the group, approaching with caution.

Clementine had crawled to Sasha undetected. She held out her hand. Sasha lurched forward into Clemmie's arms. Tears were streaming down her face. Her mascara carved a path to her chin. Securing Sasha, they scrambled like rats, rushing toward Halona. She dragged Sasha behind her, and the three huddled beside Rebecca. Clementine grabbed Rebecca's hand, squeezing it tightly.

"Deep breath. It's just the police… not your crazy-ass mom," Clementine whispered into Becca's ear with a smirk.

Rebecca scoffed. "Well, if I'm gonna get arrested and miss Mother's mandatory Sunday dinner tomorrow, at least I'm with my favorite people." She tried to laugh off her panic and sound brave. She gulped the hard knot in her throat down as she feigned a laugh. Clementine saw the panic in her eyes and squeezed her hand tighter.

"Atta girl," Clementine cheered her on. Her eyes were light and pleading, like a worried mother, coaxing a terrified child. "Now there's a healthy perspective!"

Quickly and quietly, the girls and the photographer were ushered outside into the parking lot. As the men stepped out of the silhouette of the doorway, the girls got a good look at their uniforms. Two or three officers came back through the door, along with their battering ram, wearing full tactical gear and helmets. However, a couple of the men were also incredibly well-dressed in tailored suits, including the gruff-voiced man who announced their presence and fired his weapon. If it weren't for the flashes of badges, bullets, and guns, you'd think they would have been off to the next executive board meeting at Boeing.

Regardless, there was no indication they were anything other than the finest law enforcement officers the city of Palm Dunes' had to offer. Especially considering the excessive show of force for a group of girls trespassing in an abandoned building. Waves of blue and red light flashed from the multiple vehicles in the parking lot. Two undercover SUV cruisers and a single undercover Dodge Charger blocked the entrance to the club. The police presence surrounded the girls and the photographer.

"MATTHIAS GREENE," the man with the robust voice called out, "Is there any condemned building in this town we WON'T find you in?"

All eyes fell on the shifty man with the camera.

Matt… that's what his damn name was, Rebecca thought.

"Just documentin' our local history for posterity, ya' honor," Matt quipped with a sheepish grin.

"Yeah," the man said as he started towards Matt & Desiree. He slid his gun into the holster and took a good, long look at the girls, ogling them in their state of undress on his way over. "I can see that," he said with a lecherous grin. The girls shifted uneasily in their stilettos and platform heels. They bunched closer together to hide their nakedness. Shame crept over them.

"It looks to me like trespassing is now a prerequisite for your base charges," the cop chuckled.

"Oh, come on! Ya know, no one has been at the Cabana for nearly a decade."

"Matthias, we go over this every time." The robust officer glanced at the building for a quick once-over, before continuing, "and based on that smashed window in the back, I'm gonna go ahead and say the breaking and entering belongs to you, too."

Matt threw his hands in the air, "No one lives 'ere! You know that!" His voice became rigid and strained. "We. Weren't. Hurting. Nobody! And that ol' man who owns it won't restore it anyway, busted window or nah. What's his name, anyways? Rigamaroll, Rainsomething… He's a cheapskate. What's it gonna hurt for me to get a few snaps in there?"

Matt's train of thought continued in his accented ramble, almost as if he were reading from a script of how to fail miserably at negotiations. The troupe stood by and watched the farce continue — huddled, still in costume, getting increasingly colder. Even with the morning sun moving towards afternoon, the weather was unseasonably crisp for Florida, and the lack of fabric was becoming increasingly more noticeable. The girls looked at each other, quizzically, wondering when the melodrama of the photographer would finally cross the line far enough for Desiree to step in. His theatrics had bewildered them. But what struck the girls most was that for the first time in their collective experience in the troupe, Desiree was stunningly, eerily silent.

Matt cleared his throat for his next salvo, "I mean, we're already here. Can't I just snap a couple of photos with some beautiful girls, and we'll be on our way? I'll make it worth your while…"

The girl's widened their eyes and dropped their jaws in shock and horror. They knew a bribe attempt when they heard one, and as a wad of cash made its way out of Matt's pocket and clearly into the field of vision of Palm Dune's finest, their voices rang out as one in equal protest.

"Whoa, whoa, whoa, whoa!" They cried in unison.

"He is NOT our—"

"What the fuck, man?! I didn't sign up—"

"We did not ask for—"

"Oh, my god—"

"Des! SAY SOMETHING!"

The calamity of their din echoed in the parking lot.

"HEY!" Robust Cop shouted, quieting the troupe instantly, "Keep your Kentucky fried fuckin' voices down, ya hens. Lest you forget—as far as I know, y'all are accomplices to this mess, and I have ZERO problem having you all turned in and booked for indecent exposure right now! So, calm. The fuck. DOWN."

Sasha shuddered into compliance. Meanwhile, Halona glared, mouth agape at being called a "hen." Desiree remained disconcertingly silent. She was still, like a living statue awaiting final judgment. Becca and Clem, however, shook their heads at each other, as if they were reading each other's minds, as they so often did. Their conversation from earlier echoed in Becca's mind, *Vibes don't lie.* She couldn't place her finger on it but there was something very off about the entire scene. Clementine's voice seemed to whisper in her head, *The cop's language. The photog's confidence.*

Robust Cop continued, "Matthias, I am in one helluva mood today, and I didn't bring these boys out here for nothing, so I'll tell you what... why don't you go ahead and pass me that roll so we can finish this?"

Matt smiled like a Cheshire cat and placed the roll of hundred-dollar bills in the cop's hand. "I was hoping you'd see a way through this," he sleazed.

"I sure do," Robust Cop replied, only to follow up his retort with a swift punch with his free hand to Matt's face, knocking him to the ground, "Trespassing, B and E, and now, bribery! Thank you SO MUCH for the evidence. You got any drugs on you while you're at it? Go ahead—GIVE ME something else to pin on you."

Two uniformed cops ran forward, handcuffed, and began patting Matt down. The girls exhaled a collective sigh of relief, as though they were all saying, "Finally, a reasonable move from Palm Dunes: SVU."

The second well-dressed officer — a tall, black gentleman who could've been a dead ringer for Idris Elba — stepped between the girls and the scuffle on the ground. His tone was calm and collected, almost soothing in comparison to the gruff brashness that emitted from the Officer-In-Charge.

"You'll have to excuse my partner's manners," he started in, "If I can be honest, Mr. Greene has been a thorn in our side for some time."

Becca opened her mouth to offer a very coquettish, Southern platitude of understanding, that would impress her well-bred mother, only to be interrupted by Clementine.

"I'm not gonna lie," Clementine lashed out, "this whole thing feels fuckin' OFF! I mean... did y'all really need to bring out ALL these people for one guy? You're actin' like you caught us in a ritual murder not gettin' ready for killer photos!"

"I appreciate you being forthcoming," the handsome officer's tone was calm and professional. "We received an anonymous tip fitting Mr. Greene's description, allegedly leading a gang into the Copacabana. In situations such as these, and given Mr. Greene's history, we must follow protocol," the calm cop continued. "Unfortunately, the 'gang' portion wasn't exactly described as 'five women in feather boas… and varying degrees of nudity.'"

His eyes drifted to Becca's curved breasts, capped with glittering pasties, and raised an eyebrow. She blushed, and began toying with her hair. Matthias yelled as the uniformed officers lifted him off the ground and lead him toward the Charger. The handsome cop continued, "Given Mr. Greene's said criminal history, the overall condition of the building, and now the breaking and entering, we have no choice but to call this a crime scene."

"Wait, what?" shouted Halona, "HE'S the one that broke in, NOT US!"

"And I'm sure given proper review and questioning down at the station, that'll be proven as such," said the cop flatly. He outreached his arms to begin corralling the women towards the unmarked SUVs, "If you ladies will kindly come this way."

Something tickled at the back of Becca's mind, *Vibes don't lie. Something is not right.* She had had enough. She spun around to face the officer, her voice no longer flirtatious, "Can I at least get something to cover—."

"Crime scene," he intoned professionally, immediately cutting her off. "All possessions in the building will be treated as evidence until cleared." He continued walking forward, herding the women to the vehicle, "We'll get you covered at the station, ma'am."

"But, all of our stuff is in there. Phones… IDs… Everything. We can't even get our IDs to prove who we are?"

"Like I said, ma'am, it's a crime scene."

Becca huffed and stumbled over her heels as she attempted to walk backward. Crossing her arms in a tantrum, she turned around, and briskly caught up with Clementine. But internally, a voice nagged at her, *Vibes don't lie. Something is not right.*

Sasha seemed to shrink into Halona the closer they got to the vehicle. Halona pulled her in trying to comfort her. "Hal, I'm scared," she whispered. Hal caressed her hair, and patted her gently on the back.

As suddenly as she seemed to take a vow of silence earlier during the theatrics, Desiree began screaming like she was Joan of Arc being burned at the stake. She thrashed against one of the tactical officers — weakly and not nearly enough to get away, but exactly enough to make a scene. The girls looked startled, then puzzled. They knew Desiree to be domineering, not dangerous. This was not typical behavior for her, but circumstances often brought out the worst in people. Seeing Desiree tug at the officers hair, and snatch her arm free, the robust officer came running back from loading Matt into his vehicle.

"Hey! Hey! None of that shit. Cuff her! Book her for resisting arrest."

"Wait, I thought we were only going in for questioning," Halona yelled.

"And it'll only be questioning UNLESS you wanna end up like your friends here," retorted Robust Cop loudly, "Now, move your asses."

The handsome cop grabbed Clementine by the arm and pulled her toward the open doors of one SUV, while Desiree got cuffed by another tactical officer and placed in a separate SUV. Clementine was already in full momma bear mode; fierce, professional, and attempting to talk her way out of a mess.

"THIS IS HORSESHIT," she proclaimed. The handsome cop eyed her suspiciously, as if she were dangerously close to receiving the same treatment as Desiree. She shirked, and added, "RESPECTFULLY," as he shoved her into the back seat.

Halona and Sasha were next. Halona unwrapped her arm from around Sasha's waist. She knew that Sasha was barely 19 and had never gotten in any type of trouble, so she did her best to comfort her as she cried. They held hands as they slid into the back of the SUV. Becca was last, surrounded by doubt and a constant nagging in her heart, *Vibes don't lie.* But her weakness for guilt and shame — especially the kind spewed by her devout Christian mother with prudent pursed lips and no patience for independent thought — overtook and outcried any of her gut instincts. She waved them away like all of the other realities and truths that had whispered in her heart since she was a young girl. Maybe that was the uniting factor; there was solidarity among the girls as they all knew what it was like growing up with oppression and fighting an inherent desire to be different in a world where everyone was the same.

CHAPTER FIVE
HELP I'M ALIVE

The SUVs turned off their lights and cleared out of the parking lot with a swiftness typically reserved for presidential convoys. The undercover Charger and its passenger, criminal trespasser Matthias Greene, stayed behind. Its driver, the cop with the robust voice, watched as the SUVs faded into the distance. The cop oversaw the area. No public presence, no protesting nuisances. This portion of downtown Palm Dunes remained ghostly, and all was quiet on the Copacabana front. The robust officer closed his eyes and drank in the silence and afternoon sun. This was what he lived for — those moments after the chaos, when he could revel in the bust and take the time to reset before moving forward with the next duty. He pulled a pack of Lucky Strikes out of his suit coat, ejected a cigarette from the pack with a flick of the wrist, and placed it in his mouth. He then put the pack back into his coat, grabbed his lighter out of his pants pocket, and gave it a few flicks before a butane flame appeared. Just as he went to light the cigarette, a muffled voice called out from inside the vehicle.

"Hey! Heyyyyyyyyyyyy! I think they're gone. Can you let me out now? These seats fucking suck, man."

The interruption deflated the robust man's ritual; his dream bubble of noir nostalgia burst. With the flame still hovering close to the tip of the cigarette, he lit it quickly, took a drag, and opened the Charger door, allowing Mr. Matthias Greene to scoot out of the backseat and stand up.

"Uggggh! Thanks, man. My ass was killing me," Matt thankfully sighed, his nondescript accent now completely gone, "Do you mind? They're a little tighter than usual." Matt gestured towards his cuffed hands. Robust Cop laughed.

"You WERE resisting arrest after all. I could still have you taken in," the cop chuckled, his own robust bravado having faded away. He took another slow drag of his Lucky Strike.

"You and I both know that's not happening," Matt replied, with another silent head nod to his bound wrists.

Robust Cop sighed out plumes of smoke, another deflated note of defeat. "Yeah. I absolutely hate it when you're right," he gruffly resigned while using his free hand to pull his keys out, "I gotta ask as per usual, you aren't gonna do anything stupid, are you?" The cop stuck his cigarette between gritted teeth and began to unlock the handcuffs.

"Not on your life. The boss pays too well," Matt retorted, rubbing his free wrists, "Speaking of, you still got that roll? I'll need it for the next time we do this dog-and-pony show. And speaking of next time, can you NOT slug me in the face? Damn, man, that shit hurt." He rubbed at his sore chin, wincing as his thumb grazed over a purpling bruise.

"Like you said, dog-and-pony show. If we're gonna keep doing these sorts of favors for the boss, we gotta make it look convincing." He paused, taking a long drag from his cigarette, "For any potential onlooking public too," the cop took his arm around Matt and started leading him back into the club, "Come on, no one's out today. Let's go ahead and get this place reset for next time."

The two men re-entered the club. Robust Cop offered Matthias a pair of latex gloves. Upon placing the gloves onto their hands, they immediately became silent partners of their own clean-up crew, and knew each other's moves like they had been doing this for years. The cop dragged over a barrel to the center of the golden R in the floor, while Matthias began throwing pieces of feathered headgear into it, shooting like a basketball player. They gathered all of the troupe's belongings — clothes, purses, makeup, even phones — into a pile that eventually filled the barrel to the brim.

"Hey, man," Matt said, breaking the working silence as he brought the last couple of heavy pieces of the girl's belongings to the barrel, "I did want to say... I'm sorry I forgot my keys this time. You have a more direct line to the boss. You think he can forgive a single broken window for the sake of getting these girls to him?"

The cop took a heavy drag of his cigarette. The ash glowed bright red as the tip of the cigarette threatened to crumble to the ground. His face looked concerned, as if he were pondering that simple question like he was pondering the origin of the universe. After a couple of beats, he spoke.

"I don't know, Matt. The window? Maybe. I imagine that's easy for him to replace, and he's got the means. But those doors? I'm fairly certain those doors were original to the building. Pretty antique. 'A wonder of 20th-century architecture,' or whatever he'd call it. Had you not broken the window, we wouldn't have had to break in; we could've just walked in and called it done. That, Matt? That may take some convincing."

Nervousness crept into Matt's throat. "Oh.... ohhh," he stuttered. "I... didn't mean for all that to happen. Had I known y'all were gonna go through those big doors instead of the side, I would've found the time—"

The cop raised his hand, with the lit cigarette still intact and wedged between the tips of his fingers, pausing another pre-scripted Matthias ramble of excuses. "I know you would've, Matt," sighed Robust Cop, "I know you would've."

With a swift flick of his wrist, the cop dropped his cigarette hand, drew his weapon, and fired a shot directly into Matthias's temple. Matt's body went limp and crumbled onto the Neo-Byzantine floor. The arterial spray lingered in the light as it mixed with the dusty air. The cop sighed again. "Sorry, Matt," he said to the body still twitching on the floor, "You done good, but you got sloppy. The boss decided to let you go. Not my call."

Almost as if on cue, the cop's phone started vibrating in his pocket. He flicked the still-lit cigarette into the barrel, holstered his weapon, and took the call.

"Hello?"

The sultry voice of an older woman purred on the other end, "Is it done?"

"Yeah. We got a clean up on aisle three over here, but the grocery getters are on their way."

"Leave it. I'll have the crew come collect the dog food. You have more important things to deal with," she replied sternly, with an immediate click afterwards.

"Yes, fuckin', ma'am," the cop replied sarcastically into the ether as he put his phone away, "Fuckin' nice morning for a murder anyway."

As the cop began making his way out of the Copacabana, smoke billowed from the barrel; the last embers of his Lucky Strike were reborn into flame against the sequins and feathers. The flames licking the inside of that barrel became hot enough to destroy everything within it. Fabric to ash. Makeup to molten lava. Plastic and glass, and SIM cards melted into a singular, unrecognizable pile. Everything else would fall into the atmosphere — more dust with the rest of the ash that covered the Copacabana. This was now the site of the burlesque troupe's final performance — a magic act for the ages; five women disappearing without a trace, and the only evidence was a dead photographer swimming in a glittery pool of his own blood.

PART THREE

DO I WANNA KNOW

CHAPTER SIX
ROAD TRIPPIN

As the SUV pulled out of the parking lot, Becca looked behind her to catch a glimpse of Desiree and Matt. But there was no sign of either of them. The other black SUV that Desiree had been stuffed into turned the opposite direction as it hit the highway. The cruiser that held Matthias Greene was still parked in front of the Copacabana. Even Hot Cop who had escorted her out of the club earlier, had vanished into thin air, presumably, and to her dismay, in the SUV that carried Desiree. Becca swooned over how undeniably attractive he was, well-dressed in a pressed black suit, a gold Gucci wristwatch, and polished leather monk-strap Jimmy Choo shoes. He seemed so charming before, unlike his partner, Robust Cop, who roughly referred to them as hens. He was firm and authoritative, but had a strange calmness that allured her. She had wanted to be confrontational with him about getting her things. She had wanted to fight against the injustice of being treated like a criminal, but instead, she felt her anger slither away and become replaced with the throb of desire when he shut her down earlier.

However, the man who was driving the SUV was far less attractive to Becca. Officer Jones had mousy brown, slicked-back hair, chalky white teeth, and an odor like onions. Crude and simple. She squinted her eyes suspiciously as she watched him in the rear-view mirror. He noticed her eyes watching him intently and flashed a chalky smile at her.

That smile…

It unsettled her. It was eerily similar to the one that was proudly on display in a gilded frame on the Coleman family mantel, and it had been there since her sister, Ruth, graduated from high school more than a decade ago. The image of that photo flashed in her memory. Two pimply teenagers, awkwardly posed in evening wear with a fake backdrop of the Eiffel Tower behind them, and the coarse light of a school gymnasium casting marring shadows around them. She could almost smell the musky cologne blending with a mist of Aqua-net and the rotting sweetness of a wilting corsage. *An Evening in Paris,* Becca mused. As a kid, it seemed so glamorous to her. Now, she felt a twinge of embarrassment for her sister as if the boy behind that chalky smile and musty cologne might have been Ruth's peak romantic interest.

A hunger pang reverberated in her belly. Rebecca's head began to swim with delirium. Her stomach lurched with queasiness as the SUV crossed over a rough set of train tracks. Looking out the dark-tinted window of the SUV, she saw the Palm Dunes Police Station just past the next traffic light. The SUV slowed to a stop at the light. They were almost there and could get this mess sorted out. She could state her case to someone reasonable and they would be released and taken back to their cars parked at the Copacabana. The traffic light flashed green, and the SUV accelerated. She felt the engine shift from first to second gear as they gained speed. But instead of slowing to turn into the police station parking lot, the engine shifted into third gear. Becca's mouth fell agape as she realized they were turning onto the highway, headed out of Palm Dunes, instead of stopping at their intended destination.

"You passed the station," Clementine blurted.

"Now, don't you worry your pretty little head about that."

The girls nervously glanced at each other.

"Where are you taking us, if not to the police station?" Halona pushed on, "You said you were taking us into the police station."

"Did I say that? You must be mistaken."

"Um… no. We were specifically told that we were being taken in for questioning," Becca's voice was strained as she gulped her panic down.

The officer chuckled, "I'm taking you in for questioning, alright. But I'm not taking you ladies to the police station."

Panic fully settled in the pit of Becca's stomach like a clump of hard, dry cement and her mind began slowly unraveling.

NOW I'm panicking! Vibes don't lie. We're not being taken in for questioning. I'm not gonna make it to Mother's house for Sunday dinner. She'll know something is wrong…. My poor mother! She'll die from shame… I can see it now, she and Ruth will find out about the news over the spiral honey-baked ham. She'll blame herself… Oh God! And say she was a bad mother. Or that she must have done something to fail me. She'll say she can't believe I could do something so callous. She'll say that I'm selfish. She'll lament about how I've let the family down… and how she can't hold her head up high in church anymore. Fuck… And worst of all, she'll condemn me to the full weight of her God-damned guilt. Her eyes staring, silently judging, with those lips… ugh… always faithfully pursed with condescension. I can hear her now…'You're from a good family, Rebecca Lynne, and here you are acting like common low-life trash! You were raised better.' She'll huff and pout. And Sexy Jesus in his slutty little loincloth will watch lustily from the cross hung over the dining room table. And Ruth! Ugh, Ruth will have a field day with how much of a disappointment I am.

Clementine leaned toward Rebecca and whispered, "This might be worse than we imagined. We're going in the wrong direction. It looks like we are heading out of town."

Tears slowly rolled down Becca's round, rouged cheeks, "Mother is going to lose her shit when I don't show up for Sunday dinner tomorrow," she murmured.

"Wherever we are going, at least we are all together," Clementine whispered, as tears welled up in her eyes. Rebecca gave Clementine a weak smile. Her eyes were red and puffy as she tried to wipe away the tears. But they had already streaked down her face, leaving coarse lines of black mascara and glitter.

Of all the messes to get yourself into, Rebecca thought as she returned her gaze to the passenger window of the SUV. Spindly pine trees blurred. Memories of her childhood flooded her brain. All she could think about was how Russell, her brother, was always in and out of trouble, and how she was so much like him and yet completely different. Her tears blurred along with the trees as her memories became clearer.

Her older siblings, Russell and Ruth, were always accusing her of being "mother's favorite." Throughout her life, her opinion of that accusation had shifted from pride to annoyance to disgust. Being the youngest of three and the favorite of those three was a heavy burden to bear when Mother had such high expectations. For every time Russell slammed a door in anger, Rebecca did the chores without being asked. Every time Russell got caught smoking cigarettes in the boys' bathroom at school, Rebecca brought home a straight-A report card. When Russell and his friends were picked up by the cops for breaking into the high school gym, Rebecca was home with Mother, memorizing Bible verses.

Ye have heard that it hath been said, An eye for an eye, and a tooth for a tooth: But I say unto you, That ye resist not evil: but whosoever shall smite thee on thy right cheek, turn to him the other also… Matthew 5, 38-39.

Maybe it wasn't exactly tit-for-tat, but Rebecca felt the overwhelming responsibility of perfection because she was 'the baby' and 'Mother's favorite.' Her mother would say, "God blessed me with you, Rebecca Lynne. I prayed for an angel and God gave me you."

Her whole life, Rebecca had the reputation of being an overachiever on a quest for perfection. She worked endlessly for good grades, always tried to be a model Christian, and never went to any of the parties that her peers went to (or anywhere at all without Mother, for that matter). So, the guilt of not actually being perfect was a hard pill to swallow, especially knowing that her image of goodness was brought about by her guilt-ridden overcompensations to please Mother and, as such, was a complete and utter lie.

Perfection was a figment of Becca's imagination. Just like Becca's belief in God was a figment of Mother's imagination. Rebecca believed no more in God's existence than she did in her own goodness. Even her baptism was performative, an attempt to placate Mother, who questioned her relentlessly about why she was over the age of ten and still had not accepted Jesus Christ into her heart. So, the summer Rebecca turned eleven, she answered the call to the altar on the last night of Christian Camp.

The Devil was an angel too, she mused.

Deep down, some reckless part of her was jealous of Russell. Mother never nagged him about going to Sunday School. He was feral and wild, and most importantly, free to make his own choices. She secretly loved the idea of shattering that fake Rebecca, who memorized Bible verses and replacing her permanently with a Rebecca that was bold, confident, and the exact opposite of who she was raised to be – just like her burlesque persona, Bella Valentina. It was a silly, made-up name, inspired by a character from her favorite movie. Becca knew how it felt to live life as a small-town girl who felt trapped, and surrounded by toxic masculinity, but also she really loved libraries. But there was something about having an alter-ego that made her feel invincible.

Officer Jones continued to look in the rear-view mirror, attempting to make eye contact with Rebecca, but was unable to capture her attention. She was lost in the haze of her nostalgia when he interrupted, "Hey, you in the nipple hats! You look familiar. Do I know you?"

"Who, me?" Rebecca's voice rasped as she spoke. She coughed to clear her dry throat.

"Yeah, YOU. What's your name?"

"Um… Rebecca."

"You got a last name, Um-Rebecca?"

"Oh, um. Coleman. It… It's, um, Coleman."

"You from around here, Um-Rebecca-Um-Coleman?"

"Yeah."

"Yeah? That's it? Ok, like from where?"

"Where?"

"Yeah, where? Where are you from?"

"East Creekview. I was raised in East Creekview."

"Yeah, I thought so." He flashed that chalky smile again, but there was something sinister behind it. "I knew you looked familiar. I used to date your sister… what's-her-name?"

That smile! Becca's heart hardened. "Ruth," she said flatly. "My sister's name is Ruth."

"Right. Right. That's her. I can't believe you're Ruth's baby sister. 'Course she wasn't as pretty as you. Never was. What a small world. I mean…I didn't know I was pickin' you up today."

The blood drained from Rebecca's face. She felt the urge to cover herself so she could maintain at least a little of the modesty she had left. She brought her arms awkwardly up to her chest and attempted to create a barrier between her and the leering eyes of Officer Jones. Instead, her hands fumbled together helplessly and connected as if in prayer.

"I remember you from Sunday School. Your momma used to be at church every time the doors were open. Your sister, too! You used to be a good kid. How'd you get in with this riff-raff?"

Rebecca couldn't bring herself to answer. She hung her head in shame, as tears welled up in her eyes again. She looked past her praying hands with her fingers tightly interlaced, past the supple curve of her cleavage and the thin glittery edge of her pasties that kept her from indecency, and down at her pale legs covered only by the transparent layer of her nude thigh-high pantyhose, and felt the last drops of goodness within her drip away.

As the SUV slowed down and took a turn off the highway, Officer Jones chuckled to himself, "Ruth Coleman's baby sister, how 'bout dat?" He drove the SUV slowly, winding down the dirt road. They had crept along for what seemed like an hour when, just past a curve, they saw an open metal gate with the insignia of an 'R' on it. Officer Jones drove through and continued down the dirt road for several miles. After he passed another large bend in the road, he stopped the car and looked in the rear-view again.

"Look, I don't wanna cause any drama with your family. I used to be in good with Ruth, ya know. Hell, I'm the man who popped her cherry." His eyes twinkled in the rearview mirror, "And I know you used to be a good kid."

"Can you please just take us back to our cars? I told you already. We weren't doing nothin' wrong," Clementine interrupted. Her face was set with a suspicious contempt as she glared at the cop. She was leaning past Becca, as if she were a protective barrier.

"I… I'm still a good person," Rebecca squeaked into her praying hands. Her words were barely a whisper, more like a prayer than she intended. "Please… just don't tell Mother you saw me like this. She'll be so brokenhearted!"

Feeling Clementine hovering near her, Rebecca lifted her head with renewed gumption. She stared intently into the rear-view mirror. Her gaze locked with Jones' dull brown eyes. Having lived life on a pedestal, she'd never begged for anything, but now it was time.

"How can we convince you? What will it take? I promise we won't say anything to anybody. Just let us go," Becca hesitated, "And don't tell Mother… or Ruth."

"I'll make a deal with you if you do a little favor for me. I'll let you go, and we can pretend this didn't happen." Officer Jones let out a mischievous laugh, "Mrs. Coleman and good ol' Ruth won't know nothing 'bout it."

"Whatever you want," cried Sasha, interrupting the negotiation. Her voice shook. She and the other girls had watched the saga between Rebecca and Officer Jones with bated breath. But at the opportunity of release, Sasha, Halona, and Clementine all began talking over each other, pleading for their freedom.

"Capt'n was right. Y'all are a bunch a damn hens! Now, hush up and let me speak."

The din of their voices filled the cabin of the SUV. Officer Jones whirled around and glared at them beyond the black steel cage that divided the front seat from the back seat. The ferocity of his glare caught them mid-lament and hastily ended the noise.

He drew a deep breath, "As I was sayin' before ya'll started squawking, if you do a favor for me, I'll release you. I cain't take you back to your cars, but I'm sure you can find your own way. All you hafta do is deliver this envelope to the cabin at the end of this road." Officer Jones lifted a manila envelope out of the passenger seat and flashed another insidious, chalky smile.

"Done!" Sasha shouted. Nervous laughter erupted from her throat as she let out a sigh of relief. "That's so easy. We'll do it!"

"That's it? That's all we have to do? Deliver an envelope?" Rebecca's eyes narrowed as she searched Officer Jones' face for some hidden agenda. She looked to the other girls, "Are we sure about this?" Sasha nodded her head vigorously. Halona's eyes widened as if to suggest there was no other choice.

"You're gonna let all of us go? Just like that?" Clementine cut her eyes at Jones, "And then what?"

"Oh, don't worry. You'll be well taken care of at the Chalet. Ms. Antoinette is a gracious host."

"Ok, fine, we'll do it," Becca quickly agreed. "As long as you promise you won't mention a word of this... to anyone! Especially Mother and Ruth."

Officer Jones stepped out of the SUV and opened the back door to release the four women. Cautiously, Sasha, Halona, and Clementine shimmied out of the SUV. As they stood in the soft dirt, their heels dug in, and they wobbled to balance themselves. Officer Jones watched Becca closely as she slid out of the passenger seat.

"Remember, if you keep your end of the deal, I'll keep mine." He held out his hand as she attempted to balance in the soft sand. As she took his hand, he pulled her closer and whispered, "But if you don't, I'll find you, and you'll have more to worry about than your mommy finding out you're a fuckin' whore."

Officer Jones shoved the manila envelope into Rebecca's hands. He turned on his heels and looked at the other women, "Give Ms. Antoinette my regards. Tell her I said the pharmacy is closed."

Without waiting for a response, he got back into the driver's seat of the Escalade, and whipped a U-turn, heading back toward the highway.

The dust kicked up by the SUV's tires sent an orangish-brown cloud wafting toward Halona, Rebecca, Clementine, and Sasha. The four women stood in the middle of the dirt road in a haze, nearly naked, and contemplating what they should do next. Rebecca's long legs wobbled as she tried to maintain her balance in high heels as she stood in the soft russet sand. Feeling unsteady, she attempted to balance on the gray gravel interspersed amongst the sand. Clementine giggled as she watched Becca totter from side to side.

"You look like a big titty flamingo on one foot!" Clemmie laughed so hard she snorted as Becca tried to steady herself. "Here, take your heels off," she said as she reached down and unbuckled Becca's heels and slid them off her feet one after the other. "You won't be able to walk like that anyway." The gravel she used for support earlier stabbed into the soft arches of her feet and tore runs into her pantyhose, causing them to ladder up to her knees.

"Well, what'll we do now?" Sasha asked, "How're we gonna get that delivered and then get us back home?"

Rebecca stared at the long path in front of her. She squinted her eyes, trying to see as far down the road as she could, but the cloud of dust distorted her vision. She thought about her brother again and laughed, *What would Russell do? He was so conniving… and brave. He was in the Army for five years before he died. He'd know exactly how to take care of himself. Russell would know what to do.* Rebecca desperately missed her brother and wished with all of her heart that he was still alive, so he could swoop in and save her. She closed her eyes for a moment and whispered a tiny prayer to him, begging for some ingenious plan.

Maybe there is a heaven. Maybe he's looking down on us now… watching me… stand in the middle of the road, nearly naked, like a damn fool. And maybe, Rebecca let out a deep sigh, *You're just talking to yourself.*

CHAPTER SEVEN
TAKE ME HOME, COUNTRY ROADS

Country roads were a foundational aspect of life for anyone who was raised in a small town. Much like Rebecca's hometown, East Creekview, all those dirt roads seemed to bind the community together in unexpected ways. Like a web of sand, clay, and stone that offered refuge to any teenager who wanted adventure, but most importantly, secrecy. Rebecca remembered the gossip from high school and the stories she heard from Russell about how it was the place where boys hung out all night drinking beer and looking for trouble. Most of Russell's stories either ended with some dude throwing up or passing out in the bushes. He talked about it like it was a rite of passage. The entrance from childhood to adulthood. Somehow, consuming ridiculous amounts of alcohol and not dying from it is what made boys into men. Sometimes the stories ended with car crashes. Drunk driving that resulted in dead bodies and the community lamenting the stolen lives of their promising, young men. But through the devastation of lives lost, no one ever made a change or even suggested a remedy. That was just the way it was; an accepted tragedy of country society. "Boys will be boys," the old folks would say.

For so many young girls, those country roads were the birthplace of womanhood, where virginity was lost, broken families were formed, and lives were changed. Unlike the boys, the girls were judged harshly for their behavior. Whispered words behind backs; "whore," and "slut" were commonplace. Even grown folks blamed the girls for their poor decisions, because they "shouldn't have been dressed that way," or "shouldn't have been in the woods," or "shouldn't have been drinking." Too many girls accepted their high school diplomas with swollen pregnant bellies.

But unlike the situation with the boys, the public outcry was echoed by teenage pregnancy statistics passed down from the State of Florida. The governor fervently called for sex education in schools and an increased availability of condoms at the health department. Somehow, the State of Florida had to protect those girls from themselves. The churches took a different approach to save those heathen girls from their sinful ways. Instead of teaching safe sex, they preached about abstinence, handed out promise rings, and formed special youth groups for girls who were 'saving themselves for marriage.' These groups were bursting at the seams with compliant, proper, young girls. The boys were still drinking in the woods.

Rebecca's own introduction to womanhood happened several years after she slipped that promise ring on her finger at the "See You at The Pole" rally in front of her high school. She gave her virginity away after she began college. But it still happened in those same woods in a cramped four-door sedan, to a boy who went to church every Sunday, and away to college on a music scholarship for trombone. There was no late-night party or copious amounts of alcohol or a scantily dressed Rebecca; just two eighteen-year-olds lost in their hormones.

Even though the women of the dance troupe were far from Rebecca's hometown, the country road and woods around them looked the same. The noonday sun was mostly blocked by the canopy of the forest, dappling the road. A breeze stirred through the trees, reminding Rebecca of her near-nakedness. She was still wearing her photoshoot outfit. She held the large manila envelope close to her. She wished she had grabbed a t-shirt or a hoodie or anything before being escorted out of the Copacabana. But Hot Cop's diligence left her standing in the middle of the forest in a set of sparkly pasties, a pair of snagged thigh-high pantyhose, a sequined thong, and a pair of gold slingback high heels, which dangled from her wrist. She felt a surge of injustice swirl in her belly.

Not exactly dressed for a hike in the woods, Rebecca, she thought, blaming herself.

Sasha pointed toward the direction of the cabin, "Do you think whoever is at that house will give me a ride to St. Augustine, or better yet, Palm Dunes, since all my stuff is still at the Copa. I've got a date with a new dude tonight." She batted her eyelashes, attempting to be coquettish.

"Uh… I kinda doubt it," replied Clementine. "Your stuff is probably long gone. Either the cops bagged it as evidence or someone from that homeless tent city nabbed it."

"Really?"

"Um, yeah. Either way, you're not getting dick from this new dude tonight."

"Seriously?! This guy has been sending me dick pics for days. And it's legit the biggest dong I've ever seen. I wish I had my phone! I would show you this guy's huge cock."

"Sasha, be real. That's what you wish you had your phone for? To show me pics of a guy's dick?"

"Well… you don't believe me. And it's huge! Really!"

"A phone could be used for lotsa better things right now."

"You know… I bet that hot cop has a big dick, too. He was kinda cute. But I can't date black guys. My dad would lose his shit."

"Racist," Halona interjected, rolling her eyes at Sasha. "You only think he has a big dick because he's black."

"You're a grown woman, Sasha. You can date whoever you want," Rebecca chimed.

"Well, you know what they say…" Sasha's eyes grew wide as she motioned with her hands. "And if everyone says it, it must be at least a little true."

"That's literally racism, Sasha," Halona said flatly.

"Well, what about that Jones guy?"

"Can y'all just stop? I really don't want to think about that guy's dick right now. He gave me the creeps, AND he dated my sister. Eww. Just eww." Rebecca shuddered as she pulled the envelope away from her chest and felt the lumps and grooves.

"Correction! He fucked your sister," Halona mocked, laughing.

"Definitely tiny dick energy," Sasha cackled.

"Oh my god! Stop!" Rebecca shook the large envelope like she was inspecting a present on Christmas morning. It gave little hint of the contents except for the sound of paper moving against paper.

"Whaddya think is in it?" said Clementine.

"I… I don't really know. But it's hard… and big."

"Like a dick!" Sasha giggled, opening her hand toward the package, "Here, hand it to me! I know what to do with it."

"I'm sure you do, honey," replied Rebecca, turning the package over in her hands. The envelope was new, without crinkles or creases, although it was large and bulky. Both the top and bottom had been sealed with several layers of thick, clear tape. There was no writing anywhere on it.

Impatiently, Sasha yanked the envelope from Rebecca's hands. She turned it over and, with one smooth sweep, she ripped it open. The envelope split open with gagged tears, and the contents fell to the ground. A silver pistol with a pearl handle, several large stacks of cash, and a small bag of pills landed in the dirt with a thud. Sasha reached down and grabbed the pistol by the handle, firmly placing her index finger on the trigger.

Everyone ducked as Sasha gripped the gun.

"What the fuck are you thinking, Sasha!" Rebecca's face was bright red as she screeched, "Put it back!"

Sasha's face was awash with astonishment at Rebecca's outburst. Her mouth fell agape, and she dropped the gun.

"What're we gonna do now?" Clementine shouted, standing up once Sasha was no longer armed and dangerous. "Of all the stupid things to do, Sasha! Now, how are we gonna give them their stuff? We can't just walk up to that house with a gun and a shit-ton of cash in our hands and say, 'Here ya go. Sorry, it looks like trash. Promise we didn't take any.'"

"You don't have to cuss her out like that," Halona replied.

"Fuck! Fuck-fuck-fuck!" Rebecca paced back and forth, her face had become even more flushed as she thought of what to do. "I'm sorry I yelled at you, Sasha. I'm just really freaking out right now. And… and… we need an idea."

"I've never heard you yell like that." Sasha's voice trembled as she spoke.

But Becca didn't notice, "Pick up the money! We'll just put it back as best we can and leave it at the front door. Maybe we can get out of there before anyone sees us!"

"A ding-dong-ditch?" Halona's voice was incredulous. "You must be joking."

Sasha slowly began picking up the stacks of cash, putting them back in the envelope one by one. But the rips in the tattered envelope began to open further, and the cash tumbled to the ground again.

"I'm sorry, guys! I'm really sorry. I didn't mean to. I just wanted to see what was in there."

Unable to hold her emotions back, Sasha cried. Fat tears rolled down her cheeks. She gasped for breath and dabbed her wet face with a stack of 100-dollar bills.

"Fuck you, Sasha!" Clementine blurted, "Don't try that crocodile tear bullshit on us. You are always doing shit like this. Cuz you never think. You just do whatever pops in your head. You're not sorry! You're wiping your fucking face with money."

"I said I'm sorry. I really am. Just stop yelling at me," Sasha said as she grabbed up the fallen cash, dabbing her tears with them, and then handing the damp cash to Halona.

"Fuck you, Clementine!" Halona shouted, "You think you're so much smarter than everyone. Why don't you figure it out instead of being a bitch to Sasha about it?"

"What? How can you defend her? She gonna come up in here like a dumbass and rip open the envelope, and I'm not supposed to tell her that she's being a dumbass? You're crazy, Hal. Always quick to call someone on their bullshit, but you can't handle being called on your own."

"That's it. I'm out. You're not gonna cuss me out either. This is some white-girl bullshit. That man ain't got nothing on me anyway. And he's not here to stop me. Yeah, no, y'all can figure it out. I'm going home." Halona shoved the armload of cash at Rebecca, dropping several stacks, then turned and walked back the way they had come.

"Halona, stop! You can't do this! You heard what Jones said. He'll come find us. You can't leave!" Rebecca pleaded, but Halona never turned around to see.

"Fuck her. I'm not getting caught up…"

"Clementine, don't be like that. Everyone is just stressed out right now. Let's just figure this out." Rebecca took a deep breath in and slowly breathed out. "I'm the one who got us in this mess in the first place. I had a gut feeling. I just knew something was off. I should have done something. I should have tried. But I didn't listen. I was too worried about Mother finding out. But this is way, way worse than that ever could be." Becca took a heavy breath as her voice began to tremble, "I should have done something."

"Fine. I'll stop being a bitch. One calming breath, and..." Clementine drew in a deep breath, held it for a moment, and blew it out. "How much cash you think is here anyway?" Clementine was focused and counting the cash on the ground as well as what Rebecca and Sasha were holding.

"There's probably another three stacks of cash still in here," Rebecca said, gesturing to the ripped envelope. "It's hundreds too!"

Looking into the envelope, Clementine replied, "There must be ten thousand dollars here! Where'd this money come from?"

"I bet it's drug money," Sasha said as she narrowed her eyes. "That Jones guy looked sketchy... like a drug dealer."

"Wait. I've got an idea! Sasha, take off your bustle. We can put the money in that and tie it up."

"What? No, this bustle cost me forty bucks at the dancer swap meet in Jax."

"Seriously?! What else have we got? You can buy a new bustle. Hell, I'll buy you a new bustle! And not to be a Petty-Betty but THIS," she said, pointing at the ripped envelope, "is your fault."

The three girls began surveying the resources they had between them. The bustle was the biggest piece of clothing they had. Spreading it on the ground, they wrapped the gun in the paper envelope and placed the rolls of money and the bag of pills around it. Then, they folded the remaining satin fabric over the package and tied it with the waist ribbon.

With the package securely wrapped like a present, Clementine, Sasha, and Rebecca walked toward the cabin. Only Rebecca looked over her shoulder to see how far Halona had walked away from them.

She squinted her eyes, searching. But Halona looked so small along the winding path of the road, as if she were nothing more than a mirage, a trick of the eyes caused by the shadows of the pine and fir trees mingled with the glaring sun, towering high above them. She disappeared into the woods.

PART FOUR

WELCOME TO PARADISE

CHAPTER EIGHT
THE HOUSE OF THE RISING SUN

Despite their eventful day and the drudgery of walking through sand and stone in heels or bare feet, the pleasantness and calm of the forest offered a moment of reprieve – even if it was only a brief one. Under the canopy of autumn leaves, the girls walked in silence for some time before coming to the final curve that revealed the cabin they were headed toward. Once they rounded the corner, they saw a large three-story chalet surrounded by a forest of tall fir trees. The driveway was about a quarter of a mile long and paved with stone. The entrance was blocked by another wrought iron gate. Similar to the one they drove through, which seemed like miles ago, it had a large gold crest with the letter 'R' encircled on it. On either side of the gate, there were two large golden lion statues, ready for battle, frozen on their hind legs with an open, roaring maw. There was a gated area beside the house with a large swimming pool. At the front of the house, there were two black Escalade SUVs parked in the paved circular driveway beside what looked like an empty helicopter landing pad. This was no ordinary cabin in the woods.

The girls exchanged looks, realizing that their ding-dong-ditch plan of leaving the bustle-wrapped cash and gun at the front door wasn't going to work.

"Ok, so, let's all agree that this is not what we expected to find out here," Rebecca conceded. Clementine and Sasha nodded their heads.

"So, what's plan B?" Clementine asked.

"I have no clue." Rebecca sighed, defeated. She started to pass the package to Sasha; however, just as Sasha reached out, she stopped herself and gave the package to Clementine. "Actually, you better hold this… for safekeeping." She arched her back and twisted from side to side to stretch. "But my back is killing me, and my feet are raw from walking barefoot. I'm tired. I'm hungry. And I don't wanna do this anymore. Maybe Halona had the right idea."

Becca slouched forward. Her shoulders caved under the weight of her defeat.

"Come on, Rebecca. You hafta have a plan," whined Sasha.

"Yeah, Becca! Come on," Clementine mimicked Sasha as she linked arms with Becca. "We can't give up now. We are literally in the driveway."

"See!" Sasha clapped her hands and linked arms with Clementine, "We're like The Three Musketeers! But, I'm still gonna ask if they can take me back to the Copa."

"Priorities, Sasha," Becca mothered.

Clementine had to bite her tongue. Because if she hadn't, the owner of the house would have come out to find her screaming and cussing at Sasha again. She and Rebecca began hobbling slowly toward the wrought iron gates with the gilded 'R'. As they approached, they saw a camera and a speaker. Sasha pushed the shiny gold button below the speaker.

"Yes?" A sultry feminine voice purred over the speaker, "Who is it?"

"Uh… um… we have a thing," Sasha nervously chattered. "A delivery. But, um, not like pizza or anything."

Rebecca stepped forward, "We have a delivery… from Officer Jones… He, um… said…"

Interrupting, Clemmie said, "He said to tell you that the pharmacy is closed."

A pause, and then an audible sigh came through the speaker before clicking off. The hard disconnect alarmed the girls.

"…are we sure that cop said 'pharmacy,'" Sasha nervously rattled.

Without warning, the gates opened. Clementine passed the bustle hurriedly back to Becca as if she had been shocked. Rebecca felt like Dorothy from "The Wizard of Oz," entering the gates of the Emerald City after having just awoken from a nap in the poppy fields. The three girls entered the gates, arms linked together, just like the Cowardly Lion, the Tin Man, and Dorothy, with the bustle of cash and pills as Toto. The front of the house was a mosaic of large, gleaming, glass windows whose beauty was further set off by the contrast of black cedar plank and thick slabs of slate. The sloping roof accentuated the strong lines of the A-frame house. The second-floor loggia was wrapped around the exterior of the house with intricately carved handrails and burnished end brackets. The structure was a craftsman's dream. But the picturesque chalet reflecting the setting sun looked more suitable as a winter retreat in the Swiss Alps rather than the 'cabin' it was earlier portrayed to be.

A tall, thin woman, with a large bust and long, smooth blonde hair pulled up in a pony-tail, stepped through the French doors of the chalet. She was wearing a tight black pencil skirt, a crisp white button-down shirt with the top three buttons left open to reveal her ample cleavage, and large, expensive-looking gold jewelry. She appeared to be carefully constructed and immaculately dressed. No hair out of place. No wrinkles in her crisp shirt. Almost as if she had been a piece of artwork curated for a gallery.

With a bright, pristine white smile on her face, she extended her hands as a warm welcome, as if greeting old friends, "Welcome! Welcome! You must be the new girls! I'm Antoinette. Come in. I expected you hours ago. You look positively withered. Let's get you all freshened up."

"Um, I'm not sure what you're talking about. We're just supposed to drop off this package and leave. I think you have us confused with someone else," Clementine said as she nudged Rebecca to hand over the package.

Rebecca sheepishly offered the dusty satin bundle to Antoinette. She pursed her lips, as if disgusted, but accepted the delivery as Becca placed Sasha's prized swap-meet bustle into her outstretched hands. She held it far away from her pristine clothes, like it were a contagious child.

Sasha stepped past Antoinette and into the house. Her mouth was wide open as she gawked at the high ceilings and lavish décor inside the house.

"Where are we? This place is... amazing." Sasha spun around slowly, taking in all she could see, "Who lives here? Is it just you? Can you adopt me?" Sasha laughed at her own joke as Antoinette watched her approvingly from the front entrance.

Outside the door, Clementine interrupted, "We had a bit of an... uh... accident. That's why it's wrapped like... that. But it's all there! Promise!"

Antoinette's attention was pulled back to the grimy bundle in her hands. She pursed her lips again, but attempted to regain her composure by smiling blankly at Clementine and Rebecca.

Clementine motioned at Sasha like she was a small child who had wandered too far away from her mother at the playground. But Sasha was oblivious and didn't come back. Instead, she ignored Clementine and wandered deeper into the house, and further away from the protective hands motioning for her to return.

"Don't worry about that. Come in! Come in! We can sort everything out after you are cleaned up. Mr. Rainaldi doesn't like for his girls to look messy."

"Um… thanks, but no. That's a really nice offer, but we are just supposed to deliver the package and go," explained Rebecca in her best Southern Lady accent. She, too, began motioning for Sasha as she stepped backward.

"Although we would love a ride back to Palm Dunes, if you don't mind," Sasha shouted as she wandered around the inner corridor that separated the kitchen and living room. Turning a corner, she said, "Oh! Hello!" as she found herself eye level with an erotic painting of a woman in mid-climax, as she was being devoured by three men. The gold plaque below read, "La Femme Damnee, Octave Tassaert, 1859."

"All in good time. Come in. Clean up. Rest for a bit," Antoinette said as her arm slithered around Clementine's shoulders. Constricted as she was, Clementine walked through the French doors. Dissatisfaction never broke Antoinette's porcelain face, but her words carried the ominous weight of an annoyed mother commanding her feral children.

Rebecca stood outside the doors of the chalet. Her friends stood inside. She glanced over her shoulder, as if she were searching for Halona one last time.

"Later, Marco can escort you wherever you'd like," Antoinette said as she placed Clementine in a chair.

"But… I…"

"Later. Later," Antoinette dismissed. Without stepping outside of the chalet, she extended an open hand to Rebecca. Looking down at Antoinette's smooth, pale hand, Becca hesitated in the doorway for a moment. Something insidious nagged at her, *Vibes don't lie,* echoed in her head. She looked past Antoinette and saw Clementine resting comfortably. *We have to stick together,* she thought and accepted

Antoinette's hand, allowing herself to be ushered into the living room, where her friends waited.

"Come, my dear! Refreshments. I know you are exhausted," Antoinette intoned.

In the large industrial kitchen, a short, round man with a large, hooked nose and a receding hairline stood in front of the sink, drying his hands on a crisp white towel. Four crystal glasses had been set out. Sasha watched him intently as he lifted a decanter and filled the glasses. The ice cubes popped and fractured inside the glass.

"Come, you must be parched!" Antoinette said as Marco entered the living room with a silver charger. She dropped the bustle to her side and gestured toward the refreshment that he had prepared for them. "Marco has made you all something refreshing to drink."

Marco glanced at Antoinette and raised an eyebrow at the heap of satin that she dangled from her hand. Then, he picked up the crystal glasses one at a time and served the girls. First, he handed a glass to Rebecca, then one to Clementine, and last to Sasha. As if on autopilot, Rebecca's lifelong Southern etiquette training took over, and she graciously accepted the water. She drank a long, slow sip. Clementine hesitated, but ultimately followed her lead and drained the cool liquid from the cup in one gulp, parched from the walk and the day. Like a bride with a new engagement ring, Sasha oohed and ahhed over the lavish house, ogling the opulence.

"This place is amazing! I mean… look at it," Sasha took a long sip from the crystal glass, and looked out the large, clear window at the glittering water of the pool. "Who would ever want to leave?"

Antoinette laughed mechanically. "Why, thank you! I know you would love it here. We have everything one could ever want." Her eyes locked with Rebecca's for a moment. Antoinette continued to watch intently as Becca placed the half-empty glass on the marbled quartz table. Without taking her eyes off of Becca, she said, "Finish your refreshments, my dear. You wouldn't want it to go to waste." Becca picked the glass back up and drained it, as if it were a command from her own mother.

Marco silently collected the other glasses and quickly busied himself with cleaning the kitchen, although the only items in need of cleaning were the glasses used by the three girls. Marco poured the contents of the fourth unused cup down the drain.

Sasha let out a loud yawn, "I'm so tired all of a sudden."

As if right on cue, Rebecca yawned immediately after Sasha.

We have been walking in nothing but heels and pasties for some time. Maybe the sun…, she thought.

Antionette's motherly dictation interrupted her train of thought.

"Well, my dear, you've walked a long way to get here," she mused.

Clementine rested her head on the overstuffed armchair, "I'm feeling it, too. I guess it's catching up with us."

"Come then, let me show you the second floor," Antoinette said as she escorted Clementine, Sasha, and Rebecca upstairs.

Leading each girl to a separate bedroom, "Here are your rooms. Make yourself at home while you freshen up. I think you and I are about the same size," she remarked to Rebecca. "And you two look like you could be a size 6 or maybe a size 8. I'll have some clothes set out for you while you rest."

Antoinette flashed an affectionate smile as the girls sleepily entered their rooms and closed the doors behind them. With a heavy click, the doors locked from the outside.

Rebecca flopped on the small bed with a grunt. Lying on her back, she placed her hands by her side and stared up at the tall white ceiling. Her vision blurred as the room began to spin. The room was stark – unlike the rest of the house. It was small, with the customary 'landlord white' paint job from floor to ceiling, with no art or embellishment, and it smelled of fresh bleach.

Rebecca closed her eyes for a moment to squelch the nausea creeping up her throat. She rolled onto her side, curling herself inward, and began to cry. Tears streaked through the layers of dust and makeup on her face and left faded black mascara droplets on the crisp white sheet beneath her.

"How did things get so out of hand?" Rebecca hid her face in her hands and sobbed until she fell asleep.

CHAPTER NINE
SYMPATHY FOR THE DEVIL

The morning sun poured pale beams of radiant light through the small, round double-pane window in Rebecca's bedroom at the Chalet. Though the window was small, the light from it filled the room. Rebecca lay across the middle of the twin-sized bed, curled like a newborn with her battered and bruised feet dangling just off the edge of the mattress. Her nude thigh highs were ripped and laddered, and the inside of her thighs were red and chaffed from the friction of the sequined thongs and the rough sand of the long, dusty trek rubbing against her tender skin. Beads of perspiration had left pale lines running down her breastbone, cutting through the ocher grime of red clay dust. The sequined pasties had fallen off during the night, revealing her large tawny nipples. Her long, sandy blond hair cascaded off the opposite side of the small bed. Her face, still hidden by clasped hands, was streaked with mascara and tears. Rebecca was awoken by the sound of Antoinette unlocking the door.

"Good morning, Rebecca dear, it's time for you to wake up," Antoinette stood just inside the doorway and stared at the rumpled and disheveled sight of Rebecca. Antoinette was crisp, professional, and authoritative. "Oh, no, this will not do! You need to get up immediately and shower! Mr. Rainaldi is here, and he does not like for the girls to look a mess."

Rebecca sat up on the side of the bed, heavy and disoriented, blinking the sleep from her eyes. Antoinette poked at her with a wooden hanger, making sure not to touch her in her unclean state, as she was already smartly dressed to welcome the boss home.

"You'll wear this," she said, showing Rebecca a sea foam green chiffon dress that was previously displayed on the wooden hanger. Gesturing toward a black paper shopping bag by the bedroom door, she continued, "Your shoes and undergarments are in here. You are due at the breakfast table downstairs in 30 minutes."

Antoinette stared sharply at Rebecca as if waiting for her to salute or respond with a 'yes, ma'am,' but she didn't. Rebecca couldn't focus and answered with a confused, "HUH?"

"NOW." Antoinette poked at Rebecca again with the wooden hanger, this time sharply jabbing her shoulder. With a yelp and a scowl, Rebecca leapt up and walked to the doorless bathroom across from the bed as if she were a small lamb being herded by the farmer's dog. "And DO NOT show up downstairs with wet hair," Antoinette gave her final command before leaving the room.

Rebecca could do all but blink and jump at the sounds of a firmly shut and relocked door. The grogginess she felt was not unlike a hangover, and her confusion was double that. Disconnected, she took a moment to process the room and that strange woman ordering her around.

Ok, think think think. Where am I? Why does my head hurt? Fuck, I didn't get THAT drunk at the show last night, did I? No…there was a man…wait…no, no, I didn't get to drink….what the hell… Her head throbbed, almost as if it were operating as an internal punishment for trying to remember. She shook her head, then caught a glimpse of herself in the bathroom mirror. She didn't know what day it was, but whatever the day in question, based on her state of undress and makeup, which were holding on for dear life, it must have been the night after a show. *No… we didn't have a gig. That was two days ago. We were at the Copa…taking photos, then…oh, God…* The sudden realization of the day's events came flooding back. The arrest. The drop-off. The gun and the drugs. Entering this version of Oz. The woman. The water. *THE WATER. HOLY FUCK. SASHA. CLEM!*

Becca bolted for the door, hoping against hope to either break through on impact or, at the very least, muster up the strength to rip the handle off the well-constructed wood. Neither provided any sort of budge against her current lack of physical strength and excessive grogginess. She stumbled back to the center of the room, hoping the sudden rush of adrenaline would heighten her senses enough to provide her with a clever enough way out. She remembered what woke her up in the first place. "The window," she said out loud to herself.

She slowed herself down and regained her composure as she walked briskly to the window to examine it. Feeling around the frame, there was no lock or opening. Just round, double-paned, and no way to open it. *I could try and break it,* she thought, and then looked down.

She approximated a 30-foot drop between the potential window ledge and the ground. Becca's talent for overthinking everything paid off, as she had no issue visualizing the worst-case scenario. *Presuming I don't cut myself on any shards if I find a way to break through, I'd definitely hurt or break something of mine landing on the concrete. Even if that's clean, what about that gate? Maybe Halona is still on the other side and got….wait….wasn't there ANOTHER gate we went through before we started walking…*

Her internal monologue drifted away, and was replaced with a sudden, cold drop of panic that caught in her throat, then proceeded to fill her gut. She was trapped…they all were. She was being held against her will, by all accounts drugged, and had no way out of the small bedroom, the house, or even the property until that resident school marm – *Antionette, was her name?* – showed back up in 25 minutes. *Okay, okay. Get a grip, Becca. Get a grip. We can figure this out. We can get out of here. We got this. We just gotta…not be…me. Prim…proper….me.*

Becca slumped to the ground against the window, feeling the warmth of the glass and the morning chase away the cold pit inside her. However, she was beginning to muse to herself out loud to keep the anxiety of the moment away. It was a helluva coping mechanism, and one she often used to plot through anything that needed one of her signature 'best laid plans.'

"Okay, then. Let's get up, let's think. What would James Bond do?"

Becca was irked at herself, saying that out loud as she started to pace around the tight room. She highly doubted Ian Fleming could've concocted any sort of comparing situation for his misogynist hero, as much as she admired both the artist and his creation. She found a clock and noted the time. 23 minutes to go. She paced. Back and forth. Back and forth, wearing a path in the carpet tread. The soft beauty of the chiffon dress caught the corner of her eye. After the third passing flash of green, she suddenly stopped. She was in front of the bathroom again, right at the spot where Antionette herded her to start the day. She took one more look in the bathroom mirror and then focused intently on the dress.

"No. Not Bond. What would Bella Valentina do?"

Amidst the chaos of the last 24 hours, Becca finally jumped in the shower; even one in a prison still felt invigorating. It gave her the clarity of mind to craft Bella further. That name always gave her a sense of immense power on the stage, but it was also her way out now – her character, her dissociative identity, and her muse. Becca Coleman lived in fear of her mother; Bella Valentina would've condemned and cussed her own mother out for being a hypocrite. Becca Coleman lusted awkwardly after Hot Cop and Sexy Jesus on Mother's wall; Bella

Valentina would've found a way to fuck Sexy Jesus while making Hot Cop watch. And Becca Coleman would've sheepishly bowed to these kidnappers' demands if it meant a way out, whereas Bella Valentina would've used every ounce of her feminine wiles to fight her way out tooth and nail.

There's no possibility they know who I am, she thought to herself, *so, why not give them someone unafraid of them?* She finished her shower and blow-dried her hair, then Becca looked at the time. Two minutes to go. *Shit,* she thought, *I took too long!* She bolted for the bag by the door to start with the undergarments. And undergarments they were – a matching bra, panty, and garter set. Lingerie in its finest form. *There's no way this could get put together in…,* she thought while looking at the clock.

One minute.

"FUCK."

Becca quickly removed the bra and panties from the overtly complicated packaging and put them on her body in a few swift motions. She threw the rest – garter, thigh highs, and all the trimmings – back in the bag. Just as she finished clasping the bra, Becca suddenly heard the bells from a grandfather clock chime outside the door. 9 AM on the dot. Becca quickly slipped into the well-tailored chiffon dress just as the door began to open.

"Showtime," she whispered to herself.

CHAPTER TEN

BREAKFAST IN AMERICA

Antoinette and Rebecca were making their way down the obscenely long staircase when Antoinette broke the awkward silence that lingered between them.

"You're not wearing the garter."

Becca was distracted, silently inspecting the chalet, now that she had a slightly more sober state of mind. Her sole focus was on finding any possible means of escape. The aside broke her concentration, but not enough to fully comprehend.

"Excuse me?" She asked.

"The garter? The thigh-highs?" Antoinette repeated, "You're not wearing them."

"Yeah, sorry. Just… couldn't make them work. Damned things got all tangled up."

"Given your stature as a dancer, I find that incredibly hard to believe."

The comment took Becca aback. Her mind started racing. *A dancer? How could they…? I guess the outfits from yesterday, but we could've been anybody. Strippers, hookers. How in the fuck did they…?*

"A word to the wise," Antoinette continued, "When Mr. Rainaldi offers up the finest in Italian lingerie, you'd do well to ensure every piece is on your body. He's not a man who misses much."

Before Becca could even retort, her foot landed on the last step of the staircase. The foyer opened up to a large breakfast table. There, Rebecca saw an older man sitting at the head of the table – he was in his late 40s or early 50s, with cold, dark brown eyes and a rich umber tan. His salt and pepper hair was trimmed, precisely parted along the side, and smoothly gelled in place. He was well-dressed in a bluish-gray sport coat, a crisp white-collar shirt, and wore expensive gold chains around his neck and large gold rings on his hands.

He looked up from his newspaper to see Rebecca paused on the final step of the staircase. He glared at her as if inspecting her to ensure his newest recruit met the proper dress code. With as sharp as he glared, it came as a shock when his expression quickly changed into a Cheshire smile. He set down his paper, stood, and exclaimed, "Bella Valentina! The belle of the ball."

His smile hit her like a freight train. His eyes met hers, and Rebecca recognized him almost immediately. He was the handsome man from the club two nights ago. *The silver fox,* she thought. The beacon of culture, placed squarely in exactly the type of environment Becca had always dreamed of – outside of this current hostage scenario, that is. And suddenly, it all started to make sense, especially the "dancer" comment from Antoinette earlier. This man saw her show at The Treasure Cove. This must be all his doing. It had to be.

Becca snapped herself out of detective mode and quickly brought her alter ego to the surface. This gentleman called her "Bella." By God, he was gonna get her.

"In the flesh!" She stepped off the staircase with a flourish of her chiffon skirt. "Of course, not as much as yesterday," Becca quipped with a flirtatious wink and smile, "You must be the infamous Mr. Rainaldi that I keep hearing so much about."

"Guilty, but never charged," he quipped back with a chuckle, "Please. Have a seat."

Antoinette pulled a seat from the table, beckoning Rebecca to sit. As she walked toward the table, she noticed that behind Mr. Rainaldi, there were expressively carved French doors leading out onto the property. Glancing toward the French doors, then back at Rainaldi, she walked to the table and sat as instructed. Rainaldi took back his seat as well. Antoinette walked firmly back to the kitchen, then seemingly returned instantaneously with a prepared urn of coffee.

"No garters?" Rainaldi asked the room as he picked his paper up again.

Becca opened her mouth in shock, only to find Antoinette's voice interrupting. "No, sir," Antoinette answered, "Ms. Valentina had some trouble getting them together. I had figured you'd prefer her mostly dressed rather than partly late."

"I see," he said with little affectation. The earlier charm in his voice had fallen strangely flat, but quickly bounced back. "Well, I'll make sure my man in Italy provides instructions next time," Rainaldi continued with a grin.

Antoinette tipped the polished silver goose-neck urn into the mouth of a delicate gilded porcelain mug. She added a cube of sugar and a splash of cream. Then, set the coffee cup in front of Rebecca.

She followed by offering a top-up to Mr. Rainaldi, who declined, and brushed her away in haste while continuing to read his newspaper. Antoinette scurried across the large room back to the kitchen and fussed at Marco about the coffee not being strong enough for Mr. Rainaldi.

"He didn't accept a second cup. He always accepts a second cup," Antoinette nagged under her breath at Marco.

Overhearing their forced whispers, Becca sipped at her coffee with ladylike delicacy.

"I trust you slept well," Mr. Rainaldi stated compassionately, "To hear Antoinette tell it, you and your friends apparently had quite the journey getting here."

"Mmm, yes," Rebecca said mid-sip, remembering which persona was supposed to be front and center, "It's certainly not every day you think you're getting arrested when you're actually being brought to a palatial mansion in the middle of nowhere. If you wanted to get a hold of me, you didn't need the cops and the sirens. Maybe the handcuffs, but not the rest."

Rainaldi smirked, but did not laugh nor look up from his paper. "My apologies for how that was handled. My security… they certainly do act like the police, don't they?" he half-heartedly stated in a low tone.

Act like police?! Becca thought, *We were told they were the police. They had the badges, the lights, the cars…we were being brought in for questioning for breaking and entering…the photographer…Am I remembering that wrong? No, I can't be…*

"The truth of the matter, Miss Valentina," he continued, finally setting his paper down enough to lean in and talk to Becca directly, "is that this is fate. This is our destiny. You and me. I saw you there. In that shack they called a bar, and you were performing as if you were on Broadway. I knew you were destined to be something more. And then, when I heard that you and your troupe were entering my old venue…"

"The Copa." Becca interrupted, "Oh my god. That's yours."

Mr. Rainaldi grinned again, accepting the interruption begrudgingly and continuing, "Fate, Miss Valentina. Destiny. Serendipity. Or coincidence. Call it whatever you like. You could've chosen any venue, but you and your group chose mine. And now," he proudly announced, "you and your group will fulfill that destiny with my guiding hand playing the part of fate."

Becca sat stunned. She couldn't believe what she was hearing. The world's most confident talk of fate and destiny when all she wanted to know was why she was taken from her home in such a brute manner, and when she could go back to her own, normal life. As if he were reading her thoughts, he continued.

"I hope you will be quite comfortable here," Mr. Rainaldi said as he brought the paper back up to his face. "Given what I've seen, you truly have a lot of potential to be successful."

"I… I'm sorry, but I just don't understand what you mean." Becca batted her eyelashes, attempting to cover her anxiety with Bella's coquettish charm. "Where exactly is here? And, where are my friends? Are they joining us for breakfast soon?"

"No, your traveling companions will not be joining us this morning," he said flatly.

"Why?" Becca's hand trembled slightly as she set her coffee cup on the table. She stared at the newspaper covering part of Mr. Rainaldi's face.

"Marco has already seen to their travel arrangements." His face was placid, like a calm lake.

"So, they aren't here?" Her anxiety rising, Rebecca took a deep breath. She felt her belly tremble and worried that her voice would crack or that she would burst into tears. "You took them back without me? I… I…"

"I know, I know," Mr. Rainaldi stated, "I hate that you didn't get an opportunity to say goodbye, but we also didn't want to interrupt your rest. We made them offers - not nearly as lavish as what we'll discuss - but they graciously accepted and are moving onward and forward."

Becca just could not believe what she was hearing. Sasha running off on some half-baked adventure seemed like par for her course…but Clementine? Accepting some sort of job offer from here? Nothing felt further from right. Slowly, the realization that she was alone, in this house, with a man who had only seen her for the first time two nights prior, and who had only spoken to her this morning crept over her like a plague. She felt the fog of panic rising within her. The blood drained from her face, and she thought she would faint. Setting her jaw, she mustered up her courage, "I would like to leave," she stated firmly.

Mr. Rainaldi lowered his newspaper and paused for a moment. His eyes had that same chaotic glint to them, just like when she saw him watching her at The Treasure Cove. It was like she could feel his eyes burning into her skin. The pressure of his gaze made her uncomfortable. She couldn't bear it. Her resolve began to waver, and she looked down at the table, fidgeting with the fabric of her dress.

"You are a guest in my home. Have I not offered you and your friends everything that you need? You came to me naked, dirty, and tired. I gave you beds to sleep in, clothes to wear. I provided warm showers and refreshments for you." His voice curled around her like a poisonous smoke ring, choking her. His question shamed her for being ungrateful for his kindness. "Indeed, I have. You should be thanking me. So, why would you want to leave? Is there something you lack?" He looked at Rebecca quizzically, astonished at the notion anyone would choose to leave, and uncertain of the source of her ingratitude.

Becca thought through a thousand different responses. A courageous *you kidnapped me and made me walk out here naked* or a flippant *fuck you and whatever crazed cult shit you're on* would've sufficed. The many voices of 'Bella' were well in retreat. All that eked out of Becca was "Well, I appreciate your hospit–"

"You lack nothing," he interrupted. "You want for nothing here. I have seen to it. Your friends have been given wonderful opportunities. They will want for nothing. They will be well cared for," he continued, "...as will you."

His patronizing left Rebecca wanting to protest, to argue, to demand her release, but he made her feel like her simple inquiries amounted to the severity of a toddler stomping her foot mid-tantrum. Mr. Rainaldi had a calm magnetism about him – a primal cunning. Rebecca took a deep breath, preparing to attempt to argue her position. But he even smelled powerful, like a man who was always in control. An aroma of sandalwood, smoky pipe tobacco, and fresh orange blossoms circled her nostrils and quieted her raging mind. She felt powerless around him as she drank in the deep, rich tone of his voice, lulling her into submission.

NO! Vibes don't lie. Why would he take them back and not me? I have to get out of here! Becca screamed internally.

The tension in Becca's gut had mounted to a fever pitch. She glanced across the room at the French doors where Antoinette had ushered her in the day before. It was a short sprint. If she kicked off her heels under the breakfast table, she could make a break for it. But she would have to be fast. Faster than fast.

Marco silently appeared beside her and set an exquisitely prepared breakfast in polished silver chaffing dishes on the table. Antoinette scuttled forward, eager to quickly serve Mr. Rainaldi. Marco bowed respectfully and returned to the kitchen without a word.

"Now then," Mr. Rainaldi said, glancing down at the meal. "You have two choices at hand. You can eat your breakfast, and we can discuss your upcoming duties under my employ in the study after I've eaten. Or… if you truly feel like we've taken you prisoner here, you can always walk out these doors behind me. We'll notify your friends that you won't be joining them, and that'll be that."

Rebecca snapped back into the conversation. The mental choking stopped, and the tension eased. "I… I can leave? Just like that?" she asked.

"Just like that," Rainaldi replied as he delicately placed a bite of food in his mouth.

Rebecca hesitantly poked at the runny egg on her plate with her fork. She watched the sunshine yellow goo ooze into a pool. The house was still, like all the air had disappeared, and the only sound was the ticking of the grandfather clock. Antoinette stood poised behind Mr. Rainaldi, waiting to leap into use at his earliest convenience.

Rebecca's eyes grew wide as she watched the egg yolk creep across the plate. *This is my chance. I have to make a run for it.* She glanced up at the doors and back again at the runny egg. In an instant, she kicked off her shoes and bolted for the large French doors of the chalet. Clearing the room in a matter of moments, she grabbed the handle and was knocked back by a jolt of electricity that coursed through her body.

Rainaldi sighed and swallowed his food. He took a moment to watch Rebecca uncontrollably twitch on the floor, then picked up a folded cloth napkin to wipe his mouth. "I'm glad you took the time to see it my way," he stated flatly before tossing the napkin on the table.

As Rainaldi took his leave, Marco calmly stepped around the kitchen island, where he had been tidying. He made his way toward the front door with a stoic attentiveness.

"Is there somewhere the misses needs to be escorted? I can have Arnoldo pull the car around."

Dazed and holding her electrocuted hand, Rebecca opened her mouth in shock, but again, Antoinette rounded the corner of the table and responded for her, "No, thank you, Marco." She coolly commanded, "She and Mr. Rainaldi still have much to discuss."

CHAPTER ELEVEN
GRANITE

A dazed, disoriented Rebecca shook off the jitters of what felt like 1000 watts coursing through her nervous system, only to find her scenery had changed anew. She faintly recalled being carried by Marco to the next room – Mr. Rainaldi's private study, as Antoinette called it – and was instructed to wait there for him in the leather-bound chair she was placed in. In her own subtle act of rebellion, she stood. She was still wobbly from the shock, but upright, nonetheless. She started slowly finding her steps and rubbed her electrified hand, hoping some blood flow would help her eyesight come into clearer focus.

As she looked around the room, she noticed it was finely furnished with antique leather chairs, a polished teak writing desk, and a large built-in bookcase brimming with books of all shapes and sizes. She inched closer to the wall of books to see leather-bound tomes on psychology, law, and business. Some were ancient and looked their age, with yellowed pages and sun-bleached fabric covers. It had the comforting but moody feel of old academia, not at all what Rebecca would have expected from someone who looked like Mr. Rainaldi. He certainly commanded a room, but Rebecca never would have considered him an intellectual. Well-read, yes, but academic, no. *He's a monster, but at least he likes to read,* ruminated Rebecca internally.

As if the thought was too much to bear, an aftershock of electricity ran a shiver down her spine. She slowly steadied herself, then moved to sit down in the plush leather Queen Anne chair. *Shit. Shit. Shit. Okay. Deep breath. You're okay. Just try and calm yourself,* she thought. Using her good hand, she grabbed a book sitting on the small, round table next to her and began thumbing through it. A worn, leather-bound copy of Meditations by Marcus Aurelius. She found herself focused on a line: 'Reject your sense of injury and the injury itself disappears.'

"If only it were that easy, Marcus," she quipped to herself.

On the opposite side of the room, a large boar's head hung above a stone mantle. The glassy eyes stared at Rebecca, making her feel uncomfortable. The boar seemed to smirk at her with a rueful mouth that was permanently set in an open grimace, with two long tusks jutting out. If Rebecca believed in the afterlife, it would have been easy to imagine this dead animal haunting its murderer, seeking vengeance for being unjustly condemned to an eternity as a decapitated trophy. She shuddered and turned her eyes away from the animal, looking back at the book in her hands. Even though she had been raised in a small town where hunting and fishing were a preferred local pastime, it never really made sense to her why some people enjoyed killing things. She felt sorry for the dead boar, hanging there on the wall, and wondered how it must have felt moments before its death. She turned back and looked at the trophy on the wall once more, its glassy eyes glinting in the soft yellow light of the study. What had it done to deserve this? Maybe if she looked deep enough into those eyes, she could see their final moments, imprinted in the soft, milky white tissue. Death was such an unnerving subject for her to think on. It always brought her back to Russell. His own death may have been similar to that of the boar. Both hunted. Both hunting. Both dead before their time. One was a wild animal, and the other was a young soldier fighting in a war he didn't understand. Neither were alive to tell their story.

Rebecca was still staring deeply into the eyes of the boar, pondering life's greatest mysteries, when Mr. Rainaldi entered the room. She didn't realize that she had walked closer to the mounted head or that she was no longer alone in the room. Mr. Rainaldi stood in the doorway observing her for a long moment before clearing his throat to announce his entrance. Rebecca jumped at the noise and stood rigidly erect. Russell would've called it "at attention." Rainaldi strode across the room and took his seat at the teakwood desk. Placing his elbows on the edge of the desk, he leaned forward as if he were preparing to barter.

"Well, what do you think of it, Bella?"

"Of what?"

"The boar, of course! Isn't it a fine specimen?"

"Oh. Well, I don't really know," she cautiously replied. Between the breakfast conversation and the incident with the door, she was already on edge and did not want to stoke anyone's ire any further. "I was just looking. It almost seems not real with how big it is," she said, realizing afterwards that her trying to feign awe sounded too real.

Mr. Rainaldi smirked, then turned to look up at it, "For better context, most of the wild hogs you'll see on this property are fairly standard-sized. Farm pigs, really. No harm to us here unless you provoke them. This one… this one was a really nasty one we found in Africa. Big game hunting trip. You'd be surprised how hard it is to track in a rainforest something this…" He paused, seemingly looking for the right word. He looked back to Becca, and continued, "this significant. Seemingly larger than life itself."

Rebecca tried to maintain the tremble in her voice. "You… you killed it yourself?"

Rainaldi watched Becca intently, as if he were scrutinizing every shift in her facial expressions. It seemed to her that he could look right through her, his eyes seeing all of her insecurities and shortcomings. He drew a steady breath and continued on his philosophical streak.

"There comes a day, Ms. Valentina, when you have to decide for yourself. You can either hunt and devour... or be hunted and devoured." He gestured toward the boar, "That was a life I had to take in order to continue my own. I carry that reality with me, and I keep this trophy above me as a reminder... I am, indeed, that hunter. I am that devourer."

Rebecca's shocked hand started shaking. She wasn't sure if it was aftershocks or fear. Maybe both.

Mr. Rainaldi's mood suddenly shifted. His face and voice went back to the pleasant tone and demeanor he had earlier that morning. "Well, on to business then. I've opened a spot for you at my club in Jacksonville. You'll start preparing immediately. I've worked it out for your first performance to be next week. You'll headline, of course, as our belle of the ball. That should be enough time for a professional like yourself to work out a new routine. And for Antoinette to order costuming or whatever else you require. I think you'll like my club as it's much, much nicer than the dive I rescued you from. You'll be quite successful with my clients, I'm sure."

Rebecca's soft mouth gaped. The constant switches in outward behavior left her in perpetual whiplash, and a heavy breath escaped as she stared at him.

"That's it? All of... this... and you're offering me a dancing gig? I don't need to live here to work at your club. I have my own place and my own car. Why do I have to be kept here?"

"What can I say? I like to keep my assets safe. And you WILL be safe here...and comfortable."

"But I could just–"

"I take care of what is mine, Bella. Have no doubt of that," he interrupted, with a dismissive wave of his hand. He turned to a notepad and began writing.

All Rebecca could do was internally seethe. Her emotions were evolving from emotional whiplash and started turning into righteous indignation. *The arrogance of this man. The objectivity and the possessiveness. And calling me by my stage name. And the back and fucking forth,* she thought.

Rebecca steeled her nerves. His ire be damned, she couldn't take this anymore. She needed out. Rebecca finally got up the courage to say, and with an intentionally flippant tone, "I'm sorry. But this all just seems like I'm being… kidnapped."

Rainaldi and his pen stopped in their tracks. His eyes slowly moved up, tracking from the pad of paper to the desk, then to Rebecca's impressive bodice before stopping directly at her face, and then staring directly into her eyes. The look of intention returned, this time scaring Rebecca with its intensity. With an impressive grin, he finally spoke, "Oh, my dear Miss Valentina… that's because you are."

Rebecca's stomach sank to the sub-floor. *You are being kidnapped.* She let the words roll around in her brain. Finally, a statement – no, a confirmation – of purpose to everything that's happened over the last 12 hours. Still, the feeling of actually knowing was somehow worse than the thought of it happening. Her jitters returned, and all she could muster out of her voice was an exasperated, "What…?"

"Of course. You think in an operation like mine, you get an audition?" Rainaldi replied with a laugh, "No, no. To keep things fresh for what I do, you unfortunately have to come by high performers by… other means."

Rebecca started to feel herself getting nauseous. Like a parrot, she was only picking up on certain words and just repeating them back. "high… performers…?" she eked out.

"Sex, mainly," Rainaldi flatly replied, "Fucking, and a lot of it. You honestly wouldn't believe the appetite in this state for it, even if I ran you the numbers of what I make on it. And business towards that end is BOOMING."

Rebecca's bile started to rise and choke her. Her breathing became ragged, and she felt a panic attack coming on strong. Seeing her reaction, Rainaldi's expression quickly reverted to concern. He stood up and walked around the desk to her. Sitting on the front edge of his desk, he took her hurt hand into both of his.

"Oh, Bella," he cooed, "I'm so sorry. I didn't mean to frighten you. I wasn't meaning that's what you specifically would be doing."

Rebecca looked up at him. Confused, she tried to slow down her breathing enough to talk. "Wait… wait… what do you mean?"

"You're here to dance, and to be under my charge from now until your featured scheduled performances are done. That's it. You… you are my prized possession. The piece of the puzzle that I've been missing. I would never have anyone defile you," Rainaldi claimed with the utmost sincerity.

"I… I can't believe this…," Rebecca said, still shocked but feeling her anxieties slowing down.

"I know. Isn't it great? You are to be the crowning jewel to grace my stages with your presence. It's the other girls who take care of my clients in that way. Like your friends, for example."

Rainaldi finished this sentence with a squeeze of Rebecca's pained hand before starting his walk back around to his seat at the desk, as if to accentuate the pain of that final sentence. *Like your friends, for example.* Her anxieties all came rushing back. All she could do was think about her friends and what they may be going through. *Sasha. Desiree. Did they get to Halona? Oh, god, not Clem…*

"Yes, yes," Rainaldi continued, seemingly reading Becca's mind, "Of course, seeing you in that dive, I knew without a doubt in my mind that

I had to have you. And when that Mathias informed me that he would be taking pictures of you with the group… well, I couldn't let that interfere with our date with destiny. So, I called it a bonus."

"The photographer…," she mumbled just audibly enough to hear, "Oh my god… he was working with you."

"Guilty but never charged," he quipped again.

He opened the desk drawer and pulled out a small black box. He handed it to Rebecca. Taking the box in her hands, she slowly removed the lid. Inside was a silver necklace with a dangling heart pendant engraved with the letter 'R.' Rebecca stood staring at the necklace for a long time before looking up at Mr. Rainaldi. In her stupor, it almost seemed as if his face molded into something with a touch of sincerity. He had a slight smile on his face and a look of admiration.

"What is this for?"

"Consider it a small trinket to show my appreciation for your… cooperation going forward."

"Thank you, but I can't…"

"Please. Put it on, Bella," his deep voice hardened. "I'm sure it will look quite lovely on you."

The smile that Rebecca believed to have seen inching across his face earlier was nowhere to be seen now. He resumed the stern, stoic expression he wore when she first saw him sitting at the breakfast table. He had that same chaotic glint in his eye when she tried to escape through the French doors, only to be knocked back inside by a jolt of electricity. She touched the heart pendant, still in the box, and saw her reflection as the shiny metal sparkled in the light. Rebecca fumbled with the box awkwardly as Mr. Rainaldi watched her. He stood and walked closer to her, his tall stature looming.

"Here, let me."

She turned her face upward to him and could feel the intensity of his presence emanating toward her. Slowly, she stood, making their bodies parallel. The heat from his tan skin warmed her. It was like lying on warm beach sand on a cool Spring day. Her pale skin flushed pink. She was already loopy enough from the ups and downs of the day, but now felt dizzy as she breathed in his intoxicating aroma. He stared into her green eyes and caressed her jawline with his warm hand, his index finger lingering on her chin, lifting her face upward toward his own. He finally spoke.

"You know… I knew from the moment I saw you, I knew you were it. I knew you were going to join me on this journey of mine."

The electricity sparking from the French doors' handle she had touched earlier that morning was no match for the charge that was forming between Mr. Rainaldi and Rebecca. He brushed past the wayward strands of her long, blond hair, letting them drape over the back of his hand. He gripped the back of her neck, firm and authoritative. He slowly turned her around and pulled her backward, body to body, as he leaned closer. She felt his breath on her neck as he commanded her.

"Turn around. I will do it for you."

Her heart drumming in her chest, goosebumps crept over her delicate skin as she passed the necklace box to him. He pulled the necklace from its box with one hand and finally loosened his grip on her neck with the other. He held the ends of the clasps. Slowly, the necklace trailed across her breasts to her neck, as Mr. Rainaldi's steady hands grazed against her skin, intensifying the goosebumps. The clasp linked together at the nape of her neck as his hand rested on her again.

"I need you to understand. You are not a permanent prisoner. I would very much like for us to fulfill this partnership as dutifully and honorably as feasible, given the circumstances. You dance for some powerful people; I reap the benefits of having those people in our presence. That's it. Just follow my lead and everything will go smoothly."

Just as Rebecca let out a heavy breath, his hand shot up like a lightning bolt, grabbing a fistful of hair at the base of her skull. She gasped as she felt his fingers intertwining. Fear crept over her as his voice growled.

"But if you dare try to leave before I say you can, if you even think about walking off this property without me… I will hunt you down, and I… will… devour… everything you hold dear just to watch you suffer. I will decimate your world and leave you in ruin before finally dealing with you. Is that understood?"

She felt herself shuddering in fear as the grip tightened further, finding herself nodding in agreement out of both obedience and fear of what this madman might do. She felt his breath heavy on her neck as he leaned closer and closer. He then gently kissed her. He chuckled, with her still in his mouth.

"Good girl," he whispered into her ear as he loosened his grip. He stepped back to his desk and resumed his paperwork. "That is all. Antoinette manages scheduling. Marco will escort you to your appointments. Close the door on your way out."

Rebecca stood in shock once more, granite in her chest and her spine trembling at the sudden, swift actions that continued to befall her. Another line in the Aurelius book she thumbed a moment ago came back into her mental focus: *Life is neither good or evil, but only a place for good and evil.* And in this moment, she found herself slowly losing the ability to tell the difference between the two.

CHAPTER TWELVE
UNDISCLOSED DESIRES

After Becca was dismissed from Mr. Rainaldi's private study, Antoinette entered the room. She was angry at first, but found her calm as she strode closer to his desk. Her steps landed heavily with purpose. At first, Mr. Rainaldi didn't pay much attention to her. He continued to read from "Meditations" by Marcus Aurelius. Staring intently at the page that Becca had been reading earlier, his eyebrows knit together as he was lost in thought.

"Sir," Antoinette said, "I wonder if I might have a moment of your time?"

Mr. Rainaldi looked up from the leather-bound book, puzzled by the distraction. "Yes, what is it?" He stared at Antoinette blankly as if the mere interruption of his thoughts about Bella were a quite audacious inconvenience. "Well?"

"Sir, it's just that I'm concerned about the *new* girl. She—"

"What do you mean? Has something happened?" He asked impatiently. "Well? Speak up, Antoinette."

"Nothing has happened, per se, sir. It's just that I am worried about her being here at The Chalet. We've never had a girl here. They usually go to the warehouses, as you are well aware, sir. However, I'm quite concerned that we've made ourselves vulnerable by allowing her here."

Antoinette paused for a moment, waiting for a response. But, Mr. Rainaldi only reclined in his office chair as he watched Antoinette speak. She drew a long breath and continued.

"I fear that the operation might be in jeopardy. Four girls all at one time sir. We've never pulled so many new girls at one time, and especially from one place. It seems reckless, considering that they all know each other. A pull like this could certainly look suspicious to the authorities. And we don't—"

"Antoinette," he interrupted, "do you doubt my ability to run my own business?" His face had hardened, and his tone was flat. "Because it sounds like you are questioning my ability to run my own business. And I certainly would be shocked to have such a loyal employee lose faith in me."

Antoinette blanched, "Oh! Oh no, sir. I am not inferring anything like that. It's just that I worry about the safety of the operation. Pulling four girls at once, and specifically having one here, just seems… out of character… for you, sir."

"Out of character? How bold of you, Antoinette. Have you any other concerns about how I run my business?"

"Sir, I didn't mean to suggest that. I merely wondered if Ms. Valentina would be better off permanently relocated to The Mortimer, or perhaps, another club. Ybor, maybe?"

"And yet, you clearly have doubts about the calls I have made. Must I remind you that I am in charge of this operation and am more than capable of running it as I see fit? I built this business from the ground up. From nothing, Antoinette, and now you stand here questioning whether or not my choices are 'out of character.' I hardly think so."

"Of course not, sir." She fluttered her eyelashes at him, "I am only concerned for you, sir. I would never question your authority. You are more than capable, but it just seems… risky. And we have one missing? There is no telling how this could play out. It just seems… reckless."

"Reckless? Risky? Antoinette, you have gotten far too comfortable. You work for me. Loyal employee or not. And I do not keep you around to give your opinions on business strategy or question my authority. You've said enough. Bella isn't going anywhere. And maybe, just maybe, you should pay more attention to your own duties instead of being part of the problem. Am I clear?"

"Sir, you know I am more than simply a loyal employee. I have been absolutely devoted to you from the start. And I have done everything that you've asked of me, including managing your *jewels* at The Mortimer, but having one here? This seems risky. Why not keep her with your others?"

"You've stated your case, Antoinette. However, I am quite unconcerned with your concerns. I know what I am doing. I brought this business to life from nothing. And it is by my authority that it is so successful. I am not concerned with the authorities. I am the Authorities, and you would do well to remember that. You'll train Bella, work with her on costuming and choreography, and continue to do exactly as I tell you. Understood?"

"Yes, Mr. Rainaldi."

"Now, be a good girl and fetch Marco for me. I want his brother, Arnoldo, on the hunt for our missing whore. I want her found immediately. Dead or alive, makes no difference to me, as long as she is under my control."

With her unspoken fears pressed firmly against her clenched teeth, Antoinette turned on her heels and marched out of Rainaldi's private study. She stopped by the kitchen momentarily to deliver his message to Marco. Mumbling at him dismissively about him doing his duty for once.

* * *

Antoinette returned to her small room at the back of The Chalet. It was dimly lit, cozy, and pale compared to the harshly bleached rooms on the second floor. Once inside the room, she placed her hand against the seal of the door, slowly easing it closed without a sound. She put her ear to the door jam, listening for following footsteps. But hearing none, she reached her hand into the inside of her shirt and pulled a small pistol from her bra. The metal was warm in her hand. She set it down on the bed and opened the nightstand drawer. A tiny smile inched across her face as she gazed at a pink handkerchief with small embroidered yellow roses. She nudged it to the side to reveal the bag of pills that the girls delivered to her the previous day. She shook her head and whispered to herself, "Men are so stupid. So sloppy."

Pursing her lips again, she reached for the Tracfone hidden in the back of the drawer and dialed Officer Jones' number.

"Hullo?"

"Jones, what are you playing at? Why would you have the girl deliver the prototype to me? That was sloppy."

"Annie, you worry too much. Trust me, tha girl ain't gonna buck. Just be cool about it."

"Be serious. I'm not worried about *his* new tart. Marco saw that ridiculous bundle they delivered it in. He could tell Rainaldi what he saw. You've got to be more cautious."

"Pfftt, that prissy man slave? What's he gonna do?"

"Damn it, Jones. Listen to me! Marco is loyal. And I can't have another man going soft on me. I already have Rainaldi acting like a love-sick puppy over this girl."

"It'll be fine. Trust me. Okay?"

"We can't be sloppy. Not when everything we've planned is at stake."

"Ah, loosen up, Annie. Ya worry too much."

"No! You *tighten* up. We can't afford any more hiccups. Your negligence is why we have a missing girl on the grounds. You should have delivered them to the warehouse like I told you to."

"Boss's orders. You know that. I cain't very well just tell Mr. Rainaldi no."

Antoinette let out a long sigh. "Fine," she conceded, "but no more mishaps! Find the girl. Before one of his lackeys does."

"A'ight. A'ight. I'll find tha girl."

Click.

Antoinette drew in a deep breath and sighed, "They never listen, do they?" She tossed the phone in the back of the drawer and picked the pistol up off the bed. She turned the gun over in her hands watching the metal glint in the sun light. "But they will," she said as she slid it back into her bra.

Part Five

Private Dancer

CHAPTER THIRTEEN
FANCY

Becca felt just like the young woman in Reba McIntyre's classic country song, "Fancy." Unlike the song, there was no roach crawling across the toe of her high-heeled shoe. She was, however, being shepherded into the hands of wealthy men with the promise that if she was good to the gentlemen, then they'd be good to her. Antoinette served as the proverbial mother, sharing this wisdom with her débutante daughter, as she passed down sage advice such as "never collect your own tips… the kitten does that." However, instead of a tar paper shack, this lesson was given from the comfort of a plush leather seat in the back of an Escalade. Mr. Rainaldi's manservant, Marco, steered the smooth, black Escalade into the valet parking lane of the lush private gentlemen's club.

The Mortimer was every bit the analogous equivalent to the limousine in the country song. Class. Grace. Decadence. But nothing about the exterior of this place screamed 'STRIP CLUB.' In fact, it was more akin to 'GOLF RESORT.' The Mortimer was a French Provincial-inspired country club, complete with an 18-hole golf course, clubhouse with upscale apartments, and a kitchen that specialized in authentic French cuisine. From the outside, den of inequity, it was not.

The SUV had barely come to a stop before a handsome young man with slicked-back hair, aviator sunglasses, and a Greek nose opened the rear passenger door. Stepping onto the paver brick, Becca wondered if this was the result of a wrong turn or some other ridiculous mistake — not unlike every other event that had led her to this point. Without a moment to linger in her thoughts, she was whisked inside. With Antoinette pushing her from behind, and 'the Greek nose' ushering her through the front door, Becca felt like she was being hustled away from prying eyes, like an incognito celebrity evading the paparazzi.

The interior was every bit as artfully designed and architecturally impressive as the exterior. Just inside the foyer beside the reception desk stood a professional-looking hostess, dressed in a crisp white button-down and a black pencil skirt. She ironically looked like she could be Antoinette's sister. Same hair. Same physical build. Same robotic emptiness. No doubt this was the company uniform. The beautiful blond hostess had an air about her as if her primary job was being pretty. However, between hair flips and vapid stares, her job was to check a carefully curated list of patrons, review personal identification, and collect the club's mandatory door fee for guests of the bar. For patrons who planned an extended stay, she also issued room keys and summoned a bell boy, who promptly carried their belongings to the elevator and escorted them upstairs.

Antoinette nodded a greeting to the young blond girl at the desk as they breezed by. It was reminiscent of the decorum exchanged between generals and enlisted men. But instead of salutes, it was head nods and empty smiles. The young lady had barely acknowledged them before Antoinette hurriedly shepherded Becca into an employee-only area of the club. Winding through a long corridor, Becca found herself somewhere in the back of the bar, behind the main stage. As they entered the open room, she saw the edge of the curtain sway gently as a breeze.

"Mr. Rainaldi was right about one thing," Becca mused, "this place is much nicer than the last club I danced in."

"Did you ever have any doubts?" Antoinette stared incredulously at Becca. "Mr. Rainaldi is a very honest man. He has no cause to misrepresent himself to you. After all Mr. Rainaldi has done for you, how can you distrust him?"

Admonished, Becca faked a smile and nodded. She knew it would do her no good to argue with Antoinette, whose blind faith in Mr. Rainaldi had been a constant over the past week. Becca's mind drifted to the derelict conditions of her last gig. Sticky carpet. Yellowed walls from years of heavy cigarette smoke. It was so helplessly poor compared to this. She wondered, lightheartedly, if management ever successfully removed all the wayward glitter dicks from the carpet. She thought of Clementine and was filled with a surge of homesickness. It had really only been a little more than a week since that show, since she last saw her best friend. Only one week ago, she was a free woman, and her biggest worry was about disappointing her pretentious mother and defending herself from her sister's judgmental glances. It was as if those intentional glares from her sister were daggers darting over the customary Sunday afternoon honey-baked ham. Her sister's sacred Christian hate was artfully hidden from the tear-stained blue eyes of a clearly-not-Israeli Sexy Jesus hanging lustily from the cross. Maybe that was better than how she had spent her previous Sunday, at the Copacabana, getting kidnapped by thugs posing as cops. As bad as this was, she had her doubts. However, instead of a pretentious mother, she now had Antoinette, her personal assistant, handler, and constant companion. Judgmental glances sold separately. But that wasn't much considering their interactions, mostly quiet, were focused on the deliberate business of preparing Bella Valentina for her debut at The Mortimer.

Mr. Rainaldi had taken great care to ensure that Bella's debut performance would be up to his impeccable expectations. Thus, he extended his range of control into song selection as well as costume design. He specifically told Antoinette what he wanted, and she, like a diligent taskmaster, ensured Rebecca's compliance. It was not in Antoinette's wheelhouse to fail.

Antoinette proved herself ever the talented assistant, as she not only managed The Chalet, but she also mothered Becca like a nagging, middle-aged, dance-mom. That first week at The Chalet was consumed with Becca bending to Antoinette's will. Becca had zero wiggle room and absolutely no voice in any decisions. Antoinette treated her like an infant in ballet slippers. She decided what she wore, ate, and did. Every hour of Rebecca's day was constructed and controlled by Antoinette's stern authority. And in the few months that Becca had been dancing with the amateur burlesque troupe, she had never been rehearsed so hard.

Beyond being a drill sergeant of a mother, she also designed and sewed Becca's costumes, paying deliberate attention to her precise measurements. She choreographed the new routine, ensuring Mr. Rainaldi's approval. A grand puppet master, she was. Antoinette all but climbed into Rebecca's skin and danced the routine for her. And as far as Becca was concerned, she would have done that too if she only had the ability to be two people at the same time. Becca highly doubted that Fancy's introduction to the gentleman was even remotely so impeccably executed. As far as mothers go, Becca's experiences included her own as condescending, Fancy's as negligent, and Antoinette as fastidious.

"Can I have a look around?" Becca asked, hoping to get a chance to locate the emergency exits, a routine she developed as a coping skill from a childhood tainted with crippling anxiety. Like the complimentary gift that comes with an out-of-order fight or flight response, she always identified exits as part of planning her escape in the event of catastrophe (like vomiting or fainting). Overthinking every possible and uniquely horrible alternative had become a hobby for Becca. No doubt, a symptom of being an overachiever, goody-two-shoes for the entirety of her early life. Mother accepted nothing less. Unfortunately, none of those skills prevented her from being abducted and trafficked as a dancer. Perhaps, they could help her escape, though.

Antoinette's sharp eyes narrowed as she searched Becca's face for some hidden agenda. Becca certainly had one. However, Antoinette did not seem to find any mischief lurking in her young ward's eyes and conceded begrudgingly with, "Just the stage area."

She nodded quickly, and with a turn of her heels, Becca set off for the stage.

"Stay where I can see you," Antoinette mothered.

Becca paused, looked over her shoulder, and responded with the traditional homespun Southern etiquette, "Yes, ma'am." It was as thick as Tupelo honey.

Becca pulled back the velvet curtain to reveal a decadent room filled with round tables covered with crisp black linens. The tables were encircled with plush burgundy cushion-back chairs. Adjacent to the main stage was a polished mahogany bar. The room was vibrant and warm. Welcoming, even. The deep colors were offset by the incandescent sheen of the velvet, reflecting the warm light of the flickering candelabras. Not at all the risqué, den of inequity she had envisioned. This was no smutty little club.

A gruff faced man with a thick, waxed mustache and hulking, tan, tattooed arms stood behind the mahogany bar. He looked up from drying the cut-crystal highball glasses; his forearm muscles flexed and pushed the folded cuff of his crisp white button-down shirt further up his arm. The sleeves of his shirt rippled as if threatening to burst a seam. Drying rag still thrust into the well of the glass, he tilted his jaw and warned, "You're not supposed to be in here! No whores until after the show."

Becca was taken aback. *Whore!?* She thought.

Before Becca could speak, Antoinette stepped through the curtain, amused, "She's with me, Trevor."

"Oh!" All hints of rugged masculinity melted from his gruff face once he saw Antoinette, her commanding presence asserting dominance from the eaves of the stage. "My... My apologies, miss. I thought she was one of the... um... working girls." He set the glass he'd been cleaning on the bar and reached for the decanter of whiskey. He smiled at Becca with the grace of a well-seasoned hospitality worker, "Can I get you something? A whiskey, perhaps?"

Becca nodded her head sheepishly and croaked, "Um... a white wine. Please."

He set the decanter on the bar and began searching for an unopened bottle of Sauvignon Blanc.

"No, thank you, Trevor," Antoinette interjected, her voice was rigid and her eyes glinted with the seduction and mischief of a dominatrix who had already warned her supplicant. "Miss Valentina is dancing tonight."

Picking up the whiskey decanter again, "I understand, madame. Your usual, then?" He was poised and ready to pour into the cut crystal glass.

"No. Thank you, Trevor. Not tonight."

CHAPTER FOURTEEN
CIRCUS

As night fell on The Mortimer, the backstage area filled with working girls, each preparing to dazzle the crowd of patrons with their variety acts or stripteases. Some girls worked the poles, others danced on tables, and only a select few performed on stage. Mr. Rainaldi was very intentional about which girls worked the stage and which worked the crowd. He made his fortune by having exquisite taste and an unyielding expectation for greatness. Nothing less would do.

Rebecca felt the whirlwind of pre-show jitters descend upon her as beautiful women surged in and out of the dressing room. That familiar bubbling in her veins. Excitement and terror combined in a rhythmic dance as blood pumped its way through her body. The fear of not being enough. Not beautiful enough. Not thin enough. Not rehearsed enough. A ribbon of insecurity laced along the folds of her brain, creating a churning of doubt in her belly as it cinched tightly like a corset against her rib cage.

The wild-eyed look of a trapped animal alerted Antoinette that her latest protégé was ready to claw her way out of her gilded cage or worse, would try to back out of her routine. Antoinette showed no glint of anxiety or interest in any of the other women in the room. She was as placid as a lake and as resolute in her duties as a cold gray mountain of rock. Antoinette turned to Becca, firmly placing her cold hands on Becca's bare shoulders, commanding yet gentle. Their eyes locked in a moment of calm, and the stern facade Antoinette exuded melted momentarily.

She whispered, "Pull yourself together." Becca nodded quickly, most of her body numb except for the tingling embrace of Antoinette's cold hands on her warm shoulders. Antoinette's rigid exterior returned as the stage manager stomped into the room, commanding her minions for their performance. Antoinette's hands tightened on Rebecca's shoulders as the dominatrix's attention returned to her supplicant. "You WILL make Mr. Rainaldi proud, Bella," Antoinette asserted as she lowered her hands and resumed her placid authority.

Becca's attention shifted to the stage manager as a familiar voice delivered instructions and assignments. As her eyes lifted to the center of the room, Becca's jaw dropped as she instantly recognized the Gothic pallor and oozing disenchantment. Becca's eyes widened as she glared at the woman's burgundy lipstick bleeding into her pale complexion, emphasizing the purple stains of red wine on her teeth as she spoke.

Their eyes locked as a flash of recognition crossed the Stage Manager's face. Her eyebrow lifted slightly before she returned her attention to her roster. The voice continued, announcing the lineup, "Le Fey is on first, then Beaucoup second…"

It was mere seconds, and yet, Becca's gut wrenched for what felt like an eternity. Her head swam like the murky mud-tinged water of the St. John's River merging with the aquamarine waves of the Atlantic Ocean. Two realities clashed. Bewildered, she looked back and forth between the familiar, pale face of her former troupe leader, Desiree to the perfectly sculpted, arched face of her handler, Antoinette. She staggered as the taste of her brackish existence soured like bile in her mouth.

"Valentina third…"

Becca only heard muffled sounds, "I… I… I thought…" She slumped against a makeup table, knocking lipstick and glitter to the floor with a clatter.

Interrupted by the noise, Desiree looked up from her roster. Antoinette stepped forward, "Pardon the interruption. However, I'm sure Mr. Rainaldi has made you aware that tonight is Miss Valentina's debut. However, I believe that you've placed her third in the lineup, and that simply will not do."

Disapproval creased the lines in Desiree's forehead. Her burgundy lips pursed, and her eyes were flat. "I see. And where exactly would you like her placed, Ms…Who are you again?"

"Uh huh. I assumed you knew." Antoinette's face mimicked Desiree's disapproval. "I'm Antoinette, Mr. Rainaldi's *personal* assistant. And I assure you, he will not be pleased with her being third in the show."

Desiree stared intently at Antoinette before conceding, "Fine. What would you suggest, as Mr. Rainaldi's *personal* assistant?"

"Obviously, Miss Valentina should be the last performer before the intermission. As Mr. Rainaldi says, 'Always leave them begging for more.' And I can personally vouch that Miss Valentina's performance will, indeed, leave them wanting more."

"Fine. Miss Valentina will be fifth, right before intermission, as you suggested." As if hearing the churning thoughts in Becca's head, Desiree spoke directly to her, "And new girl, try not to fuck things up." Desiree's attention refocused on her dancers, "La Nova fourth, DeMonaco instead of fifth, you'll be third. Mr. Rainaldi will be in the audience tonight, and he deserves our best. So, let's give him our finest performances."

Becca's face flushed as the other dancers scoffed and glared at her. She heard giggles from the edge of the room. A leggy blond shook her head and commented, "amateur" under her breath. The competition among the dancers was clear. No one was here to make friends. There was no Clementine to share a bottle of wine with behind 'Mother's' back. There were no comrades. Only competition for Mr. Rainaldi's eye. Becca looked back at Antoinette, hoping for reassurance. But there was none. Just her cold commanding presence.

"Show time, ladies!" Desiree chimed.

CHAPTER FIFTEEN
LACRIMOSA

Spotlights flooded the stage with warm, ambient light made brighter by the inky black club surrounding it. From behind the burgundy velvet curtain, Bella Valentina saw the glitter-speckled stage lined with gentlemen in suits and ladies in cocktail dresses. The glittering sequins refracting light on the velvet curtain dazzled her into a trance. The romance of bygone days swept over her — a glimpse of the past, just like when she stepped through the doors of the derelict Copacabana. Her eyes only saw the sparkle of delicate necks, ears, and wrists dripping with diamond-encrusted jewelry as their owners exuded wealth and prosperity. This crowd of patrons wanted their debauchery served with opulence. They had the best that money could buy, and their sexual appetites deserved no less. Shiny confetti glitter dicks would not satisfy their appetites. Bella would need to give them more.

She heard the clinking of glasses and the popping of corks from fresh wine bottles as Trevor and his fellow bartenders served their patrons while wearing polished, glistening smiles. Pandering to young ladies who married old men was Trevor's specialty. It didn't matter whether they were looking for excitement, liquid courage, or the best orgasm of their lives. Trevor and his fellows might not have been whores, but they were certainly on the menu. Everyone in the service of Mr. Rainaldi was on the menu…for the right price. And everyone in Mr. Rainaldi's service was employed to provide the service of pleasure.

The four acts that preceded Bella Valentina's debut at The Mortimer went quickly. In a blur, dancers entered and exited the stage with such lightning precision that Becca barely noticed how much time had passed. Antoinette stood guard as women buzzed by, even though none took notice of Becca or attempted to speak. Not even Desiree attempted to speak. Yet, Antoinette remained vigilant in keeping her ward focused on the job at hand and isolated from the others.

The crowd loved every dancer who set foot beyond that burgundy curtain. Cash was tossed to the stage as though it were simply slips of paper from a poor but adoring crowd. The kitten who collected tips was thin and graceful. Svelte like a cat, part Russian Blue and part ballerina, she moved like a shadow slinking through the darkness. The way she floated around the crowd and stretched across the stage mesmerized the audience. There was something intoxicating in how she slowly dipped to the floor to collect the treasures, blinking her jewel-like blue eyes adoringly as she arched her back. Her diamond-like collar glinted. The effortless art of her movements left the patrons salivating for more. They, too, were transfixed by her gracefulness. Rebecca wondered who she was before she became Mr. Rainaldi's pet kitten, his 'Russian Blue.'

The MC was a well-stacked woman in her late thirties, with a heritage beckoning from the Emerald Isles. She had flaming red hair, emerald eyes, and pale skin that gave her an ethereal appearance. She wore a dark forest green velvet dress and addressed the crowd with a rich, deep voice. Despite her voluptuousness, she had a dainty elegance, and much like Titania, she ruled her stage domain with the terrifying power of a midsummer night's fairy queen. Her deep voice lilted over the crowd in a sing-song spell, coaxing patrons to purchase the packaged services. She implored the distinguished guests of Mr.

Rainaldi to express their gratitude through a generous tip to their bartender and maître d'. However, her most important spell-casting was reserved for announcing the next dancer to the stage, which she did with charisma.

Her velvet voice crooned, "Laddies an' lassies, prepare yerselves fur an unforgettab'l evenin' o' glamour, allure, an' tantalizin' talent! Let me introduce ye tae the dazzlin' sensation who embodies the very essence o' burlesque elegance. Wi' a blend o' classic Italian charm an' modern flair, she captivates the audience wi' every graceful move an' sultry glance."

The scene was familiar, yet different. That seductive reminiscence of stages before. Becca felt it calling to her, like a favorite lover. She wanted the limelight. Craved it from the depths of her soul. It was her drug. Her perfect high.

The Fairy Queen, continued, "Presentin' the enchantin' an' mesmerizin' Bella Valentina, a true queen o' the stage! Wi' her radiant presence an' irresistible charisma, Bella takes ye on a journey through the golden age o' burlesque, weavin' tales o' passion, mystery, an' allure. Her performances are a harmonious dance o' sophistication an' seduction, leavin' ye breathless an' yearnin' fur more."

Becca felt her alter ego, Bella Valentina, powering up from the surge of excitement as she prepared for her opportunity in the limelight. Adrenaline pumped through her veins as she transitioned from good girl to bad. From Bruce Banner to The Incredible Hulk. From Dr. Jekyll to Mr. Hyde. From Rebecca Coleman to Bella Valentina. But something even deeper inside of her screeched. Her stomach lurched as she turned from the velvet curtain, with the echo of the MC's decadent voice summoning her. As she whirled around, she was face to face with Antoinette, stern-faced and pallid. With nowhere to go, the churning bile in her stomach lurched once more as she vomited on Antoinette's crisp white blouse.

"So sit back, relax, an' let Bella Valentina transport ye tae a world o' enchantment an' wonder, where every moment is filled wi' magic an' allure. Enjoy the show!"

Disgust, loathing, and anger flashed across Antoinette's face. Her pale skin flushed to red, and in the heat of anger, she blurted, "You stupid girl! I'll have you beaten for your obstinacy."

Desiree hustled forward, shoving past Antoinette. She looked down at Antoinette's soiled blouse and up at the dribble of vomit on Bella's bright red lips. Antoinette huffed and stomped down the stairs, mumbling under her breath, "I CANNOT be seen like this. Mr. Rainaldi would not approve. I need a new blouse, NOW!"

Antoinette pushed past the other dancers toward the back of the dressing room, where the reception phone was. Desiree quickly cleaned the dribble from Bella's mouth with the sleeve of her shirt, grabbed her by the shoulders, and briskly nudged her toward the stage curtain. Hesitant to step into the limelight, Bella dug in with her heels. Rocking unsteadily, Desiree grunted, "You're not gonna ruin this for me," and gave her one final shove. Bella stumbled past the curtain and into her debut as Mr. Rainaldi's Italian Débutante.

As Bella stepped onto the stage, the first few beats of a trap remix of Mozart's Lacrimosa thudded through the speakers. The violin melody snapped her back into the precision of her choreography. All the nervous churning of her belly had disappeared to the melodic summons of Mozart. As the spotlight flooded radiant light onto her skin, Bella's movements were intricately delivered like that of a well-trained show pony, exactly as Antoinette had instructed her. She strutted, toward the metal chair that awaited her center stage, to the rhythmic intonation of a symphony. As she glanced across the crowd, she saw a sea of eyes locked on her. But that sea was sorely lacking two specific sets of eyes: Antoinette and Mr. Rainaldi. Becca had practiced her routine over and over. With Antoinette making sure that every move, every shimmy, every hair flip was perfectly in sync with the music that Mr. Rainaldi had chosen. Becca had painstakingly learned every nuance of the choreography with precision. And now, emboldened by the limelight, she threw all of that away.

As the beat dropped, instead of rolling into a hair flip as Antoinette had taught her, she turned her back to the crowd and slowly began to twerk as she bent at the hip. The rhythmic bouncing of her curves excited the crowd as they cheered for more. She slowed her twerk to a gentle shimmy as she looked over her shoulder and traced the imprint of her black lace thong against her skin. On the up-tempo, she flipped her hair, turned to face the crowd once again, and began grinding her hips in unison with the music. She slowly pushed the strap of her bra to the edge of her shoulder, tempting the crowd with a view of her large, round breasts. With every shoulder shimmy, she felt the crowd hold its breath. She turned to her side, shoved the bra strap off her shoulder, and turned her face downstage. Her back to the crowd once again, she looked over her shoulder and slowly began unhooking the band of her black lace bra. As the final hook released, she whirled around and began wildly spinning the tassels of her pasties.

She felt the patron's eyes laser-focused solely on her. Eyes full of desire, mouths begging for a taste, as wallets openly poured cash onto the stage. All for her. All for Bella Valentina. Remembering the first rule that Antoinette taught her in the Escalade, she caught a glimpse of a twenty-dollar bill near her foot. She lowered to the stage floor on her knees, bending forward as if into a downward dog position. Her pasties dangled just above the floor, tassels twirling as she shimmied her shoulders. As all eyes were on her buxom breasts teasing the crowd, she reached for the folded bill near her foot and slid it slowly into the lace folds of her thong until it was tucked securely between her legs.

She felt a surge of adrenaline as the thrill of success flooded over her. She was only just getting started. She felt that old lover pulling her closer again. The intoxication of the limelight, where she revealed her deepest yearnings. The stage was where she fed her desires. And this moment was no different. She leaned into each movement as though she was pleasuring someone — her body responding to the kinetic touch of her lover. With every nuance of her body. Every touch. Every grind. Every hair flip. Every shimmy. She was making love to the crowd. Giving them what they wanted. Her ecstasy. Her climax. With each tempo change, she responded in turn, her body responding to the beats with pure erotic desire. And the crowd loved her. They begged for more. Insatiable for the raw desire she poured over them.

She was drunk. Intoxicated by her power. Delirious with her success. She was proud of her performance. It was the best she'd ever given. And she felt fully transformed. She was Bella Valentina.

Lacrimosa was coming to an end as Bella looked across the room, past the patrons, past the circle tables with their crisp black linen tablecloths, she saw Antoinette seated at the bar. She was wearing a clean white blouse, and Trevor had just handed her a fresh crystal highball of whiskey. Antoinette's red lips puckered as she sipped on the amber liquid. She closed her eyes as she felt the liquor trickle down her throat. As Bella watched Antoinette from the stage, she thought of the crisp money folded between the thin layer of her lace thong. Antoinette's rules echoed in her head.

With the last tug of her stocking, Bella was nude, except for pasties and a thong. She dropped the thigh-high stocking to the stage floor at the cheers of an adoring crowd. Then, she blew a kiss, took a bow, and strutted off the stage.

As if prancing to the opening of Swan Lake, the Russian Blue tiptoed onto the stage to collect Bella's black lace lingerie, discarded thigh highs, and crumpled tips. The MC stood on the stairs backstage as Bella walked past.

"Aye, lassie, whit a performance," the Fairy Queen hummed. "That'll mak' Mr. Rainaldi proud, fur sure."

Bella blushed and smiled brightly, "Thank you! You really think so? It felt exhilarating to be in front of that crowd. But, I didn't see him out there."

"Aye, he sure has his ways. He's always watchin'…"

The thought of making Mr. Rainaldi proud amused her. It's what Antoinette wanted. And maybe some small part of Bella wanted it a little bit, too. She thought of the way he touched her in his private library, and the sensations that erupted from his fingertips on her skin. There was something dangerous and intoxicating about the way he touched her…the way he commanded her. She glided down the stairs and onward to her makeup table. Standing in her isolated corner of the changing room, as she put on her satin robe, her hand caressed the outer fabric of the lace thong between her thighs. She felt the crinkle of paper rough against her skin.

Part Six

Bitch Betta Have My Money

CHAPTER SIXTEEN
TERRIBLE THOUGHT

The servants' entrance door to the backstage swung open abruptly and crashed against an unused makeup table, sending brushes and rounds of eyeshadow rolling. A few of the dancers scuttled at the sound of the banging door. Unfazed, Antoinette barged into the room, her eyes ablaze as she glared at Bella. Dancers scattered for fear of being her victim. The Russian Blue stood frozen and wide-eyed at the edge of the stage, Bella's lingerie cascading through her waifish fingers. Like a creeping wildfire that destroys everything in its path, she marched toward her subordinate preparing a verbal lashing so brutal it was sure to incinerate its intended victim. Even Desiree, aware of Antoinette's authority but not of her vengeance, cowered in a remote corner of the room. The room lay silent, with only the muted sounds of the performance echoing just past the curtain. The bustle of the dressing room had come to a full halt.

Bella turned around as she felt Antoinette approach, her chin defiantly jutted forward, as if bracing for a slap. If this was to be her retribution for changing the routine, then she would take it on the chin. Her mother may have instructed her in the fragility of guilt, but she felt a renewed sense of defiance coursing through her veins. She would not give Mother Dearest the satisfaction of seeing her tremble or shirk her punishment.

"You noxious tart," Antoinette seethed, "Of all the ungrateful… disrespectful… HOW DARE YOU?"

Other dancers just entering the room turned to see what the commotion was, pausing to watch what they believed to be just another cat fight between whores. Upon realizing it was Mr. Rainaldi's right hand, they quickly bounded out of the room. Antoinette leaned forward, lowering her voice, enunciating her words with precision and authority.

"After all I have done for you. Your disrespectful insolence toward me will not go unpunished. Mr. Rainaldi will not stand for it. He'll take the strap to that pretty back of yours. And I'll…"

"Madame," the Greek Nose interrupted. Lost in her diatribe, Antoinette didn't notice he had crept up behind her. She snapped erect and rounded on him, as if she intended to extend the lashing toward him for interrupting. "Pardon," the Greek Nose leaned closer, whispering so only Antoinette could hear. "Mr. Rainaldi requests your presence in his office. He would like for you to bring the girl, as well."

"Indeed," she sneered, her eyes penetrating Bella.

Entering Mr. Rainaldi's office, Antoinette grabbed Bella's wrist and roughly shoved her through the doorway. Bella stumbled on the thick Persian carpet and caught her balance on an antique wooden chair. The chair creaked under her weight. She glared at Antoinette as she rushed by, eager to tattle. Bella straightened her posture, and smoothed the front of her dress. Mr. Rainaldi looked up from his computer screen as the ladies entered. Antoinette dashed to the edge of his large, mahogany desk.

"Sir," Antoinette almost purred at Mr. Rainaldi anticipating his satisfaction with her diligence, "Bella has been most disagreeable. She did not comply…"

"Antoinette, my dear, you talk too much. Bella was nothing less than dazzling on stage."

"Yes, sir, but she did not perform the choreography as we rehearsed."

"I am aware."

"Sir, is that not cause for punishment? She has been quite insolent and she has caused me distress, as well as a wardrobe change. I…"

"Antoinette, enough," he said as he rose from his desk chair.

"But, sir, it took ages to locate a blouse that would fit me. I know how you prefer for me to be smartly dressed, sir. I…"

"I said, ENOUGH. I will not repeat myself again. You are the one being quite insolent, Antoinette. And, you will not question my authority on this matter any further. I will decide who receives punishment, and when."

"I understand, sir. I just thought…"

"Antoinette, clearly you have mistaken your role. Again. You've been far too harsh with Bella. Go occupy yourself with some menial task. Perhaps, Leonora will have something you can do in reception or scheduling." Mr. Rainaldi dismissed her with the wave of his hand and turned toward Bella standing near the chair, just inside the door. "Now, Bella, my jewel, let me look at you."

With the fresh shock of her failure and sudden demotion, Antoinette stepped backward, abruptly turned, and exited the room. Her eyes were aflame and she mouthed the word 'cunt' as she passed Bella. The fire in her wrath temporarily squelched.

Bella stepped forward, modest but confident, from behind the antique chair that hid the voluptuousness of her curves. As she twirled slowly for him, she felt the shift and crinkle of paper between her thighs. Mixed emotions swirled within her; feeling the giddiness of a young girl seeking her father's approval, all the while knowing that she'd been naughty, and had a secret to keep.

"Positively radiant. You were spectacular on stage, Bella. You are truly a talented dancer. Such graceful movements. Such raw magnetism. You've turned out to be quite the diamond in the rough. A rare treasure I've plucked from the dirt. That hole-in-the-wall bar I rescued you from did not deserve you. But look at you now, polished and glittering. I knew from the first moment I saw you backstage that you'd outshine the rest."

Bella beamed at him. He caressed her neck, gliding his fingers down the length of the chain from the silver necklace he'd placed there a little over a week before. He scooped the heart-shaped pendant into his hand. He held the pendant, the serifs of the engraved 'R' sparkling, as he gazed into her green eyes. She trembled at the warmth of his hand hovering just above her exposed cleavage. Her breath caught in her throat as she watched him, watching her with the same focused attention of a panther on the prowl.

"The facets of your eyes take my breath away, Bella. You are truly beautiful." He gently released the engraved heart pendant. "Now, then, shall I introduce you to some of my guests, my jewel?"

She nodded her head excitedly, "I'd love to."

"Then, onward to the club, my jewel."

CHAPTER SEVENTEEN
DIAMONDS ARE FOREVER

Mr. Rainaldi opened the office door, extending out his arm for Becca to hold on to. The way that he doted on her reminded her of the classic movies that she would watch with her mother when she was young. She'd always been starstruck with that romantic era. The dashing gentleman who was bold and austere yet somehow warm and loving, was usually played by some handsome man, like Cary Grant or Rock Hudson. The leading ladies were headstrong and beautiful, strong yet vulnerable. Becca thought of the glamor of Old Hollywood, and how the ladies swooned for those gallant men. A coy smile crept across her face as she delicately wrapped her arm around Mr. Rainaldi's.

He paused, searching her face quizzically, before asking, "What is it?"

"Oh, nothing really. You just remind me of Cary Grant."

"My dear, you flatter me."

They walked slowly down the empty hallway to the secret elevator that Antoinette ushered her through earlier. Mr. Rainaldi inserted a small round key into the hidden access panel and entered the elevator. Once inside, he typed in his code to activate the controls, and set their destination to the first floor. Bella was learning that there were many hidden areas within this monumental resort.

As they entered the club, arms linked together, Antoinette sat at the front desk with Leonora, the same girl who greeted them when she first arrived. Leonora nodded to Mr. Rainaldi with a militant decorum. Antoinette, however, was sulking, appearing to be more interested in licking her emotional wounds than she was in sorting room keys and organizing files. Clearly, this was busy work. And, clearly, she was noticeably offended to be subjected to it. Bella flashed her a look of schadenfreude as she breezed by. Mr Rainaldi paid her absolutely no attention, which further ignited Antoinette's disgust.

Mr. Rainaldi pushed open the double doors to reveal a bustling club. With the show at intermission, go-go dancers had taken their places on the bar and in the table top cages around the room. Working girls had also entered the club to work the crowd. Even though the club resembled the chaotic hum of a beehive, it worked like a well-oiled machine. Everyone knew their role and performed it with the utmost efficiency. It didn't matter that a tall brunette's long legs hovered inches above Trevor as he served cocktails from the bar. He was ever alert and professional in his mixology of drinks. Each actor performed their roles with effortless ease, in tandem, without hiccup.

The club seemed different to Becca now. Less like a gilded cage, and more like the opulence she craved. East Creekview never had anything as decadent as this. She tightened her grip on Mr. Rainaldi's arm and flaunted her best showgirl pose. The pair didn't walk very far into the club before a swarm of executive looking men descended upon them. Each offering Mr. Rainaldi a firm handshake or a clap on the back, they were greeted like old college pals held in high regard. He schmoozed as she offered a gleaming smile to each new introduction. Like a procession of guests congratulating a bride and groom on their nuptials, patrons took turns waiting for their moment with Mr. Rainaldi and his new girl. It was a parade of pandering compliments aimed solely on her body or her performance. Becca had never felt more beautiful in all of her life. She had grown up thinking she was an ugly duckling. Nothing special; more focused on learning, and being her mother's pride and joy.

"Bella is truly my diamond in the rough," Mr. Rainaldi boasted to a short man with thinning, greasy, black hair and a tight sport coat over a polo shirt that barely covered his protruding belly. "An absolute treasure, I tell you."

"Rainaldi, you sho have out dun yourself this time. The whole lot of 'em are tens," the greasy man replied, eyeballing Bella intensely.

"You're too kind, Guy. Of course, I appreciate your help in the matter. Your team responded quickly."

"Of course! Of course! Them boys always happy to help." Guy lifted his whiskey glass as a toast, sloshing some of the amber liquid onto the floor. "They enjoy the spoils as much as any man who likes keepin' his dick wet." Guy winked at Mr. Rainaldi, and nudged him in the rib with his elbow. "But, we can work out the particular's to settle up anotha time, unless you'd be willin' to let me have first crack at this lil lady."

The greasy man stepped forward, grabbing Bella's free hand. His dark eyes glittered insidiously as he winked at her. Bella's gleaming pageant smile dropped. She hadn't completely been paying attention to the conversation, still awestruck with the opulence of the room, but the way the greasy man looked at her made her feel dirty and shameful. She feigned a weak smile, and gently pulled her hand free from the man's as if she were shrinking from the open maw of an alligator.

"Guy, my friend, you are emboldened with too much drink," Mr. Rainaldi stepped between the greasy man and Bella. His arm still linked tightly with Bella's, he swung her behind him. As he stood face to face with his friend, he said in a low growl, "Bella is a feast for the eyes only. No exceptions. And, we will 'settle up,' as you say, in the usual method when the job is done."

Mr. Rainaldi leaned in closer, his voice a forceful whisper, "There is one still unaccounted for, you'll remember."

"I do. I do. Don't ya fret now. I got my boy Jones on it. He's round here somewhere," Guy said as he turned to search the crowd.

Mr. Rainaldi abruptly turned, pulling Bella with him, toward the bar. With a wave of Mr. Rainaldi's hand, Trevor was pouring Vecchio Amaro del Capo into a chilled shot glass. He handed the glass directly to Mr. Rainaldi, and awaited further instruction. With another wave of Mr. Rainaldi's hand, Trevor collected the glass and returned the Italian liquor into a hidden cabinet below the bar. Mr. Rainaldi took a deep breath. Becca didn't understand why but she was certain that he was shaken up by the encounter, possibly as equally as she was. She eyed him, unsure of how to proceed. She felt the urge to soothe him. Like a new mother, she felt the need to ease his discomfort, just as she wished someone could ease her own. That sense of protection when the world around you gets too dark. She rested her hand on his shoulder, but his eyes were glazed over, much like the boar that hung on his wall. Maybe that's what separated humans from animals, the urge to nurture. She wondered why he was so unsettled; was it because of the way the greasy man treated her? She saw this moment of vulnerability as a new side of him but also questioned if the man before her had ever felt compassion for others. She couldn't decide if he was truly bad or just misunderstood. He glanced up at the dancer on the bar, and sneered. Her long legs never distracted Trevor from tending bar, but they revolted Mr. Rainaldi at this moment.

"Shouldn't you be giving someone a blow job instead of annoying me? Shoo. Go away!"

The dancer blanched and scurried off the edge of the bar. Becca eased her hand from Mr. Rainaldi's shoulder and stood awkwardly at his side, unsure of what to do.

Antoinette lurked, watching from the corner by the doors. A man faced her, leaning against the door frame, as they spoke. The shadows of the club hid them from view, like two lovers who only wanted to be lost in each other's eyes. But Antoinette's eyes weren't lost in a lovers, they were fixed on Becca and Mr. Rainaldi. She whispered into the man's ear, "Jones, do you have any of the prototype on you?"

He gently nodded his head, "Whatcha want it fer?"

"I've got an idea how we can both get something we want tonight."

"Is that right? Whatcha got in mind, Annie?"

"A little science experiment, if you will. I get to test the mixture and you can offer a little bribe to your boss for that promotion."

"Oh, well, why didn't you say so? Whaddya need me to do?"

"Just tell Guy that he can settle up in Bungalow 9 in about 15 minutes. And get the prototype to Trevor."

"I sho will, darlin'. Consider it done."

The two nodded to each other and swept away from the shadow. The Greek Nose appeared at Mr. Rainaldi's shoulder, with Antoinette right on his heels. She flashed a coquettish smile, as a sort of apology, and sat on the bar stool next to where Bella stood. The Greek Nose whispered something unintelligible into Mr. Rainaldi's ear.

"Bella, my jewel, I have some business to attend to." Mr. Rainaldi clasped her hand in his. "I'll leave you with Antoinette." Mr. Rainaldi glared at Antoinette, "That is, if you think you can handle it without incident."

Antoinette gave him a reassuring nod, "Yes, Mr. Rainaldi. Of course, Mr. Rainaldi. As you wish, sir," she simpered.

"See that you do." His eyebrow cocked in distrust. He gave Antoinette a final threatening glance and exited the club with the Greek Nose. The two men were only gone mere seconds before Antoinette turned her full attention to Bella. She smoothed the creases of her tight black pencil skirt, as if she were preparing for a marketing pitch.

"Bella, dear, I've been thinking," Antoinette purred, "Perhaps I was too harsh with you earlier. This is your debut, after all. I've been working you sun up to sun down every day for a week in preparation for this night. But, perhaps you didn't have enough time to truly learn the choreography... as I had directed." Antoinette paused, rested her elbow on the mahogany bar, and leaned closer to Bella effectively boxing her in, "Just know that you are not the first showgirl I've handled and I will take care of you." Antoinette arched her back like a cat stretching before a hunt, "We'll chalk this little mishap up to first show jitters."

"Oh. Um. That's awfully... gracious of you, Antoinette." Bella's eyes narrowed, searching Antoinette's face for some hint of guilt, but she did not see the pursed lips she was accustomed to, only the placid, confident gaze of her handler. "Are you sure you're not angry?"

"No, not at all, my dear," Antoinette crooned. "I was hasty before. Impetuous. Hot-headed. We'll let bygones be bygones. C'est la vie."

Bella watched Antoinette suspiciously for a moment before shrugging it off, "Sure... Sure. C'est la vie."

"Mr. Rainaldi was quite happy with your little performance, so I have no reason to be otherwise. In fact, let's toast to your success! Trevor, let's have a bottle. I believe the lady prefers a sweet, white wine?"

"As you wish, Antoinette." Trevor began for the wine cooler, looking for the bottle he had offered Bella earlier that afternoon.

"No, no, Trevor," her eyes locked with his laser focus as a sinister grin curled the edges of her mouth, "something special... for Bella."

"Ah! Yes, ma'am. I have just the thing."

"Would you bring it to Bungalow 9? I'll take Bella there to relax until Marco has the car ready for our return to The Chalet."

"Of course, Antoinette. As you wish."

Antoinette ushered Bella away from the bar, out of the club, and down the corridor to the private rooms. The hall seemed to go on forever. It was dimly lit and the moss colored walls were hugged by shadows appearing to melt into darkness. The stone flooring gave it a reminiscent feel like that of a French Quarter cobblestone alley, lurking with excitement, mystery, or danger. The darkness was only broken by a solitary boob light every ten feet. As the two women walked down the corridor, the only sound that accompanied their footsteps was the soft crooning of a distant saxophone. It left a lonely, haunting feeling hanging in the air, clinging to the night like a heavy fog descending over a river.

Bungalow 9 was at the end of the hall. The boob light that hung over the nearby Bungalow 10 flickered as Antoinette pulled an elaborate bronze key from her pocket and opened the door with a metallic clank. The room was cozy. It was a small suite with warm, low lights and one queen size bed with crisp linens. A woolly white robe hung on a hook next to the bathroom. With a wide smile, Antoinette invited Bella into the room.

"Make yourself comfortable, Bella. Why not take a hot shower? I'll have fresh clothes brought for you."

"Um… Wow. Thank you, Antoinette. That's really kind of you." She hesitated, insecurity bubbling in her veins. "Do you know how long we'll be here?" Bella wrung her hands, "I mean… how long before Marco takes us back?"

"No need to fret about that. Just relax. Trevor will be in with your wine soon."

"Are you sure about this?"

"Of course! Of course! Anything for Mr. Rainaldi's 'Diamond in the Rough.'"

Bella cocked her head to one side, "What did you say?"

Trevor knocked at the door and hustled forward. He poured a glass of white wine and returned the bottle to the ice bucket. Leaving, he turned to Bella, "Anything else, ma'am?"

"Not tonight, Trevor. Thank you."

"Cheers, Bella," Antoinette waved from the door.

"Yes," she lifted the wine glass into the air, "to… me!"

Bella lowered the glass to her lips, and took a large swig. Antoinette smiled wide as she and Trevor left the room together, locking the door behind them with an ominous, metallic clank. Bella poured more white wine into her glass until the liquid kissed the lip of the flute. She took another gulp, as if she were drinking a cool glass of water. The tension in her shoulders melted away as the refreshing liquid calmed her soul. She sighed as a twinge of nostalgia crossed her mind. It wasn't discount grocery store wine with Clementine, but somehow she felt honored and appreciated. Like she could ask anything of Mr. Rainaldi and it would be done. She was without comrades, and yet, felt royal, like she had finally made it. This was the biggest and nicest venue she had ever performed in and they loved her. Truly, earnestly loved her. And now she was being catered to, with a chilled bottle of good wine, and a private room. She mused, "This is what success feels like." What more could she ask for? "Another toast!" She pulled the chilled bottle of wine from the ice bath, lifted it into the air.

"To Clementine, my dearest friend… my only friend, wherever she may be," she turned the bottle up and drank the contents in four smooth gulps. Then, she returned the empty bottle to the ice bath.

Bella felt the warmth of the alcohol wrap her like a blanket. Her face flushed and she felt as if she were the sun radiating heat onto the crystal white sands of the beach. She slipped out of her body-con dress, and stood under the air conditioner vent in her underwear. Fanning her fevered face, she drank the last few drops of cool wine from the glass and set it on the table before plopping face first onto the bed. The linens felt smooth and crisp on her warm skin, like plunging into the sea. She spread her arms and legs making a snow angel with the white linens. She imagined the ice melting like the slush of a frozen margarita; condensation dripping from the bowl of the glass as she licked the salt from the rim. Suddenly, she felt a pinch between her legs along the seam of her thong. She flipped over and bolted up.

"The twenty!"

She laid back on the bed and ran her fingers along the seam of her thong, slipping them beneath the damp fabric, until she felt the bill protruding like a spent tampon. She gently pulled it loose, slowly sliding the money out, shuttering as it caressed her sensitive skin, her hips rising from the bed. Her breath caught in her throat as the corner of the bill eased past the edge of her wet thong. She held the soaked bill in the air, letting the cool breeze from the air conditioner vent dry it off. She ran the fingertips of her other hand down the length of her abdomen, lifting gently as she touched the smooth skin of her inner thigh.

The lock to Bungalow 9 clicked. The door swung open, and quickly shut. Bella barely noticed as she continued touching herself.

"Gettin' started without me, lil lady?"

The greasy Southern voice echoed in her head. Bella paused momentarily, drifting through a sea of ecstasy, as her fevered body arched and contorted.

"Well, now, what's this?" The man took the damp bill from her hand. "Oh, you're a dirty girl, aren't you? Where'd you get this from? Looks like you've been mighty naughty, lil lady."

Bella continued to caress her skin, lost in a euphoric trance, the man's words floating toward her on whiskey waves. The man loosened his belt, unbuttoned his pants, and pulled a small plastic bag from his pocket. He shook a thin white line of powder onto the table. He rolled the damp bill into a tube, and placed it under his broad nose, inhaling deeply, as if sniffing a cigar. He moaned and snorted the line of dust.

"Time to settle up."

CHAPTER EIGHTEEN
WHAT A FRIEND WE HAVE IN JESUS

It was just past mid-day when Becca felt the warm sunlight burning a hole through her eyes. A solitary beam of white hot light poured in from the round window near the ceiling. She laid face up on the starched white carpet of her bedroom at The Chalet. Frozen from a deep sleep, like rigor mortis had set in, she felt as if she'd just awoken from being dead. Her eyes squinted away the bright light. Her mouth was mossy. Her ears rang. Her head throbbed. Her body ached. She had pain in places she didn't know existed. She wiggled her toes, flexing her leg muscles slowly to get the blood flowing again. The cramping and stiffness momentarily halted her. Evading the sunlight, she rolled onto her side and into the fetal position, wincing from the pain. Like a new born baby that had just been slapped on the ass, she felt the urge to cry. If this was what being born felt like, it was terrible. Becca felt a heavy sadness churning deep inside of her. But she had no clue where it came from. Maybe she had been dead. Maybe this was her resurrection. Maybe this was hell.

Mother would say, Pray it away, Becca thought as she curled her body tighter, wrapping her arms around her knees. She felt the starched white carpet burn her tender skin. Why did everything hurt? This was the most physical pain Becca had experienced in her twenty-something years. She was weak. And tired. And she didn't know why. She tried to think back, but her memory was dark and hazy, like slices of her life had been surgically removed from her gray matter. She didn't remember how she got on the floor, or even how she got back to The Chalet.

Using an elbow for stabilization, she lifted herself from the floor. She leaned forward to sit up and the world around her lurched. Dizziness. Nausea. *I'm going to throw up,* Becca thought. She saw a vision of Antoinette's angry face and vomit covered blouse pop into her mind. *You stupid girl!* Antoinette's voice echoed in her throbbing head. She remembered going to The Mortimer; the Escalade parked just out front. She remembered hovering by the curtain. She remembered the pre-show jitters. Then, nothing. Darkness clouded her mind. Droplets of black ink into a shallow water basin. She sat up and inched closer to the bed, so she could lean against it. Her back against the bed frame, she curled into the fetal position again, rocking back and forth. Her arms were weak and wouldn't wholly envelope her knees, the clasp of her hands broken by the trembling of her muscles. She looked down at her legs and realized they were speckled with small oval bruises. *What happened to me?*

Her heart ached and her mind reeled. Tears leaked from the corners of her eyes. She couldn't help but think back to when she was twelve. Sitting just like this, in her bedroom in East Creekview, the transparent lime green curtains shimmering in the sun, while the beaded metal fan pull clanked against the frosted glass globe above. She was crying then, too. Her mother had been dealing with an impending divorce. Her father had just moved out and her mother was beside herself with grief. Mourning the loss of a marriage that was never happy. Her mother held firmly to the mantra, "When the Devil sends trouble, the only course of action is to pray it away." And it didn't matter what it was. Something in life just didn't work out— pray it away. The pain of heartache was too much to bear—pray it away. Need a green traffic light instead of a red one—pray it away. Any time her mother simply didn't know what to do, the answer for everything —from mundane to life-threatening—was, PRAY IT AWAY.

"Give it to Jesus," her mother would say, throwing her hands into the air. Praying was Mrs. Coleman's favorite coping mechanism. Giving her problems to someone else, instead of dealing with them herself, was no doubt how she ended up in the midst of divorce. Mrs. Coleman had a nasty habit of turning a blind eye when praying it away didn't work. Even Mr. Coleman, her Southern Baptist minister husband, couldn't handle the incessant nagging, denying, and blaming. But, Becca always wondered what happened when there was no answer to her prayers? What if the terrible heart break continued? What if she received the red light instead of the green? Even after she prayed and prayed and prayed. Even after she gave it to Jesus. What happened then? Well, then, it must have been God's will.

God's Will. Becca sobbed, a deep guttural noise emitting from her small frame. Her tears dripped onto her skinned knees, re-wetting the wound, so that watery blood trickled down her shins. She rested her head on the bed frame, inhaling a deep breath, *Pull yourself together, Rebecca.* She wiped her tears with the palms of her hands. Then, stood up to find the carpet where she had been sitting was stained bright red. Her hands trembled as she removed the bloody thong, and placed it in the trash can in the bathroom. The lock of her bedroom door clicked and caught her off guard. Becca jolted as Antoinette entered the room.

"Bella, my—," Antoinette called, her eyes falling to the stained floor, "Oh, dear, this will not do. Marco will need to clean this carpet at once. Mr. Rainaldi will not be pleased with this one bit. Mr. Rainaldi insists on a clean house."

Without ceremony or a response from Becca, the bedroom door slammed shut as Antoinette hurried down the steps. Within moments, the door reopened with a frantic Marco pushing a carpet steamer and a nagging Antoinette reiterating how to get blood out of white carpet.

"Now, Marco, you MUST use bleach. And hot water! Mr. Rainaldi will want absolutely NO traces of blood."

"Yes, Antoinette," Marco groaned, "Isn't that always the way I clean the floors around here?"

"Mr. Rainaldi is exceedingly clear about his requirements for The Chalet," Antoinette intoned.

"Yes, Antoinette. I know, Antoinette. You'll remember I've been in Mr. Rainaldi's employment longer than you have. Now, shoo, and leave me to it."

"I'm simply ensuring that Mr. Rainaldi's wishes are honored. But if you insist… I have Bella to tend to."

"That you do. Now, if you don't mind…"

With a churlish smile, Antoinette spun on her heel and darted to the bathroom where Becca, naked, hid behind the door.

"Bella, my dear, you look atrocious. Bathe. At once. And put on the black knit dress in the closet. The turtleneck. Then, come downstairs. Mr. Rainaldi requests your presence in the study."

Becca numbly stood still, her mouth agape, and her eyes glazed over. She swayed and staggered as her muscles began to give in from standing on the tile floor.

"AT ONCE," Antoinette demanded sharply. Becca snapped erect and stared at Antoinette, as if she had just realized she was in the room. Becca was bewildered and unable to process Antoinette's quick instruction.

Becca fumbled with the towel draped in front of her and shuffled her feet, rebalancing her weight to keep from falling over.

Antoinette snatched the towel from Becca's hand, exposing her body, and yelled, "BATHE," as if she was speaking a foreign language to someone who also happened to be deaf.

Becca awkwardly covered her bare breasts with one arm and her groin with the other.

"I've seen it before, my dear," Antoinette sneered, "and frankly, I'm not impressed."

Antoinette marched out of the bathroom, giving one final command to Marco, who was busy cleaning the carpet. The door closed with a thud behind her.

Bella closed the bathroom door, and turned on the shower. She stared at herself in the mirror for a long time before the steam fogged it over. She was bruised from top to bottom. Streaks of mascara ran down her cheeks. Red lipstick smeared around her mouth and chin, like an invisible hand silenced her. Her hair tangled and matted to her face. She traced the mysterious marks on her skin, five oval bruises aligned on her forearm. Her hands were dirty, battered, swollen. She thought of Sexy Jesus hanging above her mother's dining room table. His arms stretched to each side of the cross, his body limp and languishing. She stretched her arms out to her side, palms facing up. As a thin layer of condensation formed on the mirror, she thought she looked a bit like HIM, bearing her own crucifixion.

Was it 3 hours? Or 3 days? She thought, *maybe I've been resurrected, too.* She lowered her arms and backed away from her hazy reflection. *Or maybe I was in a car crash...But Marco and Antoinette were not injured,* she thought. She strained her memory trying to recall. But it only felt like more droplets of black ink hitting the murky water. But, somehow, she knew it was something much, much worse. She could feel it deep in her gut.

Stepping into the hot water, her body throbbed with pain, cuts and scrapes burned, blood ran pink down the drain, everything in her screamed. Like the visceral, red and orange smeared brush strokes of the sky in Edvard Munch's famous painting, her body was enraged and screeching. Existential dread filled the hollow parts inside of her, but it was too late. Her heart and her mind grew inky black and benumbed in her isolation. She had no one to turn to.

Part Seven

That's Showbiz, Baby!

CHAPTER NINETEEN
GOODBYE EARL

Antoinette checked her watch. She restlessly tapped her foot, as she stood at the bottom of the staircase. Becca saw her there as she closed the door to her room. She winced as she made her way down the staircase, apologizing to Antoinette as she passed.

"Mr. Rainaldi is waiting for you in his study."

Becca did not respond. She knew better. Antoinette's words were terse and her face made it abundantly clear that she was not fond of waiting. Becca nodded her head and immediately walked toward Mr. Rainaldi's study. Antoinette followed close behind her, hell-bent on delivering her ward directly to Mr. Rainaldi herself. The two women passed through the kitchen. Marco was there meticulously pulling and folding large strands of dough.

Attempting to regain some rapport with her coworker, Antoinette asked, "What are you making, Marco?"

But Marco didn't respond, he only looked up momentarily, then went back to his work without acknowledging Antoinette. Becca continued walking, with her head down, toward Mr. Rainaldi's office. She was more concerned with what fresh hell awaited her there.

Arriving at the closed study door, Becca paused, hesitant to enter the room where Mr. Rainaldi had first touched her, where he had first claimed her, like a prize. She was revolted, and felt her stomach churn at the thought. Antoinette pushed slightly past her and knocked delicately.

"Enter."

Antoinette entered the room first, as if escorting her prisoner to the warden on a golden leash. But Mr. Rainaldi dismissed her at once.

"Antoinette, leave us. I have no need for you right now."

She bowed her head and left the room sulking. Becca stood awkwardly just inside the door, fighting her disgust only to be overcome once again by the large game mantled on the wall. The boar's glassy eyes seemed to smile in recognition. She felt as dead as a stuffed boar's head. Her own eyes glassed over.

"Bella, my jewel," Mr. Rainaldi said as he stepped from behind his teak desk. "Come in. I have a matter to discuss with you."

She walked closer, "Um… sh… should I… um," she stuttered as she gestured toward the Queen Anne chair that sat in front of his desk.

"Sit. Make yourself comfortable."

Becca sat on the edge of the large overstuffed chair, willing to do what she had been told to but unwilling to be comfortable with it. Mr. Rainaldi returned to his own seat behind the teak desk. He leaned forward, placing his elbows on the edge of his desk, and interlaced his fingers. His chin rested on his clasped hands, as he searched her face.

"Bella, I know."

Becca's eyebrows shot up, and she stared at him incredulously, "You… know?"

"Yes," Mr. Rainaldi said as he leaned back in his chair. "I know everything."

"I… I'm sorry. I don't follow. What is it that you know?"

"Do not play coy with me. What do you take me for? A fool? I know everything. Everything! How do you think a man of my incredible worth came to be so powerful? It's because I know everything. I must, if I am to succeed. And, Bella, my jewel, failure has never been an option for me. Now tell me the truth."

"I'm sorry. But I don't know what you mean."

"Stop this charade! I know what you did. I know you stole from me. Just be honest with me about it, and all will be forgiven."

"I… I'm not."

"STOP. I will not be LIED to. And I will not be STOLEN from. Not after everything that I have done for you. You were nothing when I discovered you in that sad little bar, dancing for pennies. NOTHING. And, I told you that I would take care of you. I told you that you were mine. And you ARE mine. From the moment I placed that necklace around your neck and tasted your mouth. I OWN you, Bella. And, I will not have this insolence."

Mr. Rainaldi stood up. He loosened the collar on his black shirt and began rolling up the sleeves. His tan face grew pink, flustered with anger. He ran his fingers through his thick black hair. He looked ten feet tall from where Becca sat. Her hands began to tremble as she saw his rage building. She was unsure what he would do next, but she feared the worst. Becca sprang to her feet. She held her arms up and her palms facing him, pleading her innocence.

"I told you to sit," he growled in a low, firm voice.

Becca sank into the chair, and not on the edge this time. She pressed her back into the overstuffed Queen Anne, as if she were trying to disappear. She wanted to disassociate, dissolve, and be anywhere but there, shattering into a million bats or even stumbling down a gravel road in high heels. His face was dark and serious, and the sweetness had dropped completely from his voice. There was only the low growl of a dangerous man on the verge of doing dangerous things.

"I will give you one more chance to tell the truth, Bella. Confess now. Tell me that you stole $20 dollars. Tell me that you had sex with one of my patrons. Tell me that I introduced you in my club like a queen. And for what… for you to repay my kindness by acting like a common whore? Bella, tell the truth, and all will be forgiven."

Becca's mouth had fallen agape and her eyes were frozen in terror. Internally her mind was a tornado of thoughts, swirling and crashing against her skull. *Oh my god, so that's what happened to me? That horrible greasy man… in the Bungalow.* She began sobbing uncontrollably.

"SAY IT, BELLA. YOUR TEARS WILL NOT SAVE YOU."

"I'm sorry. I'm sorry. I didn't know. It wasn't my fa—," her words were slurred and choked by the tears streaming down her face. She shuttered and gasped a deep breath. "I… I promise… I don't know anything."

Mr. Rainaldi knelt in front of her. He held her chin in his hand, "Say it, Bella, my jewel." The sweetness was coming back to his voice. He urged her for the truth. All she had to do was confess.

Becca's body shuttered as she released a heavy sigh, "I lied to you. I stole from you. I'm sorry." Her tears ran around the edge of Mr. Rainaldi's hand on her chin. He stood and wiped his hand on a tissue.

"Thank you, Bella. Thank you for being honest with me."

Becca nodded her head, unable to speak. Mr. Rainaldi leaned against his desk and crossed his arms.

"Bella, you must trust me to take care of you. Not just for the sake of the dancing, the production… but our working relationship. I can't build a relationship on trust if you don't trust me."

He stared into her eyes, searching for reassurance. But he found only tears. After a moment, Becca lifted her hand toward him. He took it.

"Here. I will prove it to you," he said as he pulled a bottle of vermouth from the wine cooler, and a bottle of whiskey and three glasses from the bar cart behind his desk. He poured the chilled vermouth into two of the glasses, and then measured the whiskey into its own separate glass. Then, he picked up the phone, "Antoinette, come see me. At once."

Within moments, Antoinette entered the study without a knock. She was eager to hear how Bella would be punished for everything that went wrong with her debut at The Mortimer.

"A toast to you," Mr. Rainaldi raised the whiskey glass he had prepared and handed it to Antoinette. She blushed, accepting the glass with pride.

"You do me a great honor, Mr. Rainaldi. This is a special treat. What is the occasion?"

"Consider it payment for all the things you orchestrate, seen and unseen."

Antoinette smiled wide. "You are too kind, Mr. Rainaldi. It is all in your service," she purred in her usual pandering tone.

He passed the glasses of vermouth for himself and for Becca.

"Saluti!"

The three drank. Antoinette sipped her whiskey with a smile, showing her teeth to Becca.

"I've a few notes on the performance at The Mortimer, if you'll indulge me," he quipped.

Antoinette beamed and replied, "Yes! I've a few notes of my own I think you'll find interesting. Especially near the end of the performance, sir."

Becca winced, knowing that Antoinette meant the moment where she slid the cash into her thong. She blushed. Uncomfortable at the thought of her shame being on display. Mr. Rainaldi walked to his desk, picked up the remote, and turned on the TV. Black and white silent security footage came onto the screen in searing high-definition, showcasing the packed house at The Mortimer. However, the stage was empty. No unflattering views of Becca, no twenty dollar bill. Just as the camera slowly panning across the crowd, eventually landing at Becca, Mr. Rainaldi, Guy, and their moment of speaking at the bar.

"Sir," Antoinette said, clearing her throat and taking another sip of her drink, "I don't mean to interrupt, but this footage looks to be ahead of the performance. Can we go back approximately 15 min—"

Antoinette found herself distracted by a sudden imagery cut. There, in crystal clear 4K, was her standing and sulking in her corner - eyeballing Rainaldi and Becca, with Jones approaching her.

Antoinette froze, watching herself conniving with Jones onscreen. She found herself riddled with fear, but could not move. She watched the camera again as it panned out showing a new image - Antoinette making her way behind the Greek Nose and ultimately getting charge of Becca, while Jones worked his way behind the gaggle, approaching Trevor at the bar with a packet of drugs. A pregnant pause hung in thick air as Antoinette's smile faded into paralysis. She then suddenly noticed the difference in beverages between the three of them in the room, as she lost control of her hand and dropped the glass, watching it smash on the floor.

"Something wrong, Antoinette? You shouldn't let good bourbon go to waste."

Mr. Rainaldi barely finished his sentence before Antoinette's eyes grew wide and dilated. She stumbled, drunker than what two sips of whiskey could offer. Antoinette looked to Becca, then Rainaldi with a puzzled, frightened look of horror. Rainaldi reached into his pants pocket and pulled out a small bag - the exact shape and size as the one Jones proffered Trevor during the night in question, only completely empty.

"You know… I gotta hand it to you. This was incredibly clean. No trace of anything in Becca's system. But because it's so new, we also have no idea what 24 times the standard dosage will do to a person, so I guess we're about to find out."

Antoinette began to choke, and crumbled to the floor. Mr. Rainaldi stood over her and tsk tsked.

"I just can't get over the fact that you orchestrated this; the drugs, that fucking man, everything. And for what? Did you think you could take over? Do better than me?!"

Blood and bile foamed from her mouth and pooled on an intricate Persian rug that she began convulsing on.

Mr Rainaldi sighed, "And of course, your final act of defiance against me would be to ruin this fucking carpet. This was my favorite. You knew that. You picked it."

Antoinette tried to gurgle out a last response, but finally went limp.

Mr. Rainaldi picked up the phone and dialed the kitchen, "Marco, I need your assistance."

"Right away, sir."

As Marco entered the room, he saw Antoinette crumpled in her heap.

"Marco, you know the drill… Feed the dogs. Burn the firewood," Mr. Rainaldi waved his hand at Antoinette's limp body on the carpet, "And order a new rug."

"Of course, Mr. Rainaldi, but… I'm still pulling the su filindeu," Marco rang his flour dusted hands. "Can this wait until the pasta is drying on the fundu?"

Mr. Rainaldi seemed to be weighing his options; ruin his favorite Sardinian pasta or have Antoinette's body fed to the alligators.

"I know this is an inconvenience, sir. However, could Arnoldo handle feeding the dogs this once?"

Mr. Rainaldi cocked his head, "Arnoldo?!"

"Yes, sir. I believe he is up to the task."

"Fine. Fine. I trust your judgment, Marco. Just have it handled immediately."

"As you wish, Mr. Rainaldi," Marco bowed graciously out of the room, and went back to pulling his su filindeu, after calling Arnoldo to come from the woodshed.

Becca was frozen in place. She simply could not process what had just happened. Mr. Rainaldi stepped over Antoinette's still twitching legs and walked back to Becca with all the lightness and grace of Gene Kelly, singing in the reign of blood and viscera becoming darker with every ounce flowing out of Antoinette's dead eyes and mouth.

"Bella… I know this wasn't your fault. You were tricked. Tricked by Antoinette. We both were. When deception presents itself, you don't prune the stems… you poison the root and ensure it rots. And now, neither you nor I will have to worry about her deception any longer."

CHAPTER TWENTY

HURT

Arnoldo Gallucci raced out of the door, and started toward The Chalet. He was eager to jump on his first important task for Mr. Rainaldi. Even though his older brother, Marco gave him very little instruction over the phone, only mentioning to "bring the large trash bags and the Gator," Arnoldo was ready to show Mr. Rainaldi that he could be trusted. Arnoldo was young, handsome, and eager. He had only been in America for a few months. Living in a small fishing village in Sardinia seemed boring compared to the lavish lifestyle that his brother Marco had in Florida. Everything about America seemed glamorous and exciting. Six months ago, Arnoldo was a fishmonger, begging his brother to give him a chance in America, and he had every intention of proving himself in the land where dreams came true.

The Gator was parked outside of the woodshed. It still had mud and clay splattered on its cab and tires from Arnoldo's trek into the swamp earlier that week. He hopped into the driver's seat, tossed the large, black trash bags onto the blue tarp in the cargo box, and spun out, slinging mud and grass behind him.

It only took 15 minutes to cross the expansive property at full speed in the utility vehicle. Arnoldo turned the steering wheel sharply, whipping the little green vehicle to a stop in front of the pool gate. He crossed through the pool enclosure and entered the kitchen through the large glass doors. His muddy boots left an imprint on the immaculate white tile.

Looking up, Marco chided, "Ehi! Togliti le scarpe infangate, fratellino!"

"Sì, scusa," Arnoldo replied.

He paused by the door, and pulled off his boots, leaving them outside on the patio. Marco rushed over with a mop and cleaned the mud, leaving the floor once again spotless.

"Ah! Stai preparando la ricetta della nonna per il su filindeu!"

Arnoldo leaned over the fundu where the su filindeu had been drying and gazed at the intricate strands of pasta laced together. He lifted his fingers to his mouth and kissed, "perfetto!"

Marco smiled wide, "Grazie! I think Nonna would be proud, God rest her soul. But you have work to do. Mr. Rainaldi wants you to feed the dogs and burn the firewood. The kibble is in the study… as well as the wood. Take care of it, pronto, fratellino!"

"Of course," Arnoldo replied, making haste as he quickly crossed the kitchen in his socks. When Arnoldo walked in the study, he exclaimed, "DIO MIO," and made the sign of the cross. The room was empty except for the body curled on the rug in a pool of blood. Marco, came when he heard his brother, "Fratellino, we talked about this."

"Sì, però…," Arnoldo stared at the dead woman, "I did not expect so soon."

"We must do what we must do," Marco replied, "because we do not have much time and Mr. Rainaldi is counting on you."

The two brothers immediately got to work. Arnoldo opened the large trash bag and began roughly stuffing Antoinette inside feet first. Her arm flopped toward Marco, narrowly missing his face, as he helped squash the dead body into the bag.

"One final assault, eh, Antoinette," Marco joked.

Once the bag was tied off, they wrapped it in duck tape, and Marco threw it over his shoulder. Arnoldo rolled the ornate, blood-stained, Persian rug and hefted it over his shoulder, and made his way to the Gator. After placing the rug in the back seat of the little green vehicle, Marco dropped the body bag in the cargo box.

It had been a hot day but the sun was sinking in the sky. Sunset was only a couple of hours away. Arnoldo knew that he would need to get to the swamp before night fell when the temperature dropped. Otherwise, the alligators would have no interest in their dinner. He hoped that the warm sun had brought them out of their dens and into the sloughs of the St. John's River.

Arnoldo drove the utility vehicle too fast. He imagined himself to be the famous race car driver of his childhood, Mario Andretti, speeding through the canopied forest toward the inlet where he planned to dispose of Antoinette's body. It was a good place for gators to come to the shore and sun since the canopy opened to the expanse of the river. Mr. Rainaldi's land was vast and skirted the edge of the St. Johns River. So, it wasn't uncommon for multiple gators to be spotted along the shoreline, especially during a warm November, like this one.

He drove this path at least once a week. It was his job to feed the scraps from the house to the gators there, thus training them to come to his call. This was the one job that his brother Marco had entrusted him with. Marco reckoned that if Arnoldo could sling fish for the local fishmonger he worked for in Sardinia, then he could sling kitchen scraps for the alligators. The hardest part for Arnoldo was emulating the low bellowing grunts of a male gator.

He revved the engine to the small utility vehicle and pretended to cut a sharp curve as he soared over a mound of soil. A dull thud echoed through the trees. Something moving behind him caught his eyes. Arnoldo slammed on the brakes. The screeching of metal tore through the peace of the afternoon. He quickly shifted gears. Shoving the stick shift into the wrong gear. The gears ground to a halt. He jumped from the cab and immediately started scanning the slope. The sound of crunching leaves and snapping twigs put his whole body at alert.

CHAPTER TWENTY-ONE
NOVEMBER RAIN

It had been over a week since Halona last saw her burlesque tribe. She closed her eyes and shuttered at the memory of her anger from when she saw them last, from when she yelled at Clementine, Sasha, and Rebecca. She was filled with regret because she hadn't turned back to see the girls that she had called sisters disappear like mirages in the heat. Their angry words left a rift in the relationship and it was just too much for her to bear. In the heat of the moment, she never paused to consider if she was making the right choice. She never questioned herself. Instead she had let her hotheadedness control her once again. She had isolated herself.

Halona was lying in the soft pine needle bed that she had made under a grouping of evergreen trees. She was lost in her nostalgia, remembering how different each of the women were, their laughing faces parading across her memory. Clemmie was brusque, impulsive, and loud. She swore too much. She drank too much. And she generally got on Halona's nerves, but yet, she was somehow endearing. Sasha was Halona's closest friend — the person who brought her into the dance troupe after their fated meeting at a Shakespeare in the Park After Hours event. But, she was also the bubble head of the group. She was usually late to dance rehearsal. She often forgot her wallet when they went out, relied on attractive strangers to pay her way, and spent most of her waking (and non-waking) hours entertaining trifling men. She was shallow, selfish, and hyper-sexual. Even still, Halona thought the sun rose and set in Sasha's eyes. She just never got up the courage to tell her. Rebecca was different. Most of the time, she was a nun compared to the other girls. She was mousy, bookish, and too level-headed for her own good. She was the over-thinker of the group, always looking over her shoulder, worried about getting caught. She was the kind of person who would appreciate a well organized spreadsheet. However, when she was dancing, all of that changed. She was impoverished for attention. A sensual and utterly feminine siren on the prowl. A modern Jekyll and Hyde.

As the wind changed, she marveled at how they were ever even friends to begin with, let alone sisters. Each woman was unique and intense. There must be something magical about public near-nudity. It was physically freeing, mentally liberating, emotionally cathartic. And yet, it bonded them together at the same time. The camaraderie of exhibition. A sisterhood of nakedness. A coven without fully understanding the magick in their veins. The four of them may have been more dumpster fire than phoenix, but she ached to see her sisters now.

In the shifting November light, Halona's shoulders drooped as exhaustion consumed her body. She was delirious from a lack of food and weary from sleepless nights. There along the river edge, she was utterly alone with her thoughts. And they flicked and whirred like a Kodak photo slide show. She blinked and rubbed her eyes, squinting to see more clearly, as the forest surrounding her became hazy with the ghosts of her past. She thought she could smell Sasha's perfume in the breeze; Love Spell. Then closed her eyes and imagined Sasha's hair tumbling out of a messy bun. She sighed. She should have told Sasha that she had feelings for her. She should have said she was two-spirited. And now it was too late.

The silhouettes of her Lakota tribe appeared from behind tall trees that swayed in the blue sky. She saw her Unci and Gaka step out from the crowd, their shadows shimmered as she squinted her eyes tighter. Halona could almost hear them, their voices echoing on the wind, "We are known by the tracks we leave." She tried to sit up, reaching toward them. If only she could take her Unci's hand, everything would be okay. She could find her way out of this forest. Her ancestors could lead her to safety. Her Unci could guide her back to her friends, back to Sasha. She began to cry. The more she reached for her family, the farther away they seemed to be. Fat tears rained down on the parched earth under her hands and feet as she crawled toward the silhouettes of her grandparents. Their bodies contorted and shifted in the light, as if they would dissipate. Halona drew in a ragged breath, her hope was disappearing. She opened her mouth and what came out was a tormented growling tumult. The silhouettes of her tribe grew inky black and scattered like an unkindness of crows. The crows roosting high above her in the trees cawed and fluttered away too, startled by the guttural lament of a dying animal.

She collapsed on the soft forest floor. Exhausted and breathless. Her tears flowed like a raging river. She was alone in the forest, who knows where, and it was entirely her own fault. But, she was also entirely too stubborn to admit that she was wrong, something no doubt that she had inherited from her Unci, a proud woman who made her own way through the world. Black iridescent feathers drifted slowly to the ground as she looked up. Her view of the sky was mesmerizing, like an enormous twisting and twirling dream-catcher. She could see the afternoon sun sinking on the horizon. The pinks and oranges swirled before her and melted into one tangerine dream. She knew that she could not continue on like this for much longer. She would die in this forest. What she needed was a miracle. She closed her eyes and began to pray as black feathers settled on her bare chest.

She laid there for hours, staring up at the sky, imagining the forest floor creep over her like a blanket of moss. It was dusk and the golden glow of the day had faded into moody blues and purples. All that remained on the sun was a thin sliver of afterglow. In the distance, Halona heard the gravelly hum of an engine, whining wildly as it shifted gears too quickly. She slowed her breathing and closed her eyes, trying to hone in on the sound. It didn't have the same song as a car driving down the road. It sounded reckless and destructive, more like a chainsaw cutting through broken branches and dead cypress stumps. As it came closer, she heard the crunch of leaves and felt the vibration under her back as it pressed flat against the earth. Suddenly headlights bobbed over a small hill in the distance, cutting the darkness like two light sabers. The light grew closer with every passing second. The shadowy figure driving was yanking the steering wheel from one side to the other, swerving heedlessly over smooth terrain, moving too quickly. A loud thud echoed through the trees. The brakes screeched. The shifting gears ground to a halt.

A sinking feeling hit Halona's stomach. She had prayed for a miracle, but what if this wasn't help? A wave of adrenaline flowed through her as she slowly struggled to roll onto her side. She was still in her costume from the photo shoot. It was thin, tattered, and smudged with dirt. She felt the jab of every twig and heard the crunch of every brown leaf beneath her weak body. Her dulled senses were becoming more alert. She lurched as blood rushed to her head. She stumbled behind a group of shrubs. Teetering on unsteady legs, she squatted low to the ground. The brittle leaves sank their tiny claws into her already tattered fishnet stockings, hanging on for dear life. She was panting with fear. Her face grew pale and she was breathless. She peeked around the scrub brush oaks she was hidden in.

A tan, muscular man exited the vehicle. He was scanning the slope. She realized he was much closer to her than she thought. He couldn't have been more than fifteen or twenty feet away. Halona's eyes followed the receding curve of the slope the man stood on and noticed a large black bag had rolled down the side of the hill and snagged on a downed tree branch.

Halona tried to get a closer look. Shuffling her feet, she inched closer, but her legs were numb and caused her to lean into the scraggly scrub oak branches. The leaves moved and caught Arnoldo's attention. He paused and scanned the forest around him. Halona held her breath. She was quivering in anticipation of being caught. Halona crouched as low as she could against the ground. More than anything, she wanted to be invisible right now. With her eyes screwed shut, grasping a lone crow feather, she made a final plea to her ancestors for safety.

Thinking that it must be a squirrel in the brush, Arnoldo went back to searching for the lost black bag. Without a flashlight, he slid down the slope of the hill. As he did, rocks tumbled down and landed on the plastic bag making a thwack sound. Small holes were torn in the smooth black plastic, revealing glimpses of the contents. As Arnoldo grabbed the tied top of the bag, it snagged on a broken pine branch and tore loose. Antoinette's head lobbed out. He slid farther down the hill to untangle the bag from the branch. Bits of plastic stretched and tore as he broke the bag loose. With Antoinette half out of the bag, he grabbed her by the armpits and tugged her out and up the small hill. The bag slipped off as he drug her back to the utility vehicle and roughly hoisted her into the bed.

Shock swept over Halona. Her breath was ragged and her mind reeled. She clinched her jaw, afraid of making a sound as she watched the man in horror. It was a short distance to the inlet of the St. John's River. Halona could hear the water lapping against the cypress stumps from where she hid. She could make a run for the water. She wasn't a strong swimmer but maybe she could swim to safety. She had been camped along this shore for the past few days, in hopes of flagging a boater down. She didn't know how she would get away. All she knew was she didn't want to end up a corpse like the one she had just seen; bloodied and abused. Gingerly, she crawled on her knees toward the river.

The man climbed back into the driver's seat and revved up the engine. He wiped the sweat from his brow as he sat behind the steering wheel. He was almost finished with his task. All that was left was to tie a weight to Antoinette's feet, toss her into the water, and grunt for the gators. They would do the rest.

Watching from the corner of her eye, Halona crept toward the slough. Sharp sticks and rocks tore at her open palms and bare knees. It felt like crawling across Legos in a strange torture game invented by a tiny maniacal puppet. She whimpered at the pain and bit her lip to stop herself from crying out. She thought of the crow feather that she had threaded into her course, black hair after praying to her ancestors. She had to stay strong. She heard the cawing birdsong as a crow flew over head. She thought of her grandfather, and whispered, "Gaka, carry me away from here, like you did when I would climb on your shoulders as a child."

Arnoldo drained the remains of a warm bottle of water and went about his work. He drove the short distance to the shore. Night was coming fast. He would have to finish quickly if he was going to be successful and impress Mr. Rainaldi, and more importantly, make his brother, Marco, proud. Without haste, he bound Antoinette's feet with rope and tied a broken chunk of cinder block to the end. He hefted her over his shoulder, grabbed the block in the other hand, and made his way down the dock grunting loudly. As an answer to his call, a chorus of low bellowing echoed along the river edge. He saw the water ripple and heard heavy splashes as the alligators slipped off the bank and swam toward the dock. With all his might, Arnoldo lunged Antoinette's body into the flowing water. The cinder block immediately sank, pulling her feet first into the depths of the river.

Halona stood frozen among the cypress knots. She was stricken at the sight of the gators swimming toward the sinking corpse. It wasn't long before a large alligator claimed Antoinette's body and began gnashing and ripping her apart. Other alligators lurched up and began to fight for scraps. Arnoldo hurriedly left the dock, as he turned, he saw her standing there along the water's edge.

Their eyes locked. Halona spun on her heel and began to run away from the water. As she did, Arnoldo yelled out, "Ehi! Fermati! Er… Stop!"

Even though she had a head start, in her weakened state, it wasn't long before she was out of breath and slowing down. Arnoldo used this to his advantage and sprinted after her. Halona stumbled on a downed tree limb. As she fell, Arnoldo gained speed and caught up with her. Struggling to stand, Halona clawed at the earth. She threw a handful of brittle leaves and dirt at Arnoldo's face as he leaned in to grab her. She kicked him in the groin and rolled to dodge. Before she was stable on her feet, Arnoldo grabbed a broken branch from the ground and swung it at her head. Halona crumpled to the ground with a thud.

PART EIGHT

REUNITED

CHAPTER TWENTY-TWO
PLEASE, PLEASE, PLEASE

Arnoldo hurried through the pool side door into the house. He was frantically looking for his brother and knew the best place to find him would be where he was happiest; in the kitchen. Several hours had passed since Arnoldo set out to do Mr. Rainaldi's dirty work. It was late but Marco was still awake; cleaning the dishes.

Arnoldo wrung his hands, "Scusa fratello. Un problema."

Marco looked up. His face was vacant, like he'd been awoken from a deep trance. He began drying his sudsy hands on a cloth towel.

"Alright, fratellino," Marco replied, "what is it?"

"Can you, uh," Arnoldo hesitated, gesturing frantically, "come outside? Un momento?"

"Okay."

With a confused expression, Marco threw the kitchen towel over his shoulder and started for the door. Arnoldo backed out, still motioning for his brother to come with him. He glanced over his shoulder, expectantly, but continued to lure his brother out of the house. Arnoldo pointed to the fence beyond the pool, where the utility vehicle was parked, "Qui."

"Tell me. What has happened? Did you lose a limb?"

"Well... uh... not exactly. It's more like... how do you say... trovato?"

"You found a limb?" Marco paused mid-step, pinched his fingers together and flicked his wrist toward Arnoldo, "Fratellino, throw it back into the river. The dogs will take care of it."

"Come see, per favore."

"Fratellino, we've been over this. A million times! You know what to do. Just do it, eh?"

"But, fratello, this is…" Arnoldo held his hands in prayer, "ti prego."

"Seriously, you've been training for six months. How do you not fucking know?"

"Just…" Arnoldo came to the edge of the patio, and gestured toward the side-by-side.

"I swear, if this is something stupid," Marco raised his hand with mock machismo like he would slap his brother.

"It's not… Just look."

Marco followed as Arnoldo walked to the back of the vehicle. There was a large mound covered by a black tarp.

"What is this? THAT is too big to be a limb. Did you not take her to the dock?"

Arnoldo lifted the edge of the tarp to reveal the slumped body of a woman.

"DIO MIO… Who the FUCK is this?"

Marco bit the edge of his hand and glared at Arnoldo.

"Non lo so. She was by the dock. She saw me… uh… buttare via…" Arnoldo's hands gestured a throwing motion wildly, "the FOOD to the… uh… DOGS."

He massaged his temples and pinched the bridge of his nose, contemplating to himself. "Hold on," he mumbled as he noticed her attire, "that is NOT Antoinette. This must be the fourth girl."

Arnoldo's hands folded in a praying motion, "Non sapevo cosa fare. So, I come to you."

"She's alive, yes?"

"I think so, but I hit her pretty hard when she tried to run. Non volevo, but she was kicking me."

Marco moved closer, checking for a pulse, "Yes, she's alive. You stay here. I'm going for help."

"What if she wakes up and tries to run again?"

Marco paused at the gate, his fingers and thumb pinched and waving toward Arnoldo, "Did you not tie her up?"

Arnoldo shrugged, his arms stretched out with open palms facing his brother, "Non lo so."

"Fratellino, you're a henchman. This is the job. Tie her up. If she wakes, bash her in the head."

"You want me to kill her?!"

"Sì, if the need arises."

Marco stomped back to the house, muttering cuss words under his breath, his hands gesturing quickly in frustration. As Marco's footsteps faded away, Arnoldo turned towards the outdoors, looking out into the seemingly infinite dark of the night. He knew in reality it was nothing but Rainaldi property outward, but there was something about the lack of light. It quickly and dizzyingly became an abyss of nothingness that had no problem staring right back into his soul, beckoning him. Arnoldo suddenly became overwhelmed with the reality of his actions. "What have I done," he whispered. He stared at his ragged hands. They were smeared with blood and dirt. He trembled. He was startled by a frail sound, like a small dove cooing. The girl's leg twitched, and her hands were clinched tightly into a ball as she woke up.

She opened her eyes, and whispered, in a feeble voice, pleading, "Please, Gaka, help me." Halona extended out her hand, reaching toward the hazy figure in front of her.

Arnoldo took her hand. It was cold and weak, barely holding on to him. He questioned if he was doing the right thing. He felt sorry for the girl. What had she done to deserve this?

Feeling the warmth of the rough hand in hers, Halona smiled. She closed her eyes and gripped the hand as tightly as she could, even in her feeble state.

Arnoldo stood in silence. The frail, breathy, "Please," lingered in his ears. His mind was a whirlwind. He wondered what kind of help his brother was actually going for considering he left instructions to kill the girl if she tried to run again. *This is the job,* his brother's voice echoed. Suddenly, his life in Sardinia seemed much better than his life in America. Behind the glamor of wealth, stood the reality of something much more sinister. Arnoldo was no longer convinced that he was up for the task. He'd rather have a mundane life, slinging tuna for the fishmonger, than whatever he had gotten himself into. The girl squeezed his hand once more before her body trembled and went limp again.

"She doesn't deserve to die for being in the wrong place at the wrong time," Arnoldo mumbled. And he didn't want to do this anymore. But no one leaves The Chalet without Mr. Rainaldi's consent. And Mr. Rainaldi would never let him leave alive after making such a mess of things. His fate was sealed. He would be as dead as the girl clutching his hand. Arnoldo knew what he needed to do. They would have to escape if they were going to survive.

The kitchen door opened slowly as Arnoldo crept in. He scanned the house before tiptoeing toward Marco's jacket which hung on a wooden rack along the interior wall. He fumbled through each of the jacket pockets until he found a key card attached to a set of car keys. He had to move quickly. The house was quiet but Marco could reappear at any minute.

He went back to the side-by-side and scooped up the dying girl. In a rush, he carried her to the garage, scanned the key card, and limboed under the roll-up doors as they opened. He laid the girl in the back seat of the Escalade and jumped into the driver's seat. Every instinct within him screamed to speed toward the gate and crash through. But he didn't want to get caught by the security team who patrolled the grounds. So, he slowly eased down the driveway, to the front gate. The large lion-clad golden gates glittered in the headlights. He rolled down the window expecting to scan the key card again. But it wouldn't reach. He yanked and snatched. He pulled on the retractable cord with all his strength but it wouldn't break. The thin metal wire was too strong. He flipped the card in his hands and noticed a four digit code. Maybe this was the code for the key pad? He typed the four digits in and pressed the pound key. Behind him, the girl grunted and moaned, waking again.

Marco had just returned side-by-side to find that both Arnoldo and the girl were gone. "Fuck," Marco swore. Flood lights flashed on, illuminating the compound. A loud siren rang from the house. Marco heard the alarm, "Double fuck! Arnoldo, you stupid idiot."

A scramble of guards were running toward the SUV in an instant. Arnoldo lifted his hands in the air, as if to surrender, but pressed the gas, instead. The tires squalled. The grill of the Escalade crashed into the gate. But the gate didn't budge. The electronic display in the vehicle glitched and everything shut off as it rolled down the slope of the pavement. Two guards opened the passenger side doors and jumped in, guns in hand.

Mr. Rainaldi relaxed in a wing-back chair in the living room. Becca stood beside his chair, nervously picking at her fingernails, still wondering if Antoinette's viscera might've made it into the atmosphere and onto her nail polish.

"Such a nasty habit," he said, without looking up, "You should take better care of your appearance, my jewel."

Marco hovered in the kitchen, his own hands trembled as he paced back and forth in front of the sink. Two security guards entered the front door. One walked behind Arnoldo with his weapon pressed firmly into his captive's back. Arnoldo was rigid with fear. His movements were limited and mechanical. His eyes were wild. The other guard guided Halona as she hobbled along. She was barely coherent, but winced in pain as she moved awkwardly. Becca's mouth gaped open as she saw her friend enter The Chalet. She ran to Halona and hugged her. Becca immediately began sobbing as she held her friend. The two women collapsed to the floor, arms wrapped tightly around each other. Halona cried into Becca's hair, "Unci, my Unci," hallucinating the image of her grandmother. Becca didn't know what the words meant, but she gripped her tighter and whispered, "I'm here. Everything is okay. I'm here. We're together now."

Unable to relax, Marco did the one thing he mindlessly did every day. Clean. He rinsed the whiskey glass and dried it. He gingerly placed it on the counter top, as if he were holding a loaded gun. He tried to steady his hands before entering the living room. He wiped them on the dish towel. Smoothed his black hair and left the kitchen.

Mr. Rainaldi sat on the opposite side of the living room. His face was placid. No worry lines creased his brow. No sign of this disturbance ever interfering with his bedtime manner. He was wearing a long velvet and silk robe, and a pair of monogrammed slippers. Still refined and gentlemanly, hands were interlocked, resting on his crossed knee. He held Marco's gaze as he walked forward with the cadence of a man soon to be sentenced to death.

"You owe me an explanation, Marco."

"Yes, sir. You see, Arnoldo was trying to help. As you can see, he located the fourth girl for you, sir. A commendable service… as security has been unable to find her… for over a week. However, she is badly injured. I told Arnoldo that she needed medical care. He misunderstood. He doesn't know our protocols. He is still new to this business, sir, as he's only been here six months. He took the initiative, sir."

"By running directly into the gate? You can be dense, Marco, but even you can see this smacks of deception. Marco, you promised me. You said he was ready."

Marco nodded his head, "Yes, sir. It was a simple misunderstanding, I assure you. How would you like to proceed? She's in terrible condition, and needs urgent medical care… That is, if you intend to keep her. Would you like me to call Dr. Woodstock to make another house call? I know he was just here, however…"

Mr. Rainaldi lifted his interlocked hands to his chin. His pointer fingers rested just in front of his lips, "I presume she was found while Arnoldo was feeding the dogs?"

"Yes, sir."

"I see. As such, they have both become liabilities and will need to be dealt with based on our protocols."

Becca's ears pricked as Mr. Rainaldi enunciated 'liabilities.' She realized that he meant to kill Halona and dispose of her body the same way he had Antoinette's. She jumped up from the floor.

"No," she blurted, "You can't do that. You can't kill Halona."

"Bella, I will discuss this with you later. It's a matter of business, that is all."

"Please." She rushed to him and threw herself at his feet, begging, "If you want me to trust you, if you really want to prove it to me, then let her live."

"There are implications that you wouldn't understand."

"I'll do anything. Please. Don't take her from me."

His eyes narrowed, searching her face for some hidden agenda. She was doe-eyed and pleading. Her face awash with tears. Her skin was splotched red.

"You are quite ugly when you cry, my jewel. Wipe away your tears. I will agree with one caveat…"

"What is it? Name it."

"You will take Antoinette's place as my secretary and handmaiden, effective immediately. And, as such, you will be this girl's handler. She'll work at The Mortimer, in your place."

Becca inhaled deeply and exhaled slowly, "Fine." She hung her head, "I will do as you wish."

"Then, we are in agreement," he said as he lifted her chin up, "You will do exactly as I wish."

"Marco, you will contact Dr. Woodstock and have him treat her. Now," Rainaldi continued, turning his attention to the guard standing near the front door, above Halona, "take her upstairs to an empty bedroom."

The guard scooped Halona into his arms and carried her upstairs. Becca slowly stood. She balled her fists up and pressed them against her chest, "Can I…"

"You are dismissed… for now."

She nodded her head and followed after them. Marco scurried to the kitchen to arrange an emergency house call with the doctor.

"Now then," Mr. Rainaldi's attention settled on the guard holding Arnoldo, "You will take him outside. I will call you back when I am ready."

Following orders, the guard yanked at Arnoldo's arm and shoved him toward the door. The gun was still positioned ready to shoot as the two men exited the living room. It was a few minutes before Marco returned to find Mr. Rainaldi alone and in deep thought. A decanter of whiskey and two glasses sat on a serving tray on top of the ottoman.

Marco slowed his pace and hesitated to approach. He hadn't noticed the beverage tray there before. Mr. Rainaldi's face was no longer placid. It was furrowed and his brows were tightly knit together.

"There has been a serious lack of professionalism here tonight. I cannot let it go unpunished. You have been with me for a long time, Marco, and have become invaluable. But not even you are beyond reproach."

"Yes, sir. I understand, sir. This will not happen again. I will see that Arnoldo is whipped for his carelessness."

"Whipped?! No no no. Marco, this has been a major fuck up. It requires more than a lashing. This is inexcusable. This could be the death of all I have worked for. It is blood for blood. Either you will take care of it, or I will."

"But sir… he is my brother."

"So, this is how you show your loyalty? He is your brother. But I have given you everything. I made you. I found you in the gutter, addicted to angel dust. You were a writhing little worm, and I gave you a purpose. No. YOU brought him here and told me to trust him. And look what happened. YOU will make it right."

"Please, sir." Marco's voice was trembling and he shivered from a cold sweat, "Please, don't make me do this."

Mr. Rainaldi stood and motioned toward the decanter, "Just tell him you appreciate the initiative he took today. Antionette sure appreciated that approach," he said with a wry grin.

Marco's face was stricken. He turned pale as blood drained from his face. Fear swept over him and flooded his senses.

Mr. Rainaldi opened the front door, and spoke to the guard, "You are dismissed. I will not need you again tonight." The guard released Arnoldo's arm and left. Mr. Rainaldi stepped out of the doorway, signaling Arnoldo to step in.

"Come in, Arnoldo." Mr. Rainaldi's arms opened wide, ushering his guest into the room, "Let us have a drink."

CHAPTER TWENTY–THREE
NINE TO FIVE

A week had passed since the bloodbath at the Chalet, as Rebecca accepted her new role as Mr. Rainaldi's secretary. If there was one thing she was quickly learning, it was that time had no meaning here. Nothing — not even a force as powerful as death, as vicious as murder — would stop the well-oiled den of inequity she had been forced to now call home, the "business" she was now under the employ of, or the demands of her new boss. And Becca found out instantaneously just how demanding Rainaldi could be and exactly how much Antoinette actually did for him. Becca spent her days ping-ponging around The Chalet attending to Mr. Rainaldi's every whim. When she wasn't directly catering to him, she was with Marco. He trained her on matters of household management, protocols of the business, and expectations for handling new assets, such as Halona.

Even her attire changed to fit her new role. She now donned the crisp white button down shirt and tight black pencil skirt that Antoinette was always in. Like a drill sergeant, Mr. Rainaldi checked her uniform at sunrise every day. Her shirts were expected to be crisp at all times and her skirt without creases, regardless of what duties she was fulfilling. Her nails were to be trimmed, cleaned, and polished. Her hair was to be brushed, ironed straight, and bound in a ponytail. Becca had never considered herself to be a messy or unkempt person. However, remaining in pristine condition at all times wore on her nerves and required far more attention than she had to give. Like a 1950's housewife, she was to be picture perfect and coiffed even in her sleep, out of fear that she would be summoned to Mr. Rainaldi's aid in the middle of the night.

Becca rarely had time to visit with Halona. Their interactions had been reduced to delivering and receiving instructions from Mr. Rainaldi. Notably, his expectation for Halona to be healed and preparing for the stage in a matter of days. He was excited to reveal his first indigenous dancer to his patrons at The Mortimer, as he was certain that she would fetch a high price. And, like all of his assets, he wanted Halona to be unblemished and poised for her audience. He was quite inconvenienced by the healing time she needed for the nasty thump Arnoldo had given her. On Dr. Woodstock's insistence, he reluctantly gave her seven days. As her second week at The Chalet was looming, he refused to postpone any longer.

Just as Antoinette had done for Becca, now it was Becca's turn to measure Halona for costuming and choreographing a routine. That Sunday morning at the breakfast table, Mr. Rainaldi gave explicit instructions that her performance would include traditional indigenous dance as well as a feather headdress, moccasins, and a buck skin bikini. He had a particularly racist sub-section of patrons who would revel in the stereotypical colonizer/colonized kink. And he meant to cash in on it.

After receiving her orders, Becca was excused from Mr. Rainaldi's presence and set about her work. She walked upstairs and into Halona's starched white bedroom. It was nearly eight in the morning, and Halona was still sprawled across the middle of the mattress. Becca always had difficulty waking Halona as she was a deep sleeper and decidedly not a morning person. After several minutes of cajoling,

Halona was finally upright with her feet dangling above the floor. Whether she was awake or not was left to be seen. If anything was going to get her blood boiling, it would be the news of Mr. Rainaldi's lofty aims that Becca prepared to deliver. She inhaled a deep breath and blurted it out.

"Mr. Rainaldi wants you to wear a traditional warbonnet," she stepped backward, creating some distance between her and Halona, "for your first performance."

Halona's eyes popped open, "LAKOTA WOMEN DON'T WEAR WARBONNETS," she roared.

"I know. I know. But that's what he wants."

"I won't do it. That's disrespectful to our traditions."

"Hal, you have to."

"NO!"

"But…"

"Becca, I can't. That goes against my heritage."

"I know. I know. But… uh… it gets worse."

"How?"

"Well…he wants you to wear a buck skin bikini and include traditional war dances into the choreo."

"That's fucking racist."

"I know… I'm sorry. Don't be mad at me. I'm just the messenger. But you know you don't have a choice. He'll force you to do it."

"How? By poisoning me?! Like you told me he did with that lady they threw in the river? Fuck, if that's the case…I'd rather be dead."

"Don't say that. You know you don't mean that. I risked a lot to keep you alive," Becca said, the last sentence catching herself off guard. It was like Rainaldi's words were coming out of her mouth.

"Well, you shouldn't have," she huffed and crossed her arms, "Death is better than living like a caged animal. We're watched every minute of the day. We can't even shit without HIS approval."

"You might as well just accept it. It'll be easier that way. If you do what he wants, he's actually pretty nice."

Halona's face dropped aghast at the honesty in Becca's voice. This wasn't sarcasm, she was sincere. It took her a moment to pull her thoughts together. She couldn't believe that Becca actually thought that Mr. Rainaldi, the exact man who was keeping them imprisoned, was 'pretty nice.' She cleared her throat, then gently said, "Bec, do you hear yourself? Look what he's done to you? You're a puppet."

"I know he's difficult, but... when I'm alone with him, he's really good to me. I think there is more to him than the big bad boss exterior. He has a softness hidden somewhere. I just know it. And he's promised to take good care of me... and you. So far, he has kept his word."

Halona rolled her eyes and pulled her knees under her arms, tucking herself into a ball. Becca stepped closer, resting her hand on Halona's shoulder.

"Do this for me, please."

"Fuck. Why not? Apparently, I have no choice," her voice was tinged with sarcasm.

"I'll go get the measuring tape so we can start making your costume. Come on! This might be a little fun. Like the old days when we were gluing sequins on pasties together." Becca chuckled under her breath, "Remember when we measured our nipples?" She laughed out loud, "We wanted to make our own pasties but you weren't sure how big yours should be and Clem said that yours would be as big as a dinner plate?" Becca snorted, laughing. Halona sat curled in a ball.

"That wasn't me, Bec. That was you. Clemmie said that to you. Not me."

"No! It was totally you, but regardless, this'll be fun! Be right back!"

Becca hurried out the door with the excitement of a child presented with a new toy. When she got to the bottom of the stairs, Marco was cleaning breakfast service off the table. Mr. Rainaldi had retreated to his study.

Becca paused at the edge of the kitchen, "Um… Marco? Where would I find the sewing kit? I need to measure Halona."

Marco didn't look up. Nor speak. He simply pointed toward the hall closet that was past Mr. Rainaldi's study. Becca stared at him for a moment. He was so different from when she first arrived. Over the past week, he had become somber, instead of studious. No more than a shell of who he was before. Now, he only spoke when absolutely necessary. And there was no vigor in his step. Only the macabre lurking of the grim reaper. He had the gray pallor of a condemned man, carrying a Sisyphean boulder chained on his back. She frowned at his melancholy, but quietly continued down the hall. She wanted to hug him, but she knew that it wouldn't be appropriate.

Becca made her way past the study to the closet, gently turned the brass door knob, and immediately found the sewing kit sitting on the middle shelf. She grabbed it quickly, and started back towards the main hall.

"… resource in our power to find the missing girls…"

The quiet voice that emitted from the cracked door of the study as she passed made Becca stop in her tracks and drop her jaw.

It can't be…, she thought to herself.

Coming under the realization that she had already passed the study, she turned around and soft-shoed her heels as she moved to spy into the opening leading to Mr. Rainaldi's private study. He was sitting in the Queen Anne chair, watching a local news station. She heard the continued drone of the person at the podium. An older gentleman with a blue jacket and soft voice maintaining an empathetic tone. He was soothing families, and coolly demanding justice for the perpetrators of this heinous act. Standard major crime fare. Becca crept closer. Rainaldi shifted in his chair and she suddenly froze. She knew she needed to walk away, but the pictures flickering on the TV screen commanded her attention.

Rainaldi was indeed watching a breaking news announcement as the picture shifted from the empathetic person at the podium to a graphic of 4 pictures in a square grid. Recent selfies and submitted family photo close-ups with names written below them listed in order: Clementine Sullivan, Halona Lightfoot, Sasha McMurray, and Rebecca Coleman. It took everything within Becca not to cry, or make any sort of sound that would give her away. She instantly felt a weight lift off of her as the thought finally landed…*the authorities were looking for us.*

The image shifted back to the man at the podium with a news graphic underneath: Daniel Lamontagne, Special Agent, Federal Bureau of Investigations. *Holy shit, the fucking FBI is here?!* Becca thought ecstatically. It took everything within her not to jump for joy.

Agent Lamontagne continued his speech on screen. He pointed behind him to a seal featuring a large five pointed star with "St. John's County Sheriff's Office" printed at the top. "With the help of the county sheriff's office, as well as local officials, we have every confidence that the abduction of The Florida 4 will be the last in a series of, what we believe to be, connected kidnappings and abductions across the East Coast of the United States."

Camera flashes and reporter scuttlebutt followed. *Connected kidnappings? The Florida 4?? We have a media name???* Becca's thoughts kept racing as she couldn't believe what she was seeing. They were on their way to being saved. She couldn't help but notice Rainaldi staying calm and comfortable in his Queen Anne as the agent continued on.

"And with that, I'll turn it back over to Chief Hogg to answer any localized questions. Thank you very much," Lamontagne concluded.

The agent stepped aside as a greasy man with shifty eyes approached the podium and the crowd of journalists. Becca felt like the sticky, slimy mucus of a slug trail was slowly working its way across her gray matter. Becca's stomach dropped; she felt instantly nauseous. The man started his greeting; his voice, his accent, haunted her immediately. She knew who this was. The graphic on the screen confirmed: Chief of Police, Guy Hogg.

Becca's eyes drained of hope and filled with fear in an instant.

Guy.

The man standing with them at the bar in the video footage. *The man who….No…it can't be.* She couldn't help the whisper that emitted from her mouth as a reporter off-screen asked a question.

Chief Hogg responded diplomatically, "As Agent Lamontagne emphasized, tha St. John's County Sheriff's Office and our local department here is doing everythang within our powa ta locate tha missin women. We believe fully that with tha help of the FBI as well as tha new evidence that was provided to our offices this mornin', it will lead our officers ta tha kidnappa's. With tha help of DNA testing, we are confident tha human remains found in the riva will provide additional connections ta tha case."

A buzz of voices erupted with questions, but one stood out loudest, "Chief Hogg? Trent Ross, Seminole Times. Can you confirm that you are looking at every possible lead, including investigating Rainaldi Properties, the last known property owner of the location where the girls were rumored to have disappeared from?"

Rainaldi leaned forward slowly in his chair and Becca leaned forward towards the crack of the door, trying to keep herself from bursting through it as Guy answered. "I can assure you we have already spoken ta Mr. Rainaldi at length. To clear tha air, let it be known that any rumor of his involv'ment is simply that," he simply replied, "That's all we can say about tha case at tha moment. Thank ya fer comin."

As Guy turned and exited the press conference, Rainaldi slithered out of his chair with a grin not unlike one of a cat who ate a canary.

Meanwhile, Becca backed away from the door as cruel memories kept slithering across her brain. It felt like a stabbing light in her eyes. Like a brain freeze splitting her hemispheres. Like a plunge into icy water. She knew him. She knew this man and knew that he was vile. She now knew her assaulter. His voice drifted toward her through a sea of memory and whiskey. It was at one point a moment during his rapture, but now rang in her head like a death sentence, *You'a nuthin but a dirty whore…all Rainaldi's girls are. And there's not a fuckin' thing you can do about it.*

Part Nine

It Takes Two

CHAPTER TWENTY–FOUR
WE CAN WORK IT OUT

Halona was able to milk another couple of weeks of invalid care out of Dr. Woodstock, in spite of Mr. Rainaldi's irritation toward the news of the delay. While the thump she received from Arnoldo was gnarly, she had healed well and wasn't nearly as concussed as she led the doctor and Becca to believe. She feigned memory lapses and fainting spells in order to get out of dance rehearsal. She complained about minor aches and pains to the point that Becca began to feel helpless as her nurse maid when the doctor was unable to visit his patient. She often refused meals and rarely came out of her bedroom. Halona had become such a bother to Becca that she considered her to be more like an angsty teenager than a grown woman.

Nevertheless, as the fourth week of Halona's stay at The Chalet began, Becca pushed Halona as hard as she could to prepare for her debut performance at The Mortimer the following weekend. Halona, however, continued to be a source of resistance. She drug her feet at every available opportunity. Nit-picked every step and shoulder shimmy of the choreography. Minced words over the song selection and altered her costume daily. Every day brought a new hurdle for Becca to mount. She was run ragged pandering to her friend. She tried the grin-and-bear-it approach for as long as she could. But the longer Halona acted like an obstinate child, the more Becca became her demanding mother. And what other references could she draw upon, other than her own mother, Mrs. Coleman, and her handler, Antoinette. Neither inspired loyalty from her rebellious ward. The harder Becca pushed Halona to comply, the more resistant she became, and the wider the gap in their friendship grew.

Halona sat on the floor with her feet tucked under her. The red feather war bonnet lay in a heap on the floor next to her. Loose feathers fluttered to the ground, spinning like pine seeds before a rude landing. Becca hovered over the dancer, her arms folded in disapproval.

"Halona, please. You have to keep trying. The choreography isn't that hard. You're just being pig-headed." Becca threw her arms into the air, "Why do you always fight me? I'm trying to help you."

"Right. Help. That's what this is," Halona groaned under her breath. She picked up a feather and rolled it between her hands. "This isn't going to work. I don't want to do this performance."

"We've been over this. Mr. Rainaldi is counting on you to make a strong impression at the club. It's a big deal. And it could be your big break."

"The only big break I want is OUT OF THIS FUCKING HOUSE!"

"Keep your voice down!" Becca said in a hushed whisper, "I told you what I saw on the TV. We have to trust that this is our way out, but you have to trust—"

"You have to trust me that it will take time," Halona repeated back in a mocking tone.

"UGH. You're such a child." Becca's face reddened and she began to fidget with her finger nails, picking at her cuticles for the first time in a month, "After everything I've done for you, and this is what I get. I put my life on the line for you and all I get is attitude, disrespect, complaints. I've had it! Not only did I save your life, but I've been defending you to Mr. Rainaldi this whole time, because you can't get your act together. I've done my best to keep you safe. Other girls would have gotten checked by now. But I've let you act like a spoiled brat. Maybe you need to get checked."

"Fine. Try it! I'm not afraid of you, Rebecca," Halona's eyes were hard and her chin jutted forward.

"That's… That's not what I meant." Becca's shoulders softened, and her back slumped, "I'm not going to hit you. But I see girls at the club get so much worse treatment for just an eighth of what you're giving me here. It's just… you could be a little bit grateful. I do a lot for you. And I don't appreciate how hard you fight me."

"Fine. Fine. Fine. It's not like it matters anyway."

"Hal… Come on. Can you just…," Becca stopped mid sentence as Marco entered the room. He motioned for her to come, but kept his eyes on the ground. "Just a sec. And we'll take it from the top, okay?"

Halona rolled her eyes.

Becca crossed the room to where Marco stood, "What's up, Marco?"

"Mr. Rainaldi has requested you in his study," Marco droned. His face was devoid of expression and his voice was flat.

"Right. Thank you." Becca turned to Halona, "Change of plan, we'll resume this later. I guess, just go back to your room."

Halona rolled her eyes again, but sprang off the floor, and bounded up the stairs to her haven without another word. Marco nodded to Becca and returned to his duties.

As Becca rounded the corner to Mr. Rainaldi's office, she slowed her steps and drew a calming breath. She didn't want him to see her in a rush or flustered from her conversation with Halona.

What Daddy doesn't know, won't hurt him, she thought. She smoothed her skirt and dusted off her white sleeves, checking for remnants of feather. She licked her hand, slicked back her straight hair, and tightened her ponytail. When she was poised, she entered the room with a sweeping gesture, like a lady of gentility, and greeted him, "Good afternoon, sir."

"Hello, Bella. Come in. Sit."

Becca lingered at the door. She was caught up in the way his gray hair sparkled in the sunlight. He looked dashing to her. Noticing the delay, Mr. Rainaldi looked up from his papers and summoned her with a wave of his hand. She gracefully sat in the Queen Anne beside his desk, interlocking her ankles, and sitting up straight. Trying her best to look beautiful.

"Is everything ready for this weekend? I assume the new girl has learned her routine?" He paused, "What is her name, again?"

"Oh. Yes. Yes. Um… Hal… er… Turquoise Cloud, will be ready."

"Bella," his voice was flat, and he folded his hands as he fixed his eyes to her face, "I'm counting on you. I have a rather large audience scheduled for this event. A great deal of money has gone into this asset, at your behest. It would not be wise for there to be any exceptions to our plans. So, I will ask again—is she ready or not?"

"Yes, sir. She is ready. She's just been… um, hesitant, to perform. Nerves, I suppose."

"Bella, you cannot play coy with me. I know you too well. What is the issue?"

"Nothing. It's nothing. Ev—everything is good."

"Really? What are you keeping from me?"

"Honestly, it's nothing. You don't need to worry."

"Bella, we made an agreement. We must trust each other. Above all else. Have I not shown you that I am worthy of your trust?"

"You have. You have been…"

"Then, do me this service, and be completely forthcoming with me, as you agreed to be."

Becca sighed, "She's just been… I don't know. Um, she's just been a little stubborn. It's nothing, though. Everything is good."

"Bella, I know you have a rebellious streak of your own. So, I would not be surprised if the new girl does as well. However, that is nothing you cannot overcome. You must be firm with her. I'm counting on you to present her well. And I have every faith that you will do exactly that."

"Of course. Of course. The choreography is ready. The costume is good. She knows her music. She knows her cues. When the time comes, she'll do what she is supposed to," Becca's eyes grew distant and her voice softened to a near whisper. "I know she will. She's my friend. She won't let me down."

Mr. Rainaldi walked around the desk. He grabbed her hand and she stood to face him. He looked deeply into her eyes, and cupped her chin. She could feel the warmth radiating from him. He smelled intoxicating, that mixture of whiskey, sandalwood, and vanilla flooding her senses once more. Goosebumps covered her arms as she felt his breath on her neck. Her senses were flooded as he leaned closer.

"You and I only have each other. I know you would not want to disappoint me, now would you?"

"No, sir," Becca whispered as her eyes searched his.

"Good. Good. That's my good girl," Mr. Rainaldi whispered, as he leaned forward and kissed her forehead.

CHAPTER TWENTY–FIVE
TWO OUTTA THREE AIN'T BAD

Just like with Becca's first trip to The Mortimer, Halona's was handled in the same fashion. Marco escorted the two ladies to the club and parked the Escalade at the front entrance. The Greek Nose was there, right on schedule, to lead the handler and her dancer into the club. Halona gawked at the beautiful building, shocked that it didn't match her expectation, which had more to do with a dirty hole in the wall for seedy alley cat types than it did a country club for the wealthy and bored. Becca giggled at her friend's overwhelmed expression, remembering her own first encounter, and how Antoinette saturated her head with advice. Since accepting her new role with Mr. Rainaldi, Becca had been to The Mortimer many times, as she was required to attend his weekly appearances, usually as nothing more than arm candy. But this time was different in one distinct way; Bella Valentina was the new bottom bitch for the pimp.

As the two women entered the backstage door, Becca and Halona were shocked to find an incredibly familiar waistline adjusting a string bikini in front of a mirror stationed at a makeup table. Clementine Sullivan looked up from her knot tying when she heard the door creak open. Her jaw dropped when she saw Becca. The two women squealed with joy and ran toward each other. There was no hesitation. No awkward distance. Just two close friends hugging tightly, and celebrating their reunion after what felt like years, even though it had only been just over a month.

"My god, let me look at you!" Clementine grabbed Becca by the hand and twirled her around like a ballerina. "You look so different! Check out this boss bitch get-up, too! Still gorgeous, though."

"Oh, stop. Look at you! Have you lost weight?"

"Ha! It must be the cocaine. Or the fucking. Maybe, both." A high pitched cackle erupted out of Clem as the sarcasm rolled off her tongue.

Becca grimaced and hugged her friend again, "Always with the tongue in cheek sarcasm, Clem. God, I've missed you."

"I've missed you, too! But tell me… What's been doing? How'd you get to boss bitch level so fast?"

Becca guffawed and sheepishly looked at Halona, "Well, it's kind of a long story."

"Hi, Hal," Clementine said, "It's been a long time. You good? We good?"

Halona smiled weakly, "Yeah, we're good. It's good to see you, too. I, honestly, didn't think I would see anyone ever again. So, sorry about… well, you know." Her tone was somber but matter of fact. Her eyes dulled as she looked away from Clementine and Becca.

"Yeah," Clem's voice cracked a bit as she tried to sound nonchalant. "Desperate times. Desperate measures. It's whatever, now."

"Yeah," Halona feigned a smile and looked around the room. She was feeling guilty and awkward about her last encounter with Clementine and needed a distraction. She turned to Becca, "Is that the bathroom?"

Clementine grabbed Becca by the hand and pulled her to sit on a plush velvet chartreuse couch along the wall. Becca was so enthralled with her friend that she didn't respond to Halona. It was still a few hours before the show, so the bustle of dancers hadn't invaded the backstage. The room had a gentle lull, like gathering clouds before a thunder storm. It was just the three of them – three of The Florida Four – but it wouldn't be long before showgirls bombarded the space, preparing for their acts.

"How are you?" Becca winced at the thought of all the horrible experiences that Clementine must have encountered since her start. Her own litany of trauma flashing before her eyes. She wondered if the joke about cocaine and sex was actually the truth and not a joke at all. It was always hard to tell with Clementine. Her sarcasm was razor sharp and her humor was as black as molasses. But Becca worried for her friend.

"Ehhhh… I'm ok. The work doesn't bother me; as far as jobs go, it's not that bad. I've gotten some good johns and I've been comin' up." Clemmie winked at Becca, "I mean… not like you," she cackled deviously, "just look at that collar!"

Becca's hand shot up and grabbed the pendant that dangled from her neck. She cupped it in her hand, trying to hide it from view.

"How… how can you say that? How are you just so chill about this?" Halona said, shocked. "I'm ready to claw my way out of here. I can't imagine just being okay with this, like it's just a job or something." Her tone began to shift from astonished at their nonchalance to enraged for their safety. "You know you're enslaved, right? This is not some showgirl's dream world. This is actual hell."

"Honestly, Hal, it's not a bad gig. I get to dance in the go-go box and everything I need is taken care of. The other girls are ok. I mean… There are a couple you gotta watch for because they're catty as hell. But, mostly, the other girls just stay in their lane. No one wants to get checked by the bottom bitch. I mind my business and do what I'm told."

"Okay, I get that it's similar to dancing freelance but… you are literally trapped here. You are literally a slave to your handler. That doesn't bother you? How can that NOT bother you?"

Clem took a long, deep breath that spoke volumes about how tired she really was. The sarcasm that twinged her voice earlier was gone, as she said, "Really… it's just the autonomy. That's all that bothers me. I should be gettin' paid. I've been turning tricks… well, mostly, it's just couch dancing and head. But that money should be in my pocket, not going to the house. "

"Sounds like you're okay, then," Becca said grimacing, but she wasn't convinced.

"You know what…" Clem said with renewed energy, as if preparing to deliver a candidacy speech. "If I were in charge, prostitutes would be paid fairly for their services. And not this measly shit that I hear the professionals talk about. Like… we should reap the benefits of our labor. We should have agency."

"You're like a modern day Karl Marx," Becca joked, trying to lighten the atmosphere. "Where's a copy of The Manifesto when you need it, huh?"

"Yeah, I guess." Clem's face and mood had shifted again. Now she had the melancholy professionalism of a grad student preparing to defend their dissertation. "If I were the madam or shit—even remotely in charge—Each person could work as an independent agent. They could pick and choose their clients. Maybe just pay rent for the space. I think a lot of people would stay in the business, if they weren't treated like slaves. There's good money to be made here." Her disposition had darkened.

"Jokes aside…" Becca gave Clemmie a stern look, "Are you really okay? I mean… where is this coming from?"

"I don't know," she shrugged. "Maybe I've always felt this way," Clemmie said with a distant look in her eyes, "but think about it, sex is really just a service. It's no different than getting your nails done at a salon. Or a hair cut or a massage. Shit, those people are being trafficked too. Honestly, nobody is safe out there. Men, women, children. There's a Hispanic guy that works in the kitchen that I talk to sometimes. I get to practice my Spanish a little. Keeps the brain sharp. But he's not here because he wants to be. He's here because they told him they would bring his family over from Haiti. He's being trafficked, too. The only difference between me and him is he grills steak and I suck dick."

"You can't be serious," Halona quipped. "Those two things aren't remotely close to being the same. Sex should be saved for—"

"Marriage? Pffttt… get real. No one waits until marriage except the devout. For the rest of the world, sex isn't always personal. It's a human function, a release of tension, no different than scratching an itch. You don't have to be in love to have sex with someone. Hell, you don't even hafta like 'em! Shit, my mother didn't like my father, and they fucked. How do you think I'm here? Besides, how many times have you had sex with some mediocre dude you met on the apps for the price of a house margarita and a lukewarm triple-dipper from Chili's? Does sex under the guise of a relationship or the potential of a relationship make you less of a whore than anyone else?"

"Well, no, obviously… but it seems so cheap. Don't you value yourself? Besides that's not even the point. We have to get out of this." Halona crossed her arms, irritated.

"Hal, I never said I didn't want my freedom back. But valuing myself isn't about who I have sex with. My worth as a human has nothing to do with sex. And, anyway, sexual identity is a spectrum. And it's not directly connected to romantic identity. I feel like you understand this," she shrugged, "but maybe, my gay-dar needs to be re-calibrated."

"Now you sound like Jung!" Becca laughed and jabbed Clemmie in the side.

"Ok, smarty pants college student," Clemmie smiled. "But, really, Hal… I coulda sworn you had a thing for Sasha. Or, did I completely miss the mark on that?"

Halona's jaw dropped, "I… I can't believe you just said that," she said as her face went pale.

"Wait, what?" Becca leaned forward and stared at Halona, "You and Sasha?! Well… Did you?"

Halona steeled herself against their prying eyes, "Stop looking at me like that."

"Hal, tell us! Were you and Sasha… you know… a thing?" Becca raised her eyebrows and smirked at Halona, her attention fixed on what she would say next.

Halona blew out a deep breath and stared at the ceiling, "No, Sasha and I were not a thing. We are just friends… or, were. Has anyone even heard from her?"

"No. I see Desiree around sometimes, but she doesn't speak. Talk about making money!" Exclaimed Clem.

"Oh, yeah, I forgot to tell you that, Hal. Desiree manages the show. I had a run-in with her a few days ago… or weeks… gosh, I don't even remember how long ago it was. Seems like forever. So much has happened. Anyway… I missed this. Just chatting with you," Becca clasped Clemmie's hand, "…both of you." Becca looked up toward Halona and extended her free hand, but Halona didn't reach back for her.

Clementine smiled weakly at Becca and gripped her hand tighter, "Yeah, it's crazy how everything has changed. It's so fucked up, but I honestly feel like I've grown through this experience. It's a weird thing to think or say… given the context, but… like, this whole experience has really opened my eyes. I know… I know… who in their right mind would find clarity in this hellscape? In hindsight, we were brats. Shallow, vapid, self-righteous brats. There is so much more to the world. We thought we knew everything. But in reality, we knew nothing."

"I just can't understand how anyone would be okay with being caged and subjected to this kind of life… fucking who-knows-what night after night," Halona said, shaking her head. "It's just another form of repression."

"Maybe. But, look around, honey. We're already repressed, by society, by capitalism, by misogyny… Halona, women have BEEN repressed sexually for hundreds of years. Shit, thousands of years! We're damned if we enjoy sex and damned if we don't. You're either a slut or a prude. Either way, we're the villains, right? So, we might as well own it. Sex work is work… It's a job, so, why shouldn't I benefit from it? If you ask me, sex isn't the cage. Being trafficked is." Clementine stood up from the couch, "It's about time for me to go. I'm dancing on the bar tonight. It was good to see you… both. Hopefully, we can stay in touch. Especially since you have some sway with the boss, Bec."

"If I have anything to do with it, we will," Becca said as she stood and hugged Clemmie again. They lingered for a moment before letting go. Both of them blinked wildly trying to avoid ruining their makeup.

Halona sheepishly gave Clementine a forced smile before she was gone. Becca felt the awkwardness growing between them. She noticed how cold and distant Halona seemed to her as well as to Clementine. *Maybe we aren't friends anymore,* Becca thought. She sighed and looked around the empty room. She felt alone, even with Halona standing right beside her. Mr. Rainaldi's voice echoed in her head, *You must be firm with her.*

Becca steeled herself. She had to be perfect. For Mr. Rainaldi. For herself. She knew that he would not accept failure from her. It was her life or Halona's. And clearly, that didn't matter to Halona. She summoned all of the grit within her.

"Now," Becca's voice dropped an octave, as she tried to sound authoritative, "get ready for your performance." She pointed toward the makeup table she had used for her own debut, "There." Halona's eyes narrowed at Becca's tone. Becca tried to command her again, but as more of a pep-talk. "We got this. Let's get started! There is NO room for failure tonight. We WILL make Mr. Rainaldi proud."

CHAPTER TWENTY–SIX
THE FIRST CUT IS THE DEEPEST

Halona sat at the makeup table crafting her look for the performance. Becca hovered anxiously behind her like a rookie dance mom who didn't know how to not be needed. She fussed with makeup and hair tools offering Halona options that she clearly didn't want. But Halona was absorbed into her own reflection and paid Becca little attention. Realizing that she was unwanted, Becca wandered to the bar, in search of familiar faces and liquid distraction.

Halona gazed at herself in the mirror. She knew that Mr. Rainaldi wanted her in war paint and a war bonnet. It still made her sick to think about it. She was forced into this, and she had been hushed every time she spoke against it. But Halona wouldn't be silenced. She sampled the selection of eye shadows in front of her. She had a palette of red, orange, yellow, and gold. If Mr. Rainaldi wanted her ready for battle, she would give him a war. She layered and blended the eyeshadow into a beautiful sunset on her eye lids. Then, finished it with black eyeliner as sharp as an arrow. Using a red lip liner, she drew the outline of a hand covering her mouth and filled it with blood red lipstick. She braided her hair into two plaits, one along each side of her face. Placing the feather war bonnet on her head, Halona was the embodiment of vengeance. She was one with the fierce warrior whose rage burned in her belly.

Halona didn't notice that the backstage had begun to buzz with excitement as the showgirls entered from a side door and made their way to their own makeup tables. There was a camaraderie among the women. They chatted wildly while helping each other fasten costumes, locate props, and curl wigs. It resembled the hustle and bustle of a beauty salon with women at each station. The only time the women were silent was when the Greek Nose or any other man in a black suit would pass through. But once the men were gone, the chatter continued. Some of the women gasped as they walked past Halona, clearly noticing her makeup. Others paused and spoke to Halona, although it was in a language that she didn't speak. But she could tell they admired her makeup and welcomed her as a sister in this new cruel world.

Some of the familiar faces from Becca's first night at The Mortimer were still there. But there were also a few new faces, too. She found a new bartender in what would've been Trevor's customary spot behind the bar serving drinks. There were rumors around some of the more uninitiated staff of The Mortimer that Trevor was fired for over-pouring or sneaking extra tips as his or some other benign bullshit, but Becca knew better. 'The Antoinette Incident' left many in its wake, as her death sparked a few more at the hands of Rainaldi. It turned out 'poisoning the root' also killed the fruit of the vine, and Becca had to stand witness to Rainaldi catching several rats on ship trying to not to get caught with food in their claws. As Trevor was on tape cavorting with the direct conspirators trying to test out Antionette's new drug, he was certainly one of the first to go. Becca wasn't in the room when it happened; it was at her request. She begged Rainaldi not to witness it after seeing what happened to Antionette. But she certainly heard Trevor go, as she had to stand outside the room. It wasn't quick.

As for the new guy behind the bar, as usual, he maintained the Mortimer standard of polite but professional. Treyvon was his name. He poured her a glass of white wine without speaking and resumed cleaning the bar and preparing the coolers for the night. While Becca sat at the mahogany bar sipping her wine, the Russian Blue and her long, ethereal legs entered the club. She appeared to be inspecting the stage, but almost tripped as she climbed the steps. She grumbled to herself in a language only she knew. She walked to the far edge of the stage, and picked up the large martini glass that she would use to collect tips from the patrons as she kittened for the dancers. Hearing Blue's grumbles growing louder, the Fairy Queen stuck her head through the stage curtain. She placed a hand on her voluptuous hip and said, "Air ye muddlin, through there, lassie?" Her velvet Scottish accent enthralled Becca in the same way it had the club audience every time she was present for a show. Becca felt a connection to the woman, even though they had only barely spoken to each other. She secretly wondered if they would be friends, but she lacked the courage to try.

Blue paused from her rumination's, "It's the step. It still has not been mended."

"Aye, weil, don't go holdin yer breath now. Ye'd faint before she'd be dun."

Blue shook her head and laughed, "I guess you are right."

Becca hadn't noticed before, but as she glanced around the room, the club lacked the dazzling ambiance that it had her first night. There were yellowing drip marks on the ceiling tiles, the tassels on the stage curtain looked a bit tattered, and she noticed scuff marks here and there along the walls. She was puzzled. This room was opulent before. Now, it felt worn and tired. It was hollow like the hole-in-the-wall bar she performed in so many weeks ago.

Becca checked the clock behind the bar. It was almost time for the doors to open. She drained her wine glass and thanked Treyvon.

Patrons would soon enter the club and she needed to check on her dancer. There was work yet to be done.

As she entered the backstage dressing room, she felt a wave of negativity crash against her. Looking up, she saw the source. Desiree and her Gothic pallor, was there, hovering in the alcove with a silent resentment smeared across her face. Even the room full of dancers felt the shift, and responded in the same way they did when the Greek Nose breezed through. The force of the wave would have pushed her clear back to the dunes, if it had been physical. But, instead, Becca didn't hesitate. This was business and she had a job to do. She pushed forward like a linebacker hurdling toward a wall of opposing defenders.

As stage manager, Desiree made the set list. And for some reason unbeknownst to Becca, she listed Turquoise Cloud as the first act. Halona was dressed and ready to go on before anyone else. Secretly, she was ready to get it over with. In spite of being disgusted with the routine, Halona did exactly as she and Becca had rehearsed. Just as Becca had promised Mr. Rainaldi, when it was time for Halona's moment on stage, she didn't let her friend down. Becca had set out to make sure that everything was perfect. And she was pleased to see it was exactly that. When Halona stepped on stage, her war cry shook the room. She unleashed all the pain and passion that had been churning inside of her. Her guttural cries were delicious and terrifying. And the audience ate it up, without leaving a single crumb. They loved Turquoise Cloud every bit as much as they had loved Bella Valentina. Perhaps even more, not that Becca would admit it.

But most importantly, Becca was proud of herself. Beyond proud. Elated. And buzzing from all the effort she had put into this one night of success. She had taken an angsty, immature, angry girl and forced her to comply with the racist demands of a narcissist. And she looked beautiful while doing it. Her uniform was pressed and her hair neatly coiffed. She felt the distinction of being Mr. Rainaldi's favorite and reveled in the respect it commanded from others. Becca just knew that Mr. Rainaldi would congratulate her and lavish his praises on her for a job well done. She had done everything in her power to make Mr. Rainaldi proud, including abusing the trust of a friend.

When Halona stepped off stage, she immediately tore the war bonnet off her head and threw it onto the ground. The cheap feathers tore loose from the headband and floated to the ground. She glared at Becca but didn't speak before retreating to change out of her costume. Becca held her gaze for a moment before looking away. She knew Halona was angry with her. But she had to do what she had to do. As Clem said, "Desperate times. Desperate measures." Becca checked her manicure and continued musing on her well-earned success.

Desiree saw Halona stomp off and shouted, "Somebody clean that up. I don't want feathers all over my dressing room." The other dancers paused, but no one came forward to help. However, Desiree didn't notice because she had focused her attention on the next dancer, a waifish model sort with large child-like eyes in a Lolita costume. She looked stereotypically Chinese. She only had a moment or two to transition while the MC and kitten did their parts. As the next act began, Desiree crossed the room to where Becca stood. As she approached, her dark eyes flashed with a hatred that caught Becca by surprise. Her crimson lips dripped with disdain.

"I've been meaning to congratulate you on your promotion," her lips curled into a snide grin. "I'd love to know exactly how that came about. I imagine it's because you were a better whore than you were a dancer. You never were very good."

Becca stepped back, and stood erect. She was unprepared for the verbal assault that Desiree unleashed on her. Even though she was momentarily caught off-guard, she knew that she couldn't let that show. Becca had a reputation to keep now. She was the new Antoinette. She was the Bottom Bitch. And if there was one thing Becca was sure of, it was that Antoinette would never let anyone disrespect her like that.

"Excuse me?" Becca tilted her head and glared at Desiree. "I'm not sure who you think you're talking to, Desiree."

"You think you're hot shit," Desiree sneered. "But you're nothing."

Becca scoffed, "You'll need to adjust your tone, if you want to have a conversation with me. In case you haven't noticed, I have a little more authority around here now."

"I don't care how much authority you think you have, you're still just white trash. You might have the boss charmed but ask him how you got here."

"What are you talking about?"

"Oh, that's right, you don't know. Sounds like you don't have as much authority as you think."

"We all got here the same way, but what do you know about that? You weren't with us when we were taken from the Copa. Speaking of which, how did YOU get here?"

"HA! I'm paid well to be here. Just ask Mr. Rainaldi. And I was paid well for you, too."

"What? What do you mean, you were paid well for me?"

"I sold you, Rebecca, like a prize poodle. You're just the boss's new bitch. No better than a dog."

"You're fucking lying," Becca stepped forward, leaning into Desiree's face. "And you'll fucking pay for this disrespect. Just wait until I tell Mr. Rainaldi about this. He has a way of taking care of employees that betray him. Just fucking wait!"

Becca shoved past Desiree and exited out the side door. The other dancers had fallen silent as they watched the two women argue. Realizing that the room stared openly at her, Desiree barked more commands about cleaning up the feathers.

PART TEN

LOVE WILL KEEP US TOGETHER

CHAPTER TWENTY–SEVEN
LOVE WILL TEAR US APART

At the end of the night, when the stage performances were done and the club chairs were stacked on the tables, Becca and Halona loaded up in Marco's Escalade and took the long road back to The Chalet. It was a silent ride. Neither of the women were able to let go of their pride, and Marco was still somber over the loss of his brother, Arnoldo. So, Marco steered, Halona slept, and Becca stewed.

It was early morning, around 4 o'clock, when they arrived. Mr. Rainaldi had not yet returned, even though he had been flown to the club in the helicopter. It wasn't unlike him to have late night business to attend to. However, Becca had not seen him since before Halona's performance. Knowing this, she paced the floor like an expectant housewife. Her mind was a rickety ship lost in a churning, stormy sea, and she was in desperate need of the guidance of a light house. She couldn't shake the grip of Desiree's news and wanted nothing more than for Mr. Rainaldi to deny Desiree's involvement. There was no love lost between Desiree and Becca. They never got along well; however, Becca just couldn't fathom that anyone she knew – including Desiree – would be so callous as to sell her fellow woman into the sex trade.

Becca had every intention of confronting Mr. Rainaldi about it at the club after she stormed out of the dressing room. But he was nowhere to be found. So, she planted herself on the couch in the living room and planned to stay up until he came home. Like all of the best laid plans, she was disappointed. Come morning he still had not returned.

It was another three days before his helicopter landed at The Chalet. Standing in front of the large picture windows in the dining room, Becca saw the trees lurch and swirl in a fury. She heard the helicopter hovering over the house, preparing to land. She ran out to the pad to confront Mr. Rainaldi about Desiree. She had thought of nothing else over the past several days and needed more than anything to know for certain. As he stepped out of the aircraft, he paid Becca no attention. Even as she ran toward him, waving in an attempt to welcome him back, he walked right past her and into the house. She was confused and looked to the pilot for some understanding but received no explanation.

She followed him into the house. He went directly to his study and began making phone calls. She hovered uselessly by the Queen Anne, waiting for some acknowledgment, or to be offered a seat. But he only shooed her out of the room.

A few hours later, he emerged from his study and demanded dinner from Marco. Becca again followed him into his office. She had waited long enough, but Rainaldi's demeanor demanded softness if she was going to get anywhere near the truth. She cleared her throat and started as he sat back down at his desk, "I take it your absence means business is good. How was the trip?"

"Fruitful," Rainaldi said flatly. He began working on something on a piece of paper on his desk.

Becca was stunned at his monotone. Clearly, the business assistant vibes weren't going to break the ice slowly forming in the room. Maybe the Bella side could help. "Oh, sir. Surely it was more exciting than just all that."

"It wasn't."

More monotone, no eye contact. Finally, Becca cleared her throat again and blurted out, "Look, I just have to know… Did you give Desiree money for me? I mean…"

"I know what you mean," he said without looking up from his work.

"Okay." She shifted her feet, "Well… did you?"

"Why do you ask?"

"Desiree said…"

"And you believe her over me?"

"Well… I… It's not that. It's… I just need to know if it's true."

"Why does it matter?"

"I… just…," her resolve began to crumble and her voice began to shake, "I just want to know."

"To what purpose, Bella?" He let out a heavy sigh and looked up from the documents he was reviewing, "Why do you need to know? Have I not been good to you? Have I not taken care of your every need? Have I not given you allowance after allowance, like a spoiled child, even against my better judgment? And yet, you still make demands of me? Even when you know you have yet to satisfy any of my requests of you? You've made promises to me and none of them have been honored."

Becca opened her mouth in an attempt to respond. She wanted to tell him how well Halona's performance went. She had worked so hard and done everything just as he wanted. She thought he would be proud of her. But no promises honored? She was stunned. How could he say such a thing? But before she could draw another breath, Mr. Rainaldi continued berating her, "You are ungrateful, especially after all I have done for you. And I continue to trust you and put my faith in you. For what? Bella, I know you've betrayed me again."

"W-what? I haven't. I've done everything you've wanted. I wouldn't…"

"I know about the red hand print, Bella. How could you allow her to do that? You knew how important this was to me. And you let her go on stage with that red hand print painted over her mouth."

"I don't understand. It was just makeup."

"Oh, it was more than just makeup, and you know it! You let her do this! And that's not even the worst of it."

Becca had begun to cry, tears slowly slid down her bright red cheeks. "I… I just thought you'd be proud," her voice cracked as she spoke.

"PROUD?" He roared, "How could I ever be proud of you? You let me down. And you cheated on me. Again. No, Bella, dry up your tears. I won't feel sorry for you this time."

Becca continued to softly cry for a moment. She couldn't stop the tears from coming, no matter how hard she tried. And now accusations of cheating? Their relationship was always strictly business, but her developed sense of blind devotion to his whims left her compelled to defend herself, "Mr. Rainaldi, I would never! You can check the tapes. We can check them together. I was nowhere near the Bungalows or anywhere where you could think—"

"I know about HER."

That last word hit Becca square in the jaw. *HER. CLEM. He's jealous of…Clem??*

Rainaldi continued. "I saw you flirting in the dressing room. And I won't have it. The way you touched her hand," he stopped for a moment and turned his head to the side, as if his face had been slapped. "I won't have it, Bella. I won't share you with anyone. Especially HER. I saw how you looked at HER." He shook his head in disbelief, "No. No, you love me. And only me."

Becca stood, trembling, in shock. She had no words and even if she did, she knew that he wouldn't believe her. Her voice was small and weak, but she whispered, "How can I make this up to you?"

He sat in his desk chair, and pressed his thumb into the center of his palm. His voice was low and deep, but still rigid, "I don't know if you can."

Her hands were shaking as she approached him. She bent down at his side, with one knee on the ground. Her hands were clasped, as if in prayer, "I'm sorry," she wept. He turned to face her. Looking down at her with disdain, he said, "That's not good enough."

She crumbled to the floor, unsure of what to do next, her sobs growing louder.

"But it's a start," he said, his voice firm. "You aren't fit to handle the new girl. She's too full of spite and rebellion. So, I'm sending her to Yvette in Ybor. She'll whip the stubbornness out of her and maybe then, she'll be worth my investment."

Becca had stopped crying and stared incredulously at Mr. Rainaldi.

"But that's none of your concern, until further notice you will be confined to my bedroom. Clearly, that's the only way I'll be able to ensure your loyalty. Marco will orchestrate the move. Now clean your face, I really can't stand how ugly you are when you cry."

CHAPTER TWENTY–EIGHT
RING OF FIRE

Just as Mr. Rainaldi had threatened, he made good on his decision to relocate Halona to Ybor City. The two women weren't given the chance to say good-bye or even see each other. Halona was packed up and swept out of The Chalet almost as quickly as she had arrived, only this time more coherent. Marco handled her transportation into Yvette's care, who was only too happy to have a new rookie to break. That left only Mr. Rainaldi, Marco, and Becca living within the parameters of The Chalet. As for Clem, Rainaldi made it abundantly clear that his jealousy, not unlike his lust for control, knew no bounds. Becca had been informed that Clem too was also being relocated, but Rainaldi made it a point to ensure Becca would not be given the knowledge of where to find her ever again.

It had been almost two months since Mr. Rainaldi confined Becca to his bedroom. She glanced at the calendar. *Groundhog Day. Of course it was.* The never ending loop of hell. She felt the monotony of it. The repetition. Day in. Day out. Her scenery never changed any more. She was rarely out of his sight, and when she was, it was because he had left her under Marco's supervision. But even then, she wasn't trusted to do anything even as menial as take out the trash. She was a toy on the shelf, always waiting for Mr. Rainaldi to take her down and give her some sense of use. The more isolated she became the more she found herself longing for anyone's attention, any type of mental stimulation. In her desperation, she would have welcomed any task. In truth, she would have scrubbed the grout between the tiles, if only she had been allowed. Anything that would furnish a reprieve from her deep loneliness.

Her brain was assaulted with worry after worry regarding what punishment she would receive from Mr. Rainaldi. If he was capable of doing all of the heinous crimes that she had witnessed within these few short months, then he could do anything without remorse. She couldn't bear to think about it, much like the thought of death sent her into an existential crisis, the thought of his continued torments left her in a constant state of panic and paranoia. The more she feared his retribution and didn't receive it, the more unhinged she became.

All that was left now was where it all started months ago. Waking up confined to a room – only to be brought out during beckoned calls, but mostly waiting in silence. Waiting for some semblance of action. Scared that she may be just ultimately waiting for the end. The weight of it all hung heavy on her shoulders. Her thoughts swirled in the rotation of a desert sand storm when she was alone over those months.

I should have told Halona not to place the handprint. Even though I didn't even know she was going to do that. But I SHOULD HAVE known she would try something. She's so stubborn! I should've let things be with fucking Desiree! Ugh! Fucking bitch. I can't believe I let her get to me like that. I should've been better for him. Why couldn't I just be better?! Maybe they are right… Maybe I am just white trash. FUCK! My own mother never thought I was good enough. But, I'm trying! I'm trying SO hard to be what they want. And what about Clem? God, of all the insane, backwards ass…there's no way that…there's…

Her thoughts trailed off. All she could envision was Clem laughing with her – even at The Mortimer, even at the height of peril at the beginning of all this, even at her corniest jokes. And that smile of hers. That damned smile.

Becca silently wept in those moments alone. For her friends, for Clem…hell, even for her own mother and sister, whom she found herself missing dearly. She wondered if they were at that press conference she spied in on, and wondered if they felt the same. But more than anything, she wept for herself. She wanted to go home. She wanted the strength to break free of this nightmare. She wanted freedom.

Another day had come and gone as Mr. Rainaldi stood at the edge of his king size bed, loosening his necktie. Becca stood opposite of him, lost in the servitude of her nightly duties, which included fluffing his pillow and turning down his comforter for the night. He paused and held the long silk tail of the necktie in his hand as he watched Becca. There was something in the way she plumped his pillow that aroused him. He bit his lip as he continued watching her. Feeling his gaze, she looked up and blushed, embarrassed after realizing his intent. She turned and sat on the bed with her back to him. He walked to the closet door, opened the top drawer, and neatly folded his tie. His closet, like everything else in his wake, was always meticulously arranged. A place for everything and everything in its place.

Turning to face her again, "Bella," he said as he slid open a hidden compartment inside the closet, "I want you to dominate me."

Becca paused her pillow fluffing for a moment, processing the sharp flash of what exactly he had just said. "I want you to dominate me." It was as cold and calculated as any other request of his; another business transaction with no difference of gravity. Kidnapping, murder, and now sex…all the same to one, Mr. Rainaldi. She felt the blood drain from her face.

Shocked, she bolted off the bed and turned toward him. Inside the closet revealed an array of bondage gear and a large, 6 foot tall leather-padded "X" that was equipped with restraints for hands and feet. He reached into a drawer and pulled out a black leather strap-on harness with a realistic looking dildo protruding from the o-ring, "I haven't gotten a good release since before Antoinette left. Not that she could ever give me what I really need." He slid his hand down the shaft of the dildo, "I always found her lacking."

Her mouth gaped open as she stared past him fondling the dildo, and into the secret dungeon within his closet. It looked like the back room of a sex shop. Every apparatus and contraption necessary for the deepest of fetishes.

"Your reaction surprises me, Bella. I thought you would have guessed at my proclivities by now. We've shared a bed for two months and I've not once made an advance toward you. Did you not find that odd?"

It took her a few moments to compose herself. But when she thought about the passing of each night, she realized that he really had made no movements toward touching her in any way. She slept unmolested on her side of the bed each night. He had every opportunity but he had made no effort to seduce her.

"My jewel," he crooned solicitously, "I'm not interested in fucking you, especially since you've been defiled. I simply want you to fuck me. That's not too much to ask." He chuckled. His laughter was harsh and mocking.

Becca stood unmoved beside the bed. She was astounded and revolted at the same time. She felt an ick creep over her skin at the mention of her being 'defiled.' She shuttered as she waited for the bitter memory to pass over her gray matter like a storm cloud. But it didn't pass, the words, *since you've been defiled,* clattered against her skull like thunder. *That's why he hasn't touched me.*

"I've… um… never done anything like that. BDSM, I mean. I've heard of it, but I wouldn't know what to do."

"Don't play coy! Anyone who shoves money into her snatch must have some idea of what to do."

She gasped, "I…" Blushing, she was ashamed of her desperation, and the guilt of her deception. She remembered how badly she wanted to be free that night. She was willing to take chances. Bold chances. And now she hid in plain sight, afraid of being perceived, frightened of making some innocuous mistake that would set Rainaldi off, terrified of his form of punishment via poisoning.

The thought of sex disgusted her, especially with him, but she questioned what he would do to punish her if she refused him. This man wasn't the type to ask for consent. No, Mr. Rainaldi was the type of man who took what he wanted, regardless of who he hurt.

"Take off your skirt," he commanded. "I'll buckle the harness onto your waist."

She obeyed, but her body was rigid as he approached her. He cinched the leather belt tight against her abdomen. The silicone appendage brushed her inner thigh. It was an odd sensation and sent a shiver down her spine. His hands reached through the open part of her legs and adjusted the leg buckles to loop around her thighs. His proximity to her sensitive areas heightened her senses. She could feel the heat radiating from his hands but he didn't touch her, only the leather straps. The lace of her underwear peeked under the edges of the harness.

"Now, take your shirt off," he said as he unbuttoned and removed his own. After he finished undressing, he pulled a leather collar from a drawer, and fastened it around his neck. He prepared the large 'X' by adjusting the ankle cuffs.

"I want them tight," he said as he unbuckled the wrist cuffs, "when you bind me to St. Andrew's Cross." He removed a leather flogger that was hanging from the middle 'V' of the cross. "We'll start with this," he said as he handed it to Becca, "and then you can finish me off with the strap-on."

As she gripped the clear glass handle, she felt a churning in her belly. Panic swept over her.

"Can I have some water," she said, clearing her throat loudly, "before we start."

"How about a vermouth, instead?" He opened a small wine cooler, took out a glass, and poured. Becca watched him intensely. It was obvious to both of them that she was astutely aware of his habit of poisoning people. He noticed her hesitation, "Don't be ridiculous," he said as he handed her the glass, "why would I poison you now?" She took a long swig and handed the wine glass back to him, hoping the liquid courage would help her get through what she was about to do.

"Let us begin," he said as he faced away from her and positioned his chest against the cross. Becca buckled the restraints on his wrists and ankles. She backed up and gazed at Mr. Rainaldi's naked body spread eagle. She waited for the burn of the alcohol to warm her from the inside out. But her nerves were still getting the best of her.

"Begin," he said, impatiently.

Becca heard the crack of the leather tendrils clashing against Mr. Rainaldi's bare skin. Her stomach lurched.

"Harder," he instructed.

She swallowed hard and struck him with the flogger again. He groaned as he gripped the restraints on the St. Andrew's Cross. His back muscles rippled as his body tensed and relaxed in a wave of pleasure.

"Again," he muttered through clenched teeth.

The curved, glass handle of the flogger slipped in Becca's grip. She wiped the sweat from her shaking hands. Gripping the glass handle tightly, she reared her arm back and struck him harder. Mr. Rainaldi arched forward as the leather slashed across his back. Becca gulped down the rising bile in her throat.

"Again," he said, louder, forcefully through gritted teeth.

Becca was breathing heavily, her heart pounded, and the sparks of a wrathful fire ignited in her belly. She felt something sinister awakening in her. She didn't know what it was but she felt it to her marrow. He deserved to feel pain. But she hated that he was enjoying it. She wanted to hurt him. She wanted him to suffer. The rage inside of her was rising. She released a slow breath from her nostrils, stepped back, and swung the flogger with all her strength. The thin falls of leather thrashed his back with a heavy thwack. His body contorted as he curved his spine, and rose up on his toes. He clung to the restraints on his wrist. He pulled hard against the cuffs. A deep guttural moan escaped from Mr. Rainaldi's lips.

"Finally," he sneered, "You've given me what I want."

A deep hate had awoken inside of her. She hated the sound of him moaning. He didn't deserve to feel pleasure. Becca stepped forward and grabbed the metal chain on the back of the polished leather collar. She pulled it tight, cinching it against his throat. He gagged and choked.

"Stop talking," she commanded as she slowly released her grip on the metal chain.

As the leather collar loosened around his throat, Mr. Rainaldi chuckled. It was a low, devious sound that seemed to bubble out of him with delight.

"Yes, Mommy. Have I been a naughty boy?"

The inflection in his voice made her nauseous. She fought back her disgust. She hated this. And she hated him. But she couldn't lose control.

Breathe in through the nose and out through the mouth, she thought as she closed her eyes. *Inhale. Exhale.*

As her body relaxed, she thought of the gentle way Clementine's hair tumbled around her face and the softness of her skin when she held her hand at their last meeting. Clemmie's voice was a tender whisper in Becca's head, *It's a job, so, why shouldn't I benefit from it.*

She didn't want to be Mr. Rainaldi's dominatrix, but she knew there would be consequences if she didn't do exactly as he wanted. Over the past several months, he had made that abundantly clear. And somehow, beating him senseless was the only catharsis she would get.

"Now slide in, and give me what I want," he purred.

"No," Becca's voice was hard and deliberate as she refused his demands, "You have been a naughty boy. You don't deserve it."

Rejecting him was cathartic, too. She felt a surge of power flowing through her. It was so similar to when she performed, and yet so different. She felt high but it wasn't from pleasure. This didn't feel good. It felt necessary. Chills rolled over her skin, prickling the fine hairs along her arms. This was justice. This was vindication. This was retribution. She stroked the soft leather tendrils. The waves of nausea had vanished. She was girded and ready for battle.

A slow, amused laugh curled out of him as he relaxed against the cross and cooed, "Then, give me what I deserve."

The lilt of his voice angered her. She cracked the flogger in the air and released a fury of attacks on him. The falls of leather lashed at his back and sides, reddening his skin. His body tensed and released with each impact. He moaned as if she were massaging him.

"Ooooooo! Yes, Mommy, that's what I want."

"I don't care what you want. But I WILL give you what you deserve."

She walked around the cross, watching, as his body shuttered from the attack. She paced around him in a circle as she tied tiny knots along the ends of the leather tendrils of the flogger.

"Promises. Promises." He teased, "Will you break those too and disappoint me again?"

She was behind him once more, surveying the damage, but it was minimal. To her disappointment, his bare skin revealed only a general reddening, like a faint sunburn. She finished tying the knots, stepped forward, grabbing the metal chain of his collar again. She tightened it.

"I thought I told you to stop talking."

"Yes, ma'am," he grunted.

She prepared to give him another lashing, but lowered her aim. She wanted him to feel the sting of the knots on fresh skin. With the leather falls knotted the flogger resembled a cat of nine tails. Without warning she popped the falls against his bare bottom with the flick of her wrist. The first hit landed with a thud, sending a shock wave through him. He yelped as his whole body jolted from the enhanced impact. He thrashed wildly, snatching at the restraints as she continued her attack. Becca felt powerful. She reveled as she watched him writhe. Regaining his composure, a sinister laugh curdled deep in his throat.

"I knew you'd be good at this," he moaned as he stretched his back, flexing his muscles against the strain of the cuffs. "Your rage is delicious. I want more."

"And I'll feed you all of it," she said through gritted teeth, "but good boys ask nicely."

"Oh, yes, ma'am. I'll be your good boy," he said with a child-like innocence. "Please, Mommy, may I have some more?"

With this she penetrated him with the strap-on dildo. As she thrust against him, the waves of nausea returned, crashing alongside every moan he let out. His pleasure was still the dominant even under submission, and she found herself losing control once again. To her, it was no different than her first night at The Mortimer. Just another man taking control of her for his own pleasure, and she was repulsed once again as the memories of being abused flooded her mind. She grabbed the chain of his collar and pulled it tight, hoping her righteous rage would translate into a grisly end to this nightmare. Instead, it was only another pleasure trigger, as he proceeded to orgasm. She dismounted as he lost consciousness, unbuckled the harnesses, and ran from the room crying, leaving him still bound to the St. Andrew's Cross.

CHAPTER TWENTY-NINE
BEST OF YOU

Becca ran down the stairs to the main floor of the house. As she tumbled off the last step, she collapsed against the white tile floor. She was overcome as all of her repressed emotions from the past several months came surging forward. Tears streamed down her face. She pressed her cheek against the cold tile as she gasped for breath. The heavy guttural sobs poured from deep within her. She hated what she had just done. She hated that she let herself fall apart and lose control. She felt unbearably weak after feeling so incredibly powerful as she flogged Mr. Rainaldi. Her desire for revenge made her think that she could make him pay for all the suffering he had caused. Instead, she let her anger consume her and it left her feeling even more vulnerable. Dashed by her failed attempt to strangle him, she felt utterly lost and hopeless.

Alarmed by the sound of sobbing, Marco rushed around the corner of the kitchen wall. It was late and he didn't expect anyone to still be awake. He scrambled to Becca's side, and checked her over quickly to ensure she wasn't injured. Confirming that she had no broken bones nor open wounds, he lifted her from the floor and carried her to the couch. She clung to his neck and cried into his shoulder. As he sat on the couch beside her, she wrapped her arms around his waist and buried her face into his armpit. The way he cared for her reminded her of her older brother, Russell. He had the same gentle nature.

"What is it?," he questioned her. "What has happened?"

She continued to cry. She didn't have the words to explain what had happened and she couldn't control the tears as they soaked the fabric of his shirt.

Marco pulled her from his side, "Where is he?" He shook her a little, "This is important. Answer me."

She took a deep breath, "Up… upstairs."

"Is he…," Marco raised his eyebrows to insinuate something fatal.

"He's… uh… on… on the cross. I tried to…," the tears began to flow again and she covered her face with her hands before continuing, "but he just… I don't know… came and fainted."

Marco wrapped his arm around her and let her cry. Becca clung to him with all her might. After a few minutes had passed, she began to calm down and dry her tears. The awkwardness of her vulnerability caused her to pull away. But Marco didn't seem to notice it. Instead, he returned to his own standard issue diligence of managing difficulties, large and small.

"Here now, I'll get you some water and then tend to him," he said as he headed back to the kitchen. He poured her a glass of cold water and set it on the dinner table.

"Come sit," he motioned.

Becca weakly stood from the couch and hobbled to the dining room table, wincing from the tenderness of the hip she had fallen on when she tumbled down the stairs. She waited there while Marco went upstairs to uncuff Mr. Rainaldi from the St. Andrew's Cross. Having been accustomed to cleaning up after Mr. Rainaldi, he made quick work of the situation and Mr. Rainaldi barely awoke from his intensely relaxed state as he was removed from the cross and laid to rest in his bed.

When Marco reemerged, he winked and made the OK gesture with his hand, "He'll be out for a while."

Becca finished her water. He pointed at the glass and said, "Another?"

"No. Thank you."

He nodded, grabbed a rag from the counter, and began wiping the condensation that had pooled on the table.

"Marco, can I say something? I... I've got something bothering me and... well, I don't really have anyone to talk to about it... especially now that Hal is gone. And... well... you've always been kind. Never rude to me or anything like that."

Marco stopped wiping the dinner table and gave her an inquisitive look, "If you would like."

"I'm realizing some things and I don't know what to do."

"Well, I'm no priest, but I'll listen," he said as he sat next to her at the table.

"I've just... changed so much since I got here. And in ways that I never thought I would. I... I don't know. I'm afraid I'm losing myself. I don't know who I am anymore. I've never felt so repulsed by sex before. With burlesque, it was freeing. I felt empowered. And... now, I... I wanted to end it so bad that I was willing to do anything. I didn't even think, I just... just kept pulling tighter and tighter. I wanted him to die. And I was willing to kill him. I just feel so... dirty and empty. I'm ashamed that I would even be willing to take someone else's life. That's not me. Or... at least, that's not who I was. I'm just so disgusted by men. That man from the club. And now, Mr. Rainaldi. I... I honestly don't want another man to ever touch me that way ever again," she stopped, realizing who she was talking to. "I'm sorry, Marco. I don't mean you personally. Just men... in general. I don't know what to do. I just feel so used. So worthless."

Marco stroked his chin thoughtfully. His gaze was distant and melancholy. He covered his mouth with one hand and stared at the overhead light reflecting off the tile for a moment before speaking.

"There are some people in the world who only know how to take," he said with a heavy sigh. "And they take and take and take until they've taken everything you have. It doesn't matter what it is; money, family, job, future, love, pride, virtue. They won't stop until you're numb and empty and don't even have the will to live. They don't have a soul, so they turn everyone around them into shadows. We become shells. Empty skins. Just hollow versions of who we once were."

He paused. Becca reached across the table to take his hand, "I'm sorry, Marco."

"Rainaldi took everything from me," he said, his eyes focused on their cupped hands. "I thought my loyalty meant something. But it was never about loyalty. It's about him having the power to control someone so much that they destroy themselves. We're his play things, Bella. I see that now. I just wish I had seen it before he took my brother. I should have fought to save Arnoldo. But I was afraid." He stopped speaking for a moment and looked at her thoughtfully. "I bet Bella isn't even your real name."

She grimaced and hesitated, "Uhhh… I don't think I should…"

"Look at me. I'm nothing. I'm not going to reveal who you are. How could I? Who am I? No one. Just a shell, where a man once was."

Marco leaned forward in his chair and released Becca's hand. But she grabbed it, and clutched his hand firmly with both of hers. Their eyes locked for a moment that seemed to stretch on.

"No, Bella isn't my real name," she smiled at him. "It's Rebecca. Bella is just a stage name. Seems silly now, the reason why I chose it— just childish fairy tales and princess fantasies. And now it's the only identity that I have."

"Maybe not. Maybe it's not too late for you, Rebecca."

Becca mused at the irony of the situation. The words held hope within them, but the person they came from seemed so broken, so depleted of hope for himself. She shook her head and gave him a sad, half-smile.

"I don't understand how you can say that… like there's hope for me but none for yourself. If there is none for you, how can there be any for me? He's gotten the best of us."

Marco scoffed, "You don't realize the power you have, Rebecca."

"What do you mean? You literally pulled me off the floor tonight because I lost control."

"Oh, you have power, Sorellina. You just don't know how to wield it."

She searched his face, looking to find the hidden meaning somewhere within the darkness of his eyes or the depth of his crow's feet. She could tell there was wisdom behind those eyes. And she couldn't explain why, but she trusted him. There was something in that moment that comforted her. It was like a touch of home. A rare moment of calm. It felt like she was talking with her brother.

"I don't understand. What power do I have?"

"He allowed you to handcuff him tonight. Do not take that lightly."

Part Eleven

Girls Just Wanna Have Fun

CHAPTER THIRTY

COCAINE

The next morning Mr. Rainaldi was in a chipper mood. He was relaxed and jovial at the breakfast table, even to the point of complimenting Marco on the quality of the avocado toast and fresh wheatgrass juice, which Becca considered to be rather bland. He made no mention of the previous night's events, nor questioned why Becca was not in his bed when he awoke. But instead he went about his normal routine of working in his private study. The only real difference in his mood was that he was much less restrictive of Becca's movements. As long as she was in the house and came when summoned, he allowed her to roam more freely. Had Becca known that beating Mr. Rainaldi with a flog would result in a few minutes of alone time each day, she would have done it much sooner. And their regular encounters continued on that path for the next several weeks. Becca had started to learn that the best way to deal with Mr. Rainaldi was to pander to his whims, regardless of whether that was domestically, professionally, or sexually. As long as Mr. Rainaldi's demands were met, Becca was given the privilege of a longer leash.

* * *

A few weeks later, he announced at breakfast that he had some pressing business to attend to in Miami. He planned to be flown to the club there later that day and requested for Becca to accompany him.

"Bella, I'd like you to see the Dungeon at the club. I think it may spark some interest in new techniques for you. Several of the ladies there make use of the space for clients' unique needs. You may tour that while I meet with the club manager."

"As you wish," she replied simply.

Marco interrupted, "What time would you like for me to have the pilot ready for take off, sir?"

"I see no need to delay. Say, in one hour. That should be plenty of time to prepare for our departure."

Marco nodded a confirmation and went to work orchestrating the day's schedule, as well as notifying the Miami crew about their impending visit. It wasn't long before the sound of the propeller was heard overhead and the wind whipped through the tall pines that surrounded the house. As Becca stepped into the helicopter, she recognized the pilot. He was one of the guards that had detained Arnoldo and Halona. She marveled at how the guards seemed readily available and yet typically unseen. Her own access to the property was limited and she wondered where the guards hid most of the time and just how many of them there were. She thought back to the day she walked down the dirt road to The Chalet with her friends, and laughed at her own stupidity as she realized that they were never alone. She knew now that all of that land belonged to Mr. Rainaldi. There were probably guards surrounding them the entire time or at least aware of them. It seemed to her that Mr. Rainaldi liked to give people the illusion of choice. When in actuality, they had none. But that led her to an even more puzzling question: how had Halona evaded them and survived in the woods for a week? While she was at The Chalet,

Halona never opened up about her experience. It seemed too sensitive to discuss.

The helicopter flight to Miami was shorter than Becca expected. She marveled at the views from that altitude and considered it a rare treat from the hustle of the usual routine of babying Mr. Rainaldi. When they landed at the club, a group of employees, all dressed and pressed in the standard uniform, greeted them on the platform. The staff treated Mr. Rainaldi's visit like a general inspecting his troops. An ingratiating man, with a round belly and a cowboy mustache pushed through to the front of the crowd. As he came waddling from behind, he reminded Becca of a shifty used car salesman from one of those buy-here-pay-here dealerships. The ones who specialized in selling lemons or recalls.

As usual, she stood quietly behind Mr. Rainaldi, like a concubine waiting for him to require her assistance. The Cowboy Mustache didn't even acknowledge her presence. But neither did any of the employees who stood at parade rest, waiting for their own instruction. However, more often than not, that was the norm. It was rare for anyone to address her directly. She was more like a ghost that hovered behind Mr. Rainaldi everywhere he went, until he grew tired of being followed. Then, Becca was sent on some menial errand that got her out of the way while the men could attend to the real business. Even though she was treated as if she wasn't there, the men were always extraordinarily cautious about discussing business matters in front of her. And when they did discuss business in her presence, it was always through code or a foreign language.

Becca was on one of those menial errands when she found her way to the Dungeon. Just as the name suggested, it was dark, ominous, and jam packed with weapons intended to evoke pain as well as pleasure. As she entered the room, she saw a woman exploring a wall of teasers.

She looked as if she were shopping for a feather duster. At the squeak of Becca's shoe on the polished floor, the woman whirled around.

"Becca?" She said with a confused expression. "Is that you?"

Becca looked hard at the woman, but she didn't recognize her face. Her hair was jet black and chopped short in a French bob with fringed bangs. The woman's smile widened, as she came rushing forward.

"It IS you! What are you doing here?"

Becca was still confused as the woman came closer, but once she was within only a few feet, Becca caught a flirtatious glint in her eye that was hauntingly familiar.

"Don't tell me you've forgotten me already? It's only been a few months. Well, maybe longer. The last time I saw you was at that gorgeous A-frame house in the woods."

"Sasha?" Becca's face contorted as she squinted for a closer look. Her eyes were so familiar and her voice reminiscent. But nearly everything else in her appearance had changed. She looked like a new woman. "Oh my god, your hair! I didn't even recognize you! You look amazing!" The two women embraced for a long while, swaying from side to side as they hugged each other, like two old women.

Sasha pulled away and flicked at Becca's long ponytail. "I've never known you to rock the cheerleader ponytail. You look like one of the front desk girls. You're not doing maid stuff, are you? I figured you'd either be dancing or riding dick."

Becca laughed, "The hair is different but you're still the same. I'm here with Mr. Rainaldi. I'm still staying at the A-frame you loved so much."

"Ohhhhhhh. So, you're the boss's bottom bitch, now. Well, you did move up the ranks fast! Good for you, hon!"

Becca feigned a weak laugh, "Is that good? I'm not sure it's worth congratulating. But, anyway, how are you? How's everything been?"

"Oh, girl, I'm loving it. This shit is my dream job. I get to bounce on dick as often as I want. I get to try kinky shit on newbs. I got all the angel dust I can snort. I'm headlining most weekends and Federico… er… Mr. Gasparini gives me whatever I want."

"Who's Federico?"

"He's the boss here, you know… the general manager, or whatever his official title is," Sasha fanned the air, as if brushing away the unnecessary details. "Regardless, I'm his little sugar baby," she said in a babyish voice and giggled. "But seriously, though, if I want it, I got it. Just call me Ariana Grande." She giggled. "He takes care of everything, though. But I bet you got it like that too, being the big boss's girl."

"That's crazy. I definitely don't have it like THAT. But, you know I saw Clementine a few months back. And Halona. She turned up about a week after you all left. You know, I think she has a thing for you."

"Who? Clementine? Or Hal?"

"Hal. She was asking about you and got real quiet when we pressed her for details."

"Oh, ha! I've known about that since we first met. Honestly, I think it's the only reason she joined up with the dance troupe. But, I'm just not into girls. I never had the heart to tell her, though. She was always a good friend to me. I hope she's doing okay. BUT, you know it's funny you mention it. Because I definitely thought there was some scissor sister action going on between you and Clementine."

"What? Me and Clementine? No, no. We're just really good friends. But…uh…what made you think that?"

"Ha! That's what every lesbian says. There was always just something about the way you two looked at each other. But, maybe I was wrong. I mean… if you say, you're just friends." Sasha shrugged. "Then, I must have been seeing things."

"Yeah. I guess so. Anyway, I'm supposed to tour the Dungeon while Mr. Rainaldi is working. Want to show me around?"

"Oooooo! Yes, I would love to. Where would you like to start? Ass ticklers, floggers, canes, or pillories?"

Becca laughed, "You pick."

The two women were lost in the quietude of the Dungeon for hours, laughing and giggling while they explored all the available tools. The contents were vast and resembled the selection of a store. Just about anything that Becca could think of, was there and then some. Her face blanched as Sasha explained how pillories work. Sasha had a list of favorites that she recommended to Becca. She also had a list of techniques to try. Sasha demonstrated how to use different items as if she were a sales clerk working on commission. Her knowledge of BDSM gear was extensive and her passion for it oozed out of her.

As the tour was coming to an end, Becca's mood shifted and the dark, circular room began to close in on her. She fell silent for a moment, and tried to shake the feeling that she was trapped in a prison. Sasha leaned forward, and placed her hand on Becca's shoulder, "You good?"

"Yeah, yeah," Becca said with a sigh. "It's just a lot. Guess I just got overwhelmed."

Sasha looked at her thoughtfully, "I get it. It's not for everyone. To each their own, though."

"Yeah, to each their own," she smiled weakly at Sasha. "Can I ask you something?"

"Sure. What's up?"

"Do you ever think about running away? You know, like escaping this?"

"You know, it might sound odd, but no. Life before this wasn't great. My dad was a dick. My mom died when I was just a kid. We were dirt poor. And now I have everything I want. Fame. Fun. And someone to pamper the fuck outta me. What's there to go back to? I know it'll end eventually. I'll wrinkle up like an old hag and no one will want to fuck me anymore. So, I just ride the wave while I've got the looks to enjoy it."

Becca just shook her head in silence. She didn't know what to say. And she wondered if she should say anything at all. But she worried for her friend. She worried how completely okay she was with prostitution; how unbothered she was to be confined to the vapid world she lived in.

"Welp, I'm wearing thin. I think I'll go see Daddy Darling Federico for a lil pick me up. You wanna partake?"

"Oh, no. I better go find Mr. Rainaldi. He doesn't like it when I'm away for too long."

The two women hugged tightly and parted ways.

Becca located Mr. Rainaldi in the main area of the club, reviewing sales sheets with the bar manager. It wasn't long after that that he announced their pending departure. Becca felt a wave of relief, even though she didn't want to go back to The Chalet, she was ready to leave Miami.

Becca was silent during the helicopter flight home. She couldn't get Sasha's words out of her mind. She kept rolling them over and over. She wondered if her feelings for Clementine were obvious to everyone except her? First, Mr. Rainaldi mentioned it and next, Sasha. And the better question, which made her stomach knot: had Clementine realized it too?

It was late evening when Mr. Rainaldi and Becca returned to The Chalet. She followed her normal routine of pumping his pillow and turning down his bed in an effort to keep him satisfied. But she was anxious to confide in Marco. So, once Mr. Rainaldi was asleep, Becca crept downstairs to see if Marco was still awake. To her delight, as usual, he was.

"Boss asleep?" He asked as she came around the corner.

Becca nodded, "Marco, have you ever been in love?"

"Once."

"How did you know?"

"I just knew."

"But, how? Were there any signs?"

He scoffed, "Oh, there were signs. I couldn't stop thinking about her. I wanted to be with her all of the time. It didn't matter what we were doing, as long as it was with her. And I knew that I would do anything for her. Her happiness was the most important thing to me."

"That's beautiful. What happened?"

"Eh, it was a lifetime ago. And I was young and stupid."

"Oh."

"Why do you ask?"

"Eh," she said mimicking his Italian accent, "there's a girl I can't stop thinking about."

"Oh! Someone new?"

"No, actually, I've known her for a long time. I just always thought that was… I don't know… friendship, I guess. I never really had great female friendships. She was the first true friend I ever had. But, now when I think about her, it's different. I guess I'm realizing that there might be more to it."

"Have you told her?"

"No, and I'll probably never get the chance. It's not like Rainaldi is going to let me out of his sight… that is if he ever even lets me go back to The Mortimer, or wherever she ended up. He was pretty angry that I even spoke with her last time."

"I see," Marco paused thoughtfully, "Well… only God knows what the future holds, Sorellina.

God, huh. She looked at him inquisitively, "Why do you call me that? What does it mean?"

"Oh, Sorellina? It means little sister. I never had a sister, growing up, it was only me and Arnoldo. But it seems like a good fit for you."

CHAPTER THIRTY-ONE
RIOT

Just as winter thawed into spring, the days of spring flowed into summer. It had been nine months since Rebecca's abduction. Life had fallen into a rhythm and she barely noticed the passing of the months. Her duties for Mr. Rainaldi had become instinctual; they were something that she no longer had to think about and she not only complied to his demands, but anticipated them. Like a sixth sense, Becca had begun to read Mr. Rainaldi's moods by the subtle ticks of his facial expressions and nuanced inflections in his voice. She had learned to curate her responses and requests of him, because certain words or phrases would set him off. She had become hyper-vigilant to his whims because when she didn't accommodate him in exactly the manner he expected, his wrath was made known to everyone in the vicinity.

Like a toddler, smashing a block tower because he wanted sliced carrots instead of carrot sticks, Mr. Rainaldi's tantrums became more erratic and destructive. Over the past few months, he'd smashed teacups because it contained Earl Grey instead of English Breakfast. He'd groaned and moaned over pant legs that had been inappropriately folded and displayed crooked pleats. He vehemently complained if he ever had to wait for Becca for any reason at all. Keeping Mr. Rainaldi on an even keel was running Becca ragged.

Rainaldi's maladjusted attitude wasn't without reason from a business aspect. Antionette's prototype date-rape drug had since been put into full production by Rainaldi, and was being heavily used in and outside of his clubs. The problems started coming more frequently when his Cuban competitors in Miami got a hold of a sample or two, and found out what it could do when used in excess doses. As such, the direct ties to the drug were becoming harder to shake. Becca had passed by his study one fateful evening to hear Rainaldi screaming on speakerphone at Chief Guy Hogg to get the FBI and Agent Lamontagne off his scent.

Even though he was becoming more easily incensed, Mr. Rainaldi had begun to trust her more and more since she had begun to dominate him in the bedroom. With every lashing, she believed that she had earned greater freedom and he believed that he had gained a greater hold on her loyalty. While she still shared a bedroom with him, he no longer required her constant presence.

While Becca learned how to wear the mask convincingly, Marco's mask had begun to slip. Growing tired of pandering to Mr. Rainaldi and cleaning up his messes, Marco began to resent every action that was in service to him. His melancholy had grown into a deep loathing. And it was becoming more and more difficult for him to hide his emotions. Marco found tiny ways to rebel against Mr. Rainaldi. He had never been passive aggressive before, but his evening chats with Becca had renewed a sense of justice and morality in him that hadn't been present for a long time. He wanted vengeance for his brother. But he also wanted to keep Becca safe. She had become like a little sister to him, and he couldn't bear the thought of losing someone else.

At dinner that night, the tension hung in the air as the three of them were quieter than normal. Mr. Rainaldi was the first to break the silence.

"Marco," Mr. Rainaldi announced, "Bella and I will be traveling to Ybor tomorrow."

"Yes, sir. When do you plan to return, sir?"

"Some time tomorrow night, I haven't nailed down a time."

"Would you like for me to have your evening meal prepared or will you be dining out, sir?"

"No need for any of that, Marco. I believe we'll have dinner out. My palate is in need of a cleanser from your usual cuisine. Just schedule my pilot, as usual, and contact the necessary parties. However, I appreciate your diligence. You're proving to be a faithful servant, after all."

A pregnant pause hung in the air. Marco nodded in acknowledgment, but fought the painful jab of being referred to as a servant. Even Becca winced at the mention of "servant." Marco had never considered himself as such. But instead, thought of himself as an assistant to the boss. There was something about the word "servant" and the way Mr. Rainaldi said it, that sent the image of a groveling man through Marco's head. Marco had been pulling away from Mr. Rainaldi since his brother's death but being referred to as a servant so nonchalantly sealed that separation. It was obvious to Marco that Mr. Rainaldi no longer held him in high regard, if he ever did at all. He felt it deep in his gut. His loyalty had been for nothing. Knowing that filled him with a deep loathing for Mr. Rainaldi.

"In that case, sir, I have some errands in town to attend to," Marco bowed ceremoniously, and said, "with your permission, of course."

"In town? I assume you are visiting the Euro Market. Ingredients for a new creation, I hope."

"Something like that, sir."

"It's been quite some time since you last surprised us with one of your culinary creations. Will it be something rare like the handmade pasta you made?"

"It is something I've never tried before. However, I prefer to keep it as a surprise, sir."

"Ah! Well, in that case, I look forward to the reveal, then."

"Yes, sir. I'm sure you will be astounded."

Becca watched the cat and mouse game being played by the two men. There was so much that was being said without words. She felt the awkwardness of the conversation, as Marco's tone had become sarcastic. She knew that he would go too far if she didn't change the subject.

"Since we are going to Ybor," Becca twirled a strand of hair between her fingers, "would it be alright for me to visit with Halona?"

"I don't think that's a good idea, Bella." Mr. Rainaldi had a stern expression, like a disapproving father, "She is a poor influence on you. And you've come too far to fall back now."

"Please, I haven't seen her in so long," she fluttered her lashes and implored, "It would be nice… just to talk with her."

"Just talk?" Mr. Rainaldi searched her face and said, "Fine, as long as you are not alone."

"As you wish," she replied.

Mr. Rainaldi sighed heavily and left the table for the comfort of his study. Later that night after he had retired to bed, Becca and Marco met in the kitchen for their nightly chat.

"Servant! Ha! He is not the only one with connections," Marco huffed as he scrubbed a stainless steel pot with his gloved hands. "He will see."

"I know you are mad," Becca consoled, "but you can't let him see that."

"And to insult my cooking! The audacity!" Marco's voice rose, "I've never made a bad meal in my life!"

"Shhh! He might hear you," she glanced over her shoulder, "and honestly, I think it encourages him to do it more. Like he enjoys finding new ways to bug the shit out of you. But you can't let him get to you."

"Oh, I know he does," Marco vented. "He is an evil, little man, who enjoys tearing people down. He likes to watch us squirm! But he is not the only one who knows how to poke the bear." His voice was pitched with intensity as he became grumbling under his breath in Italian.

"Marco, breathe! You're gonna scrub a hole in that pot."

Marco leaned away from the pot in the sink, "You are right, Sorellina." He took a long breath and exhaled slowly. "All good. All good. Now, how are you feeling about your trip to Ybor?"

"Nervous. The last time I saw Hal we weren't on the best terms. But I want to tell her I saw Sasha. Maybe it would help her to know that she seems to be happy."

"Perhaps. And, what if it were you in Halona's shoes? Would you want to be sure of your darling Clementine's happiness?"

"Of course. I worry about her. It feels like it's been 84 years since we saw each other, but I'd still want to know if she was okay... even though I honestly don't know if I'd have the courage to tell her how I feel about her."

"Eh, something to dream about while you sleep next to... him," Marco snarled as he jutted his chin toward Mr. Rainaldi's upstairs bedroom.

Becca gave a sad smile, "I guess I should get some sleep. I'll have to be up in a few hours to be ready before him. I know he'll be pissed if he has to wait on me."

"Indeed. And, I have some calls to make tonight."

The next morning, the helicopter pilot and Becca were downstairs ready and waiting for Mr. Rainaldi. It seemed like they were only in the sky for moments before landing at the club in Tampa. Becca had never been and was excited to get away from The Chalet. However, when they landed a frantic young man in a white button down and black sport coat greeted them abruptly.

"Mr. Rainaldi, sir, there's been an urgent phone call." The young man looked no more than 20-years-old and had the face of a cherub; innocent and chubby. "The boss sent me to tell you."

"What's the issue? Where is Geraldo? He usually greets me himself," an annoyed expression creased Mr. Rainaldi's brow.

"It's the Miami warehouse, sir. There's been a breach," the Chubby Cherub said as he fidgeted. "Boss thinks it's the Cubans. But they need you in Miami, sir. Immediately."

"Fine," he said in exasperation, "Tell Geraldo that I am on my way. And then take Bella back to The Chalet. At once! She isn't to be here unsupervised, do you understand?"

The Chubby Cherub nodded quickly, "Yes, sir."

Mr. Rainaldi turned his attention to Bella, as if she had not heard the entire conversation, "Bella, my jewel, you will go with Luca. He will take you home, where you will wait for my return."

Her eyes widened as he motioned for her to leave the helicopter. But she did as she was instructed, feeling the urgency of the situation. She stepped down from the aircraft, and quickly disappeared into a rooftop hallway with Luca as the helicopter lifted back into the air.

The drive back to The Chalet was a long and silent one. While it only took about an hour to fly there, it took almost three to get back via the car and the winding paths of the interstate. Becca felt awkward being escorted by a stranger. Instead of forcing conversation with Luca, she stared out the window and watched the blurred browns and greens of pine trees speed past along I-4 and I-95. Her mind was filled with regret for not being able to see Halona. Luca had followed Mr. Rainaldi's orders succinctly, and ushered her out of the club as discretely as possible. She knew she and Halona had their differences but she felt guilty for the way things ended. Even though Halona denied having feelings for Sasha, Becca knew they were there. Just as her own feelings for Clementine seemed hidden to her, and yet, others could detect them so easily. She also knew that Sasha didn't reciprocate those feelings, but that was not her truth to tell. She didn't want to deliver a heartbreak to Halona. She wanted to deliver some semblance of peace. Becca knew she struggled and wanted to give her some relief, even if it was only the knowledge that Sasha was alive and well. In her heart, she knew that she would want the same, if the tables were reversed. No matter what Clementine's feelings toward her were, she would still want her to be happy.

Luca was polite when they arrived at The Chalet, like a taxi driver delivering her to the requested destination. His face said it all. The transaction was complete, and he wanted to be on his way. He didn't escort her to the house or even open her car door. He just dropped her off and left as quickly as he came.

The Chalet was empty. Marco was still gone to town. And there was no telling how long Mr. Rainaldi would be attending to the Miami warehouse emergency, whatever that entailed. Becca was alone. For the first time in almost a year, there was no one guarding her. She hesitated at the front door, afraid to touch the door knob as the last time she did, it sent a brutal jolt of electricity through her. Confusion swept over her racing mind.

I'm alone. There's no one here. No one to stop me from leaving.

She paced in front of the doors. After a few moments, she walked around the side of the house to the pool patio. The gate was unlocked, so she went in, and sat underneath an umbrella next to the pool. The noon sun was beating down and the white concrete patio was blindingly bright. As Becca sat in the summer heat, her mind was filled with a million-and-one scenarios about how to get away and what would happen if she tried.

I could go into the woods, like Hal. Maybe I could make it to the edge of the property and find a neighbor to help. No, that won't work. If there even are neighbors, there's no telling how far I'd have to walk to get there. And I don't even know which direction to go. And they might not even be nice neighbors. What if they know Mr. Rainaldi…and tell him they found me? He'd lose his shit. There's no telling what he would do if he found out I tried to run away.

She was silent for a long time as the scenario played out over and over in her head. Her eyes were transfixed on the pines in the distance. Each rumination in her mind revealed a new and more devious punishment inflicted by Mr. Rainaldi, most involving the gear in his hidden closet or the poisoned whiskey decanter in his study.

I could go to the river. I know this path leads right to it. Marco takes it all the time. But where would I go from there? I can swim…but there are also gators. And if they will eat a dead body they find in the water, they will damn sure eat a live one, too. If only there was a boat or a jet-ski or a canoe… Jesus! Literally anything that could get me to the other side of the river.

She considered the option of swimming, which sounded pleasant in the sweltering heat, but the idea of being an alligator snack made her queasy. *Oh, what about the garage? Maybe there's another car, or even an ATV?* But as she envisioned herself finding keys, and driving away in an ATV, she still had a gnawing, nagging voice whispering in her head. It was Mr. Rainaldi's voice, deep and seductive, *Your tears won't save you. You're mine.* She was overwhelmed. Inundated by his possessiveness of her, she felt hopeless. Alone. Weak. Trapped.

Even if I could find a way out of here, the guards would bring me back. He'd find me. It's no use. And what about Marco? I can't just leave him here. I can't do this.

Becca felt lightheaded. She couldn't shake the feeling that no matter how much she wanted to leave, she just wasn't physically able to do it. She wanted so desperately to be free. That's what she had wanted since the beginning. She was yelling and screaming for her body to move. To run. But she worried that no matter what she did, he would come after her. He would find some way to retaliate.

His voice echoed in her head, *You can never leave. I own you.*

Dizziness took over. Her eyes blurred and the edges of her vision began creeping in like the dark confines of an expanding tunnel. It was an inky black that filled her eyes, capturing the light until only darkness remained. Even her unspoken consideration of running away was reason for punishment. It was as if Mr. Rainaldi could read her thoughts and somehow punish her—no matter how far away he was. She was conflicted, and sweating profusely. She tried to shake away the dizziness. But it was no use. She didn't have control over anything, not even her own body.

I'm too weak for this.

She clenched her eyes shut, and leaned her head back against the chair. As she calmed her nerves, and breathed slowly with purpose, the light appeared at the end of her tunnel vision, and continued to grow. Bright light filled her eyes. Her hands trembled as she grabbed the arms of the chair, ready to push herself forward. The metal of the chair burned her skin. She felt a churning deep in her belly. Even in the shade, the Florida summer was unscrupulous. She gazed up into the clouds beyond the fabric of the umbrella. A small brown bird soared by. The way the clouds swirled made it seem like the bird was resting on them – just floating along, nestled in the protection of the soft white embrace. It made her heart ache.

Why is this so hard? Why am I struggling? Just leave. Marco would want this for me. Clem would want this for me. There are people looking for me. It's now or never, Rebecca! LEAVE.

She pushed herself the rest of the way upward and stood from her seat. Becca walked out of the gate, and toward freedom.

256

CHAPTER THIRTY–TWO
I KISSED A GIRL

Once Becca's feet had been set in motion, they slowly picked up speed like a coal-fed locomotive. With the crunch of gravel in her ear, like the squeak of forged steel wheels on rail, she chugged along the path to the river. Her feet had reached a steady pace as she entered a canopied tunnel of the trail. Some distance behind her, she heard the hum of an engine and the squeal of brakes.

A voice called to her, "Becca! Wait!"

But she didn't slow down or even glance behind to see who was calling after her. She pressed forward, her speed peaking to a near jog. The trail before her curved through the woods, like a slithering snake, but she could still see the glisten of water as the sun shone bright light on the gentle lapping waves. It seemed so small and far away. But she had taken the first step and couldn't stop now.

"Stop! Come back," the voice shouted.

Becca's pace quickened even more. She was running as hard as her legs would carry her toward the river.

The voice was high and cracked with terror, "Rebecca!"

Becca stopped dead in her tracks. "Rebecca." Only a select few knew her real name, her friends and Marco. And she knew it couldn't be Marco. She knew the feminine voice that called to her. But how could it be? She hesitated to turn around, believing that the voice must be a figment of her imagination. Maybe it was wishful thinking. She could see the water's edge. She could see her path to freedom was clear. This was her one and only chance.

"Rebecca! Come back," the woman's voice called to her again, louder. She couldn't resist the urge to look. She had to know. She had to be certain. Before she sprinted to the water and swam to freedom, she had to take one last look behind her. She spun around on her heels, and started to cry. Adrenaline flooded her senses. Blinking away the tears, she knew the vision before her was real. It was Clementine.

Clementine jumped from the vehicle as it rolled to a halt. She landed on her feet and the Escalade door bumped hard against the hinges. The two women ran toward each other. As they crashed chest to chest, they embraced in a hug that seemed to span on for years. Becca was sobbing, as Clementine patted her back.

She whispered, "It's okay. I'm right here."

Becca squeezed her tighter, wrapping her arms around Clem's waist, "But, how? How did you get here?"

Clem pulled loose from her grip and pointed toward the Escalade that was parked haphazardly in the driveway. Marco had parked the car, and got out to close the passenger door. He stood beside the idling SUV and watched the girls embrace. It warmed his heart to see the girls together, and brought a wide smile to his face, one that hadn't been there in months.

"It was Marco," Clemmie whispered. "He came to the Mort and brought me here."

Becca looked baffled as she processed what she'd just heard. "You… you've been at the Mortimer this whole time? He never moved you?"

Clem frowned at her, "What do you mean? I've been there waiting for you to come back."

Becca looked up to see Marco's smiling face. She smiled and laughed, "He did this?! But how? Why?"

"I don't know. You'll have to ask him."

Becca hugged Clemmie once more and the two women walked toward Marco.

"You two go inside, while I park the car. I've unlocked the door with the remote. It's too hot to stay out here. The index has already hit 100 degrees."

The two women continued on to the house, retracing the steps Becca had just taken – back up the trail and through the patio gate. The cool air of the house made Becca shiver as she escorted Clementine to the kitchen, and poured each of them a glass of water. It wasn't long before Marco joined them.

"Marco," Becca said, "this is a wonderful surprise, but I don't understand why."

He smiled at her, and replied, "Sorellina, this is for Arnoldo. Getting to know you these past few months has really opened my eyes. I realized that Arnoldo tried to do the right thing by helping your friend." His smile vanished as a melancholy ache set in his eyes, "His heart always was bigger than mine. But even though he is gone, he is teaching me that compassion is what makes us human. I wasn't strong enough to help him. But maybe I can help you. I've done many things I regret in this life. Maybe this will right some of the wrongs."

Becca extended out her hand and grabbed his. She pulled him closer and hugged him.

"Thank you, Marco. This means so much to me. You've been like a big brother these past few months. You've already helped me so much. Without your friendship, I don't think I'd still be alive."

"Are you two gonna kiss?" Clem said with a sly grin.

"What?" Becca whipped around to look at Clem, "I just said he's like a brother to me. Who kisses their brother?"

Clem started laughing, "Hillbillies. Hillbillies kiss their brothers." She cackled.

Becca rolled her eyes and laughed, "Oh, stop."

"Why don't you two go upstairs and relax? I'll bring up some lunch in a bit."

"But what about Mr. Rainaldi? He could come back at any minute."

"Oh, do not worry about him," a smug look crept across Marco's face. "He won't be back for a while. My Cuban friends will see to that!"

Becca stared incredulously at Marco, "Wait…what do you mean by that?"

He laughed, "Sorellina, I told you last night. He is not the only one with connections." Marco's smile was devious, "I made a phone call to my old dealer and gave him a tip on where to find some new product."

"Oh, Marco! He'll kill you if he ever finds out it was you! What were you thinking?"

"Eh, I was thinking that he deserved a taste of his own medicine," Marco said as he shook his fist in the air. "But, do not worry about me. Go and enjoy the time you have."

Becca and Clementine locked eyes for a moment.

"Go, go, go! You have things to talk about," he said, raising his eyebrows.

"I see," Becca replied, and turned to Clem, "I'll show you around. I don't think you got to see much when you were here last."

Clem chuckled, "Nope. Don't remember much either."

Becca escorted Clem around the house, stopping at each room like a tour guide in a historic mansion, sharing interesting tidbits about each. It wasn't long before the two made their way upstairs, and into Mr. Rainaldi's bedroom.

As the women entered the room, Clementine commented, "It's a beautiful home, Becca, but I'd rather just hang out and catch up."

"Oh, yeah, good point. I don't know why I'm giving you a tour. Here, sit," she said, awkwardly motioning to the bed.

Clemmie sat on the edge of the bed, and patted the plush comforter motioning for Becca to join her.

Sitting next to her, Becca said, "Soooo, how are you? From our last convo at the Mort, you were doing well. Enjoying dancing. What's new?"

"Meh, it's ok. Ya know, a lot of that is just making face. Ya gotta tell yourself that things are good even when they aren't. What about you? You good?"

"I literally want to die most days. I was being real about Marco. I know it's sappy, but he saved my life. It's a long story," she shrugged.

"Tell me anyway," Clem goaded.

"Alright, here's the Cliff's Notes. A few months ago, I hit a wall and fell apart. Marco picked me up off the floor. Figuratively and literally. We trauma bonded and he's been my rock ever since. I think we both needed each other. We've both lost a brother. And we are both trapped here. There's more in common than I expected. But he showed me kindness, when he really didn't have to."

Clementine was silent while she listened to Becca. She reached across the bed and held Becca's hand.

"I know Rainaldi has taken everything from us," Clementine said as she looked into Becca's eyes, "but he can't break us unless we let him. And we can't let him, Bec."

Becca smiled weakly, "That reminds me of an Eleanor Roosevelt quote."

"Oh, yeah? Tell me."

"Let's see if I can remember it correctly…" Becca paused thoughtfully and began reciting the quote like a child delivering a poetry reading, "No one can make you feel inferior without your consent."

"That's it," Clemmie said, "We have to stay strong. For ourselves." She paused for a moment, "For each other."

"I guess so. It's just so hard when it feels like everything is set to break you."

"I know, girl. But we hafta hold on to every little piece of joy we find. We hafta cling to it, for our own sanity. Because joy is what makes it easier to bend when you wanna break."

"Maybe you are right. It's just that joy is few and far between around here."

"Bec, can I tell you something?"

"Sure. Anything."

"It's kinda…" Clem took a deep breath, "I better say it before I lose my nerve. Now or never, right?"

Becca scoffed, "Funny, I was just saying that to myself earlier. Just say it. You know you can tell me anything. We've been friends for a long time."

"Yeah. Friends," Clem was silent as a pregnant pause hung in the air. She felt her courage waffle. She took another deep breath, and found her resolve. "I… I have feelings for you. Like…not just friends. Like… you're my joy. Like… I don't care where I'm at, as long as it's with you."

Becca's mouth fell open as a whirlwind of emotion ran through her. Tears pooled in her eyes. In a rush, she leaned forward, grabbed Clementine's face, and kissed her passionately.

Part Twelve

Maneater

CHAPTER THIRTY-THREE
KILLER QUEEN

That one passionate kiss erupted into something much more as Clementine cupped Becca's face in her hands. She pressed her lips fully against Becca's and plunged her tongue deep into her mouth at the first gasp for air. Becca pulled Clementine closer as her arms wrapped slowly around her waist. Clem's fingers caressed Becca's neck as she tightened her grip, closing the gap between them. Clem pulled herself into Becca's lap and they fell backwards onto the bed, lost in the intensity of the softness of their lips. Chest to chest, Becca and Clem stroked each other from neck to waist until their finger tips caressed bare skin. Clem unbuttoned Becca's starched white shirt and pulled it loose from her shoulders with a rough tugging, unfazed by the sound of seams popping. Becca's roaming hands reached lower and unburdened Clem's hips from the fabric that bound her legs together. She slid her panties to her knees with hooked fingers.

"Open your legs," Becca whispered, as she traced the curves of Clem's inner thigh. "I want you to sit on my face."

Clem stood and mounted Becca. She made a small sound deep in her throat as Becca flicked the tip of her tongue against her labia. She gripped the wall to steady herself as Becca clasped her butt and drove her tongue deep inside. Clem groaned and rocked her hips in a rhythm, grinding against Becca as she licked and sucked. Encouraged by the pitch of her moans, Becca buried her face between Clem's legs, like she was eating the juicy, pink flesh of watermelon still on the rind. Her face was dripping wet from her ears to her chin, when suddenly Clem moved away. Becca felt a cold, smooth finger wiggle between the lips of her labia and slide across her clitoris.

"Oh, you're so wet," Clem whispered as she buried her fingers inside, thrusting with a 'come here' motion. Becca's eyes rolled to the back of her head and her breathing was heavy. As she began to moan louder, Clem leaned over and kissed her passionately, while she was still stroking her with her fingers. Becca's body clenched in rhythm with Clem's, bucking, and riding the wave. She moaned louder and louder until a spurt of cream filled Clem's hand. She laid on the bed beside Becca with a euphoria swimming in her head and lust still in her eyes. She forced her wet fingers into Becca's mouth. Clem bit her lip as Becca sucked the juice from her fingers. She grabbed Becca's breast, and twisted her nipple as she shuddered from her orgasm. Becca rolled toward Clem. Her face was flushed and the soft baby hairs around her temples were glistening with sweat. Becca gazed into her eyes.

"That's the most alive I've ever felt during sex," she sighed. "Honestly, it's the first time I've actually enjoyed it." Tears pooled along her eyelashes, Becca trembled as she recounted her unpleasant sexual encounters with men, even before coming to The Chalet, they paled in comparison. She wiped the tears from her face. "Clem, I want you to fuck me with the strap-on," she whispered. Her voice was pleading and fragile. Clementine caressed her cheek, and brushed the hair from her face.

"Anything for you," she said.

Becca opened the secret compartment in the closet and picked a dildo from the collection to use with the strap-on. She brought it back to the bed where Clem waited and took great care to gently buckle it in place without pinching her sensitive skin. While she was on her knees in front of Clementine, she paused, stroking her outer thighs. She traced the curves of her body. Becca took her time and savored ritual, leaving delicate kisses along her skin. This process was sacred to Becca. She thought about all the times she had been the one who was getting buckled in and how mechanical and distant Mr. Rainaldi was. There was no love in his touch. Only the efficiency of getting the job done. There was no romance in those sexual encounters. It was business. A service being performed. Even as far back as losing her virginity to her high school sweetheart. But this felt different. Becca felt like she was dressing a Goddess for battle. She marveled at Clementine's beauty and ferocity. The rough leather against her soft skin enveloped the duplicity of her life.

As she stood, Clementine held her hand, an act of chivalry, steading her, as if lifting her out of despair, a Goddess blessing her worshiper. They locked eyes. Clementine kissed Becca on the forehead.

"Gentle or Rough?" Clementine's face was placid, but warm.

"I want you to claim me," Becca said demurely. "I'm giving myself to you."

"Of course," Clemmie said as she pushed Becca onto the bed. "On your knees, ass up."

Becca kneeled on the bed, arched her back like a cat, and rested her chest on a pillow. Clem stood at the edge of the mattress, admiring the width of Becca's hips and the roundness of her butt. Her vulva was pink and puffy. She licked it, took the soft dildo into her hand, and slid it in. Becca groaned and pressed her hips against Clementine's as a solid, hardness filled her.

Clem's hands were soft and warm as they hovered over the curve of Becca's hips. She cradled them and pulled herself deeper into Becca. She gasped as Clementine began to thrust deep inside her. With every crash Becca moaned louder.

"That's it, honey, let it out," Clem grunted as she pounded against Becca.

"I'm so close. I'm gonna cum," Becca whined.

The bedroom door flung open, and Mr. Rainaldi stepped into the room. He immediately flew into a rage. He grabbed a fistful of Clementine's hair and yanked her backward, dragging her away from the bed. The dildo snatched out of Becca and she yelped as she rolled off the bed.

"You fucking whores! I'll fucking kill you both," Rainaldi screamed.

In an instant, she ran toward Mr. Rainaldi, and tried to pull him away from Clementine. He grabbed Becca by the chin and shoved her onto the ground. Clementine swatted at his face and tried to pry his hand loose from her hair. But he pressed her face into the wall, with his hand at the back of her head. She slumped to the floor, as her knees went weak.

Becca jumped up, and lunged forward, clawing at his back. Mr. Rainaldi turned just in time to stop her with a backhanded slap across the face. She tumbled to the floor, with a thud. Dazed, she struggled to stand. Blood dripped from her lip. After a moment, she pulled herself to her knees. Mr. Rainaldi held Clementine by the throat with one hand, as he pushed her back into the wall again. His attention was fully focused on choking the life out of her. She kicked at his knees and squirmed under his grip. She clawed at his hands, trying to pry his curled fingers from her throat. She began to choke and gag, as he pressed down on her windpipe. Becca heard Clem gasping for breath and charged at Mr. Rainaldi, like a linebacker about to tackle a running back. She plowed into his side as hard as she could with her shoulder and sent him crashing into a chair. An adjacent lamp turned over and shattered as it fell off the end table. Clementine crumpled to the floor, as she gasped for air, like a dying fish.

Marco heard the commotion and burst through the door. He immediately ran toward Mr. Rainaldi, who was trying to fend off Becca's slaps as well as untangling himself from the broken lamp. Marco grabbed Becca by the hips and shoved her to the side. He grabbed Mr. Rainaldi by the arm, jerked him upward, and twisted his arm hard against his back. Becca stumbled backward. Mr. Rainaldi jabbed Marco in the gut and freed his arm. The two men began throwing punches at each other. Marco landed a solid punch in Mr. Rainaldi's stomach. He doubled over and stumbled against the wall, landing on top of Clementine. Marco grabbed him by the collar and lifted him into the air, and threw him toward the bed. Becca rushed to Clem, who was crumpled on the floor, still gasping for breath. She struggled to regulate her breathing and clutched at Becca's hands, as she positioned the upended chair cushion under her head. Mr. Rainaldi rebounded and charged at Marco, like a bull in the ring. He shoved Marco's back into the wall near the closet. The two men grappled with each other, until Mr. Rainaldi wiggled from Marco's grip. Marco tripped him. As soon as Mr. Rainaldi hit the floor, Marco mounted him and punched him in the face. He gripped Mr. Rainaldi by the arm again, and twisted it backward until it snapped. Mr. Rainaldi screamed and writhed under Marco's weight. Becca was fanning Clem, who was just beginning to calm down, when Marco yelled for her.

"Go get the whiskey!" He commanded her, "Hurry! You know the one, from his study." She stared at him incredulously. "Hurry!" He urged her. She nodded, and ran down the stairs.

As she ran back into the bedroom, Marco was straddled across Mr. Rainaldi's chest and had his other hand pinned down above his head. Rainaldi's broken arm lay limp at his side.

Clementine had removed the strap-on and she was sitting on his legs, restraining him from bucking against Marco.

Becca looked at Marco with a wild expression, "Are you sure about this?"

"Yes! We are going to give him exactly what he deserves. A taste of his own medicine."

"That makes us no better than him!"

"We don't have a choice! It's us or him, Sorellina."

"He doesn't deserve your compassion," Clem nudged. "Marco is right. If we let him live, he'll kill us. There's no going back now."

Mr. Rainaldi let out a hearty chuckle as he squirmed under his restraints. Marco pressed harder on his wrist. Clem grabbed his ankles and held them together.

"You thought you could make this the Bella and Marco show and you're dead wrong," Rainaldi said through gritted teeth, "You can't do anything without me. This world doesn't EXIST without me, and I made all of you what you are today. Liars. Thieves. And now murderers. You're right, Bella, you are no different than me. So go ahead, Bella, and give me what I deserve."

Bella immediately recognized the laugh, as it had the same tone and tenor as when he was on the cross. Rainaldi took pleasure in this. Even in knowing this was his end, he wasn't going to let anyone take pleasure in this other than him. Rainaldi started to struggle again.

"Hurry, Bec. We can't hold him for much longer," Clem exclaimed.

Becca got on her knees near his head. She unplugged the crystal stopper from the decanter and locked eyes with Marco. There was an unspoken reassurance in his eyes.

"Just a little sip," Marco instructed her.

Becca's naked breasts grazed Mr. Rainaldi's forehead as she leaned forward. She locked eyes with Rainaldi. He did nothing but grin menacingly and whisper, "Have you finally decided to be the hunter and devourer, Ms. Valentina?"

"No," Becca replied, "I'm just poisoning the root."

In an instant, Becca grabbed the strap on off of the floor and shoved it into Mr. Rainaldi's face, with the dildo forced into his mouth. Without pulling the dildo from his mouth, she dribbled several large drops of the poisoned whiskey onto the shaft as the liquid ran down the realistic ridges of the fake penis. He gagged, and tried not to swallow. But Becca pushed the plastic cock deeper into his throat before pulling it back out. He gasped for breath and choked as the poison whiskey flowed into his throat. His body began to spasm.

"Should I give him more? He fed way more of this stuff to Antoinette."

"But she only put a droplet full into your wine, and look what it did to you. In small doses, it only paralyzes."

Mr. Rainaldi's body stopped twitching, but his eyes were wide open, as his pupils dilated. Becca sat back on her legs as she replaced the stopper in the decanter. Clemmie leaned around Marco to see. She let go of his legs as she saw his open eyes.

"Is he… dead?" Clem asked.

"No, he can hear us but he can't move."

"What are we going to do with him?" Becca feared the answer, but her curiosity was piqued.

"We're going to feed him to the dogs," Marco said as a sinister grin covered his face. "But he's going to be awake for every moment. He deserves to feel every ounce of terror that he has caused. Go get a tarp, a roll of duct tape, and some rope. We'll tie him up."

The girls dressed quickly and followed Marco's instructions exactly. Every item was where he said it would be. They found a tarp in the downstairs hallway closet. The duct tape was in the kitchen drawer, and they used some rope from the hidden dungeon in Mr. Rainaldi's closet. The three of them taped Mr. Rainaldi's mouth shut, wrapped him in the tarp, and tied him tightly. He was a pretty package with only a small air hole just below his nose.

It was late in the day and sunset was making way for nightfall.

"I want you two to stay inside and out of sight until we decide how to handle the guards. There are six that roam the perimeter, and two at the gate. I've closed the blinds, just in case they get near the house. If they see me, they will just assume it is business as usual. So, I will handle this part alone. Besides, I want to see him as he sinks to the bottom. He deserves to feel the pain as the alligators bite into him and tear him apart. But I am sure he will drown long before that."

"Marco, you are a dear, sweet man. And I appreciate you trying to protect us. But I want to be there when he goes under. This man has ruined my life in unspeakable ways. Call it a sick form of therapy, but I'm going with you," Becca said.

"Sorellina, are you sure?"

"Yes, very. The guards have seen me with you outside many, many times. It won't raise any suspicion. I promise."

Hesitantly, Marco looked between the two women. Before searching Clementine's face for advice. She nodded in agreement, and with that Marco conceded.

Once the forest was shrouded in dark, Marco loaded Mr. Rainaldi into the back of the utility vehicle and he and Becca drove him down to the river.

CHAPTER THIRTY–FOUR
DOOMED

The summer night held only the sound of crunching gravel, croaking frogs, and humming cicadas. The headlights from the utility vehicle bounced off the trees and cast long, spindly shadows against the forest. As the side-by-side eased up to the dock, Marco and Becca could hear the gentle lapping of water against the shore. It was peaceful out on the river at night. The heat of the day was gone and the night whispered like a breeze luring a kite to explore the stars. Out along the remote parts of the St. John's River, the light pollution was gone and the night sky sparkled like a blanket of diamonds. Each gleaming, bright, and breath-taking.

Marco stepped into the edge of the water, and pulled a small canoe that was tethered under the dock. He tossed the rope to Becca to hold, while she waited for him on shore. He hefted the tarp enshrouded Mr. Rainaldi onto his shoulder, like a 50 pound bag of dog food, and heard a grunt come from inside.

Good, he's still alive, Marco thought as he lowered the package into the canoe. He stepped into the small boat, and sat on the back bench. Following him, Becca stepped in and sat in the front, while Mr. Rainaldi was laid across the middle. Marco used the oars to push away from the shore. The moon was shining bright and reflected off the smooth surface of the water. Marco took a deep breath and sighed, as he began rowing into the river current.

"What a beautiful night, eh?" Marco said as he nudged the tarp with his foot. "It's really a shame that you are not able to see how gorgeous the sky is, sir. But it is a feast for the eyes of the living."

Marco pulled up the oars and allowed the boat to drift for a bit. He leaned forward and relaxed for a moment, just listening to the calming sounds of the water lapping against the boat. Thunder rolled in the distance, and a streak of heat lightning lit up the sky, like poison creeping through veins of electricity splitting the night.

"I can't tell you how often I've rowed out to the middle of the river and just floated while watching the moon." Marco looked at Becca and smiled, then down at Mr. Rainaldi, addressing him directly, "Feeding the dogs may have been my favorite out of all the duties you assigned to me. Oh, not because I was disposing of your skeletons or cleaning up your messes. Please, do not believe it was out of loyalty, but instead, because it was the only moment of peace I had. I've been catering to your every whim for years. And, sir, you are very demanding. Nothing was ever good enough for the great and powerful Enrico Rainaldi." Marco paused for a moment, "Eh…maybe it was out of loyalty, at first. But that all changed when you forced me to pour the whiskey that took my brother's life. Sir, the way you smiled as my hand shook. It was all over your face. So much pride and power. You knew I was too afraid of you to do anything. And you knew exactly how much it broke my heart to deliver Arnoldo's death. You were so pleased with yourself. You are a monster. Delighted by suffering. You'll do anything to turn the knife in someone's back. You are a vampire, sucking the life out of everyone around you. For years, I've watched you pull in young women and control them and break them until there was nothing left. You bled them dry. And then, sent me to dispose of the evidence. But body after body, it was never enough. You needed more. Once you took my brother, I knew it was only a matter of time before you bled me dry too."

He paused again, thoughtfully, and smiled at Becca, "But it was, you, Rebecca, who gave me my fight back," Marco sighed a breath of relief. "Eh, I ramble on. But there really is something so serene about the river at night. It connects me with nature in a way nothing else ever has."

Marco looked down at the tarp again, speaking to it, "I know you have no care for beautiful things unless they make money for you. All this raw natural beauty, and you use it as a burial ground for your sins."

"You've known him a long time haven't you?" Becca's face was enshrouded by the lace shadows of the leafy trees. She watched Marco, giving his eulogy for a man that he had spent years in servitude to. Her heart broke for him, knowing that the weight that he carried must be immense.

"Long enough." Marco said.

Becca and Marco were both quiet for a long while, just absorbing the serenity of their surroundings. Suddenly, Marco kicked the tarp again and a weak grunt came out.

"Eh, it sounds like it is about time."

Marco picked up the oars and rowed to a spot in the river where the trees hung low and blocked the light of the moon. He put the oars back in the holsters and grabbed the feet of the tarp.

"Any final words, Sorellina?"

"I'm honestly not sure. What do you say when you are murdering someone?" She paused for a moment, "Maybe a few lines of poetry?"

"What's the line by Shakespeare? You know the one? From Hamlet?"

"Ah, I know it," she said as she cleared her throat,

"To be or not to be—that is the question:

Whether 'tis nobler in the mind to suffer

The slings and arrows of outrageous fortune,

Or to take arms against a sea of troubles

And, by opposing, end them."

"Yes, that's the one. A proper monologue."

He pulled the tarp toward the edge of the boat until the tips of the feet were in the water and the lip of the boat pressed into Mr. Rainaldi's stomach. Marco held Mr. Rainaldi by the head, and said, "No more suffering the slings and arrows at your hand, we've chosen to take arms. Farewell, sir."

"Farewell, Mr. Rainaldi. I'm finally giving you what you deserve."

Marco let go of his hold on the tarp and it slid into the murky river water. Bubbling air as it slowly sank into the St. John's River.

"The king is dead. Long live the king," Marco said with a smirk.

As the final bubbles of air escaped, and Mr. Rainaldi's head sank below the surface of the water, Becca replied, "And heavy is the crown."

Part Thirteen

Epilogue

CHAPTER THIRTY-FIVE
WHERE DO WE GO FROM HERE

The lights in the house were dimmed when Marco and Becca came back from the river's edge. The air was filled with the smell of brewing tea, and fresh cut lemon. The house had a cozy bookish feel to it, unlike the bleached clinical white from before. As they stepped inside the door, Marco took off his muddy boots and left them on the patio. He cleaned his hands at the sink, making sure to scrub meticulously under his fingernails and up to his elbows. Becca did the same, only much quicker since she didn't have Marco's attention to detail.

Clementine was cuddled on the couch in the living room. A serving platter with a pot of hot tea, a jar of honey, and sliced lemon sat in front of her. Two empty teacups with scrawling rose vines imprinted on the lip remained on the tray. She sipped tea, while her mind quietly ruminated on the events of the evening, as well as imagining what the future could look like for them. Becca quietly joined her on the couch. Her own mind was reeling from the dystopia that she found herself in. It had been almost a year since The Florida Four had been trafficked. But that fact remained unspoken. The eerie truth hung in the air, unannounced, and avoided. They didn't want to say it because they knew that it meant they would have to admit a hard reality to themselves. But the realization that they could never go back to their former lives lurked in the dark shadowy corners of the room. Their past lives would only ever be an echo. Reverberating in their own nostalgia, waiting for moments to reveal its fangs and remind them of what once was.

How could we go back? Becca's thoughts circled around this one massive question. No one would understand the lives they now lived. The tears of Rebecca's well-intentioned, grieving mother would sear her skin instead of washing away the trauma. The guilt of sin would rest heavy on her brow for the remainder of her life. There were no words in the English language that could fully communicate the horror that she survived. Horrors that somehow became mundane, accepted, and expected. Her scale of right and wrong, common and uncommon, acceptable and unacceptable had been forever tipped. There was no way of un-experiencing or un-knowing a bitter reality. Once that line had been crossed, there was no going back to blissful ignorance. There was already a bite mark in the apple from the tree of knowledge. The lid to Pandora's box was already askew. There was only the new perspective of having survived it, having grown from it, and becoming the rare species of human that existed in the unearthly realms like transcendence and astral projection, or unicorns and dragons. The room was silent for a long time as understanding crept through their gray matter and down to their hearts before resting heavily in the pits of their stomachs. There was nothing to say. Only more unspoken questions on how to move forward.

Marco walked around the corner and poured himself a cup of tea. The clink of the porcelain broke the heavy silence and pulled the two women from their dissociation. Marco settled into a chair and crossed his legs, and fired the first audible salvo.

"Well, what's next, ladies?"

"I was… actually just thinking about that," Becca mumbled. "I don't honestly know."

"It's like starting over, isn't it?" Clem leaned forward to top off her tea. "What if we reinvented ourselves? New names. New looks. Everything."

Clem's half-joke landed flat for Becca as she looked at her solemnly, "They'd be looking for us. Our pictures are plastered all over the news. It's a little hard to hide from that."

Clem sighed, and looked at Marco, "What would you do if you could start over?"

Marco sighed, "I'd open my own restaurant. I've always wanted that. It's why I came to America. To become a chef." His voice was full of regret, "Instead I became a drug addict and henchman."

Becca scoffed, "I have no clue what I want to be. I don't even know who I am." Clem frowned and rubbed Becca's back for a moment, trying to soothe her.

"Workin' at the Mort always made me want to make changes. Those girls deserve better. I think I'd make prostitution ethical. Like in that movie with Dolly Parton!" Clementine giggled, "That's probably where I got it from! Did you ever see it?"

Becca shook her head, "What's it called?"

Clem smiled brightly and announced the title in her best Texan accent, "The Best Little Whorehouse in Texas! I watched it when I was a kid," she grimaced, "I don't think my parents knew about it. But I loved it! Dolly was the madame and everyone loved her and she was SO good to the girls that worked there. They were like a family. Like prostitution was illegal but everyone was accepting and respectful about it."

"So… you'd become a madam?"

"Yeah, think about it! We got everything we need to make it happen. I bet the girls at the Mort would appreciate being treated better. And we could do that! Fair wages. Health care. Maybe even retirement accounts! We could make it ethical."

"We definitely couldn't leave things the way they are," Becca frowned. "If we do, then we are no better than him. We have to give these people their lives back. We have to do what we can to make the world better. Remember? Cling to the joy."

"So, the ones who want to stay can stay and the ones who want to go can go? The choice is theirs to make. That's how people take their power back. They can be the owners of their own businesses. Their tips are theirs. Same with service fees. They can just pay us rent for the space. It's not us controlling them. They would be in control of themselves. What do you think?"

"Consent IS sexy. But… what if everything falls apart?"

"Then… we'll take the money and run. Deal?" Clem cackled. Her dark humor was ill-timed. The seriousness of the conversation weighed the room down with lead. She looked back and forth between Marco and Becca, searching their faces for a sign of confirmation. Finding none, she chose something more realistic. "Marco could have his restaurant. And you and I could do whatever we wanted."

Becca considered it, "Yeah. Okay… as long as I'm with you, I don't care what we do."

Marco looked thoughtfully at the two women, as he contemplated their idea. He wanted to craft his words respectfully before speaking.

"It's a beautiful thought. But, I don't think you two realize how big this thing is. The other club owners aren't going to just let you take over —and take their profits. This is a cut-throat business and there will be a power grab when they find out Rainaldi is dead. They'll march in here and kill us all before they let two 'whores' run the business. No offense, Sorellina, but it's their mindset. Why would they pay you when they could be the boss? Rainaldi kept them in line because he was ruthless. But they have the resources and the men to start a war. No, we can't let that happen."

"Oh, I just assumed everyone worked for Mr. Rainaldi. I guess I didn't think about them wanting to take over," Clementine grimaced. "That complicates things, doesn't it?"

"Eh," Marco shrugged, "in a perfect world, prostitutes could have autonomy over their bodies and their lives. And everyone would be paid fairly for the fruits of their labor. But this isn't a perfect world. Far from it. And those men are thugs in their own right. That's how they moved up the ranks. If we leave and they find out Rainaldi is dead, everything will collapse. It would be a blood bath."

"What if we went to the cops?" Clem asked. "They could set up a sting operation and bring them down?"

"No!" Becca exclaimed, she wrung her hands as they began to tremble, "We can't go to the cops. They… They can't be trusted. They're involved. I don't know how many. But Rainaldi is…was… way too close with the Chief of Police. He… he knows…" Becca shook her head as flashes of Guy's writhing and heaving flashed across her eyes, "He knows who we are. And he's deliberately throwing the FBI off the trail. We can't trust it. They'll find out and they'll…they'll…"

Seeing that Becca had become incensed, both Marco and Clementine leaned in to comfort her.

"It's okay, Sorellina. The best thing for us to do then, is make it look like Rainaldi is still calling the shots. No one can or will know he is dead. At the very least until we can all find our own exits. Until then, we must act in his place."

"So, the three of us are Mr. Rainaldi now?" Clem asked.

"That's it. That's how we make changes. Slowly and from within. If it is coming from him, then the others will comply. They are too afraid of him to refuse. But we must keep a firm grip on this. No one can know."

Becca nodded in unison with Clementine, the women stared into each other's eyes, and repeated Marco, "No one can know."

"Long live the king, indeed."

Acknowledgements

I've always heard that you have to know someone to get anywhere in this world. But the older I get, the more I realize that it's not about knowing powerful people. It's about having a community. We are all made by the people who touch our lives and inspire us. None of us get anywhere without a supportive community. So, no matter how high up the ladder you climb, or what feats you accomplish, give gratitude to those who made a way for you, those who held the door open, those who poured love into you. When you do, it'll take root inside you and you'll be able to give that love to the next person in need of it. This is how we grow.

And without further ado, I would like to acknowledge the people who supported me through this journey.

To Rob Perez: Thank you for being my plot whisperer, my cheerleader, and my personal antidote to imposter syndrome. Every time I convinced myself this book was terrible and I should just give up and bury it in the backyard, you talked me off the ledge. This book exists because you believed in it—and in me—even when I didn't.

To JD Justice: Thank you for your honest feedback, your enthusiasm, and for not running away screaming after reading the first draft. Your insights made this story infinitely better. And thank you for bringing Rebecca Coleman to life through cover design in a way that no one else could. You artfully captured her essence.

To Michael Lister: Thank you for taking the time to read this book. Your work has long inspired me, and having you engage with mine is an honor I don't take lightly.

To the Bay County Health Department and Freedom 180: Thank you for the vital work you do educating middle and high school students about the realities of human trafficking. The victims' stories you shared and the statistics you presented built my awareness and deepened my understanding of this crisis. This book was informed by your commitment to prevention and your refusal to let these stories go untold.

To Britt Matthews, Nicky Holt, and the entire Panama City Poetry and Spoken Word community: You taught me that vulnerability isn't weakness—it's the bedrock of honest storytelling. You gave me permission to share the uncomfortable, the raw, the real. Thank you for creating a space where writers can be brave.

To The Tupelo Honies, my burlesque troupe from a decade ago: This book is a love letter to the sisterhood we built. Thank you for the sequins, the laughter, the late nights, and the memories that shimmer even now. You showed me what it means to hold each other up, both on stage and off.

To Tim Hammond, my high school English teacher, thank you for challenging me to read "A Tale of Two Cities" by Charles Dickens. You inspired my love of classic literature and set the standard for what a good teacher looks like.

And finally, to every survivor who has ever had to become the villain to escape: I see you. This one's for us.

About the Author

Pamela G. Holmes is a writer, educator, and advocate for survivors' stories. She holds an M.A. in English and Creative Writing from Southern New Hampshire University and a B.S. in Professional Communication from Florida State University. Her work has appeared in *Emerald Coast Review*, *Philosophy Today*, and various literary journals, exploring themes of resilience, identity, and transformation.

Pamela's awareness of human trafficking began during her time teaching high school English, where she witnessed presentations by Freedom 180 and learned the sobering realities behind the statistics. What started as shock and education evolved into a mission to illuminate the psychological complexities of survival and captivity.

With over a decade of experience teaching both high school and college English courses, Pamela brings both compassion and unflinching honesty to her fiction. When she's not writing or teaching, you'll find her exploring Florida's natural springs, reading classic novels, or sipping strong coffee along the Gulf Coast, where she currently lives and writes. This is her debut novel. Follow her online at @pamelagwrites or visit www.pamelagwrites.com.